WRITTEN IN BLOOD

A FORENSIC HANDWRITING MYSTERY

BOOK 2

BY SHEILA LOWE

SUSPENSE PUBLISHING

WRITTEN IN BLOOD
By
Sheila Lowe

PAPERBACK EDITION

* * * * *

PUBLISHED BY:
Suspense Publishing

COPYRIGHT
2008 by Sheila Lowe

Cover Design: Shannon Raab
Cover Photographer: iStockphoto.com/Cameron Strathdee
Cover Photographer: iStockphoto.com/Sky_Sajjaphot

PUBLISHING HISTORY:
Suspense Publishing, Print and Digital Copy, 2016
NAL/Penguin Group, Print and Digital Copy, September 2008

ISBN-13: 978-0692641927 (Suspense Publishing)
ISBN-10: 0692641920

BOOKS BY SHEILA LOWE

FORENSIC HANDWRITING SERIES
POISON PEN
WRITTEN IN BLOOD
DEAD WRITE
LAST WRITES
INKSLINGERS BALL

STANDALONE THRILLERS
WHAT SHE SAW

NON-FICTION
THE COMPLETE IDIOT'S GUIDE TO
HANDWRITING ANALYSIS
HANDWRITING OF THE FAMOUS & INFAMOUS

DEDICATION

To Jennifer, whose brave and foolhardy spirit lives on in Annabelle.

ACKNOWLEDGMENTS

A work of fiction has many made-up elements, but some things need to be real. For those things, I'm grateful for the kind assistance of FBI agent, George Fong, and detectives Lee Lofland and Kenny Brown. Doug Lyle, MD, a mystery author in his own right, has been generous in his assistance with medical questions.

I would be lost without my friend Bob Joseph lending his experienced eye, and not being afraid to say, "That's really crap, you can do better." To the SCVMW: Bruce, New Bob, Gwen, Bad Bob—you are the best writing group in all the land. And certainly not least, working with editor Kristen Weber was a pleasure.

PRAISE FOR SHEILA LOWE

A Top-Ten pick
—Independent Mystery Booksellers Association

"Couldn't put it down—well, until my eyes drooped last night. Picked it right back up this morning and didn't start work until I'd finished."
—PopSyndicate.com

"A fascinating and complex murder mystery that keeps readers involved and guessing till the exciting climax."
—American Chronicle

"Readers will relish Sheila Lowe's fine tale."
—The Merry Genre Go Round Reviews

"Sheila Lowe's mysteries just keep getting better. Her writing is crisp, and she deftly incorporates interesting information about handwriting analysis along the way. Her characters are rich and fully developed and her plots sizzle."
—Armchair Interviews

"If you enjoy forensics, then give these *Forensic Handwriting Mysteries* a try. It's a different slant on the field wrapped in some pretty believable story lines."
—Gumshoe

WRITTEN IN BLOOD

A FORENSIC HANDWRITING MYSTERY

BY SHEILA LOWE

CHAPTER 1

Now, there's a heart attack waiting to happen.

From her office window, Claudia Rose watched the man heave himself out of the Mercedes 500SL. He kept a meaty hand on the doorframe, rocking a little until his feet settled on the asphalt. About six feet tall and just shy of obese, he had a shock of thick, wiry hair starting to grey on the sides. A short salt-and-pepper beard hid his jaw.

Despite the coolness of the fall afternoon, the man plucked a handkerchief from his breast pocket and mopped his forehead, as if the mere act of exiting the vehicle had sapped his energy. The shoulders of his suit coat strained, the belt disappearing under his belly as he buttoned it closed and went around to the back. He popped the trunk, hauled out a briefcase, every step labored.

Before he could get there, the passenger door opened. A stunning blonde stepped out of the car with a wriggling Bichon Frisé clamped under her arm and a phone to her ear. In response to the man's apparent offer of help, she shook her head and bumped the door shut with a curvy hip, then preceded him up the path. Women would kill to have that shape. Men would describe her as "smoking hot."

Paige Sorensen. The new client.

By the time the man had climbed the wooden staircase, Claudia was at the door, ready to welcome them in.

"Bert Falkenberg," he gasped, proffering a sweaty hand. He

tried to hide the fact that he was winded, but his damp forehead and flushed cheeks gave him away.

"Please come in," Claudia said, standing aside for him to precede her into the house.

At the bottom of the staircase, Paige Sorenson ended her call and ran up, as lithe and smooth as a panther.

"You must be Claudia," she said. "I'm Paige." That smile had no doubt charmed the pants off more than one admirer. She held the little dog up for Claudia's inspection. "I hope you don't mind that I brought Mikki with me. He'll be good, I promise."

"It's fine," said Claudia. She reached out to give Mikki a scratch behind the ears and invited them inside.

Paige Sorensen had sounded young and vulnerable over the phone. This well-turned-out woman made Claudia revisit her first impression.

Paige had said she was recently widowed and the headmistress of the Sorensen Academy, an exclusive Bel Air school for girls. Her late husband's will was being challenged, she had explained, and she needed a handwriting expert to authenticate his signature. Her attorney had recommended Claudia.

"It's my stepchildren," she said, once she and Bert Falkenberg were seated on the living room sofa and Claudia in the armchair. "They're accusing me of—" A tinkling sound from her Gucci handbag interrupted. Bert Falkenberg gave an audible sigh of annoyance. Paige broke off with a wry smile and apology and answered the phone.

Claudia could hear a high-pitched voice, talking fast. Paige listened for about thirty seconds before interrupting. "Annabelle, enough! Tell Brenda to send the other girls to their rooms. You can go to my office and stay there till I get back."

She clicked off and dropped the phone back into her purse. "I knew you should have stayed behind, Bert. *Somebody* needs to be in charge."

Falkenberg gave her a quelling look, and spoke to Claudia, "Let's cut to the chase before someone else has an emergency that can't wait. The situation with Mr. Sorensen's will—"

The touch of Paige's hand on his sleeve halted him mid-sentence. "Let me," she said, gently urging the Bichon's haunches into a seated

12

position on her lap. The little dog fidgeted for a moment, then laid his head on a miniature forepaw and closed his eyes. A flash of irritation lit Falkenberg's eyes, but he sat back against the cushions without protest.

"My husband passed away a month ago," Paige began, reiterating what she had told Claudia over the phone. "He had a stroke—several strokes, then he passed away. He left virtually everything to me, but his kids are saying I forged his signature on the will." Her eyes filled with tears; the pouty lips trembled. "It's just crazy. I would never do something like that!"

"Insane," Falkenberg murmured. "Utterly absurd."

Claudia nodded, giving them her best sympathetic professional face as she adjusted her impression of Paige a little more. If the husband had children old enough to accuse her of forgery, he must have been significantly older than Paige.

"I'm so sorry for your loss, Mrs. Sorensen," Claudia said. "Unfortunately, this sort of thing is pretty common in families."

"Really?"

"Many of the cases I handle are between family members disputing who gets what."

"My attorney, Stuart Parsons, said you're the best handwriting expert around."

Claudia had worked with Parsons before, and liked him. He was not shy in protecting his expert witness from the vicious attacks that opposing counsel often launched in court.

"Did you bring exemplars of your husband's genuine signature? I'll need those to compare to the questioned one."

Paige nodded to Falkenberg. "You've got the files, Bert?" She returned her gaze to Claudia. "I'm a *nice* person and they're calling me a liar. I need you to prove it's my husband's signature. There's too much at stake—my reputation."

Millions of dollars, too, Claudia thought. Paige had let that slip during their preliminary phone conversation. She glanced at Bert Falkenberg, taking note of his broad hands as he snapped open the briefcase and set it on the coffee table between them. Workman's hands with poorly manicured fingernails that seemed more fitted for outdoor work than a desk job. An affront to the Italian silk suit and tie.

13

He hasn't always worn Armani.

Falkenberg removed several file folders from his briefcase and fanned them out on the coffee table. Easing his large frame back against the cushions, he let his eyes roam the room. His gaze traveled from framed family photos on the mantel to a snapshot of Claudia in the arms of her partner, Joel Jovanic. Jovanic was leaning down so they were cheek-to-cheek, a rare grin replacing his homicide investigator's deadpan expression. Falkenberg stared a long time at the photo, but his face gave nothing away.

Paige repositioned the little dog on her lap and reached for the folders Falkenberg had placed on the table. "These are some checks and other papers that he—that Torg—my husband—" she trailed off as one fat tear welled up in each outrageously blue eye and spilled onto her cheeks. "I'm sorry." She dug in her purse and brought out a tissue to dab the tears. "It was a complete shock when I found out he'd left everything to me."

Falkenberg shifted his bulk, fidgeting. Claudia glanced over at him, sensing that the abrupt movement was intended to extinguish some internal reaction to Paige's words. She murmured something vague and spread open the folder Paige handed to her, leafing through the documents inside.

Every signature on the checks, trust deeds and business contracts had been executed in a bold, firm hand. Extra-large capital letters; elaborate, written with a flourish.

Flipping one of the checks over, Claudia ran her fingertips across the back, noting that Torg Sorensen had exerted pressure on the pen strong enough to emboss the paper. To a handwriting analyst, it all added up to an inflated ego and an aggressive need for power. Torg had been the type of man you couldn't push around. Paige's husband could not have been easy to live with.

One aspect of her handwriting analysis practice dealt with forensic behavioral profiling. In cases like this one, her job was solely to verify the authorship of a document. Sometimes it was tempting to blur the lines. No one could prevent Claudia from privately visualizing the man who had penned that showy signature, but in the courtroom her two specialties had to be kept separate. Returning the items to their folder, she replaced it on the table with a sharp reminder to herself to stay out of Sorensen's personality.

If she accepted this case, her task would be to compare the true, known signatures of Torg Sorensen with the one on his will and offer an opinion as to its authenticity. Period.

The second folder contained three checks, a grant deed, and a power of attorney. The signatures on these documents bore little resemblance to the first group. The letter forms were little more than a shaky line. The writing stroke exposed the tremor of an unsteady hand.

Claudia picked out a grant deed and studied the signature. The name, *Torg Sorensen*, rose at an extreme angle above the printed signature line, the final letters fading into a feeble trail of ink. The weakened state of this signature seemed even more than the others to beg the question of why someone in such obvious poor physical, and possibly mental, condition was signing legal documents.

"Is there any question about his competency to sign?" she asked.

"None," Falkenberg answered. "I'll testify that he was absolutely lucid when he signed it. There was no mental impairment. The children wouldn't have a leg to stand on if they tried to use that argument."

"So, all of the documents in this folder were definitely signed *after* the stroke?"

"Yes," Paige confirmed. "He *insisted* on signing those papers himself."

The third and final folder remained on the table between them. This was the crux of the case, the reason why Paige had sought the help of a handwriting expert: the key document containing the signature being contested by her stepchildren.

This folder contained a certified copy of Torg Sorensen's will. A probate court stamp on the first page indicated that the original was on file in the County of Los Angeles Superior Court. Claudia viewed the shaky scrawl with a practiced eye. Decline in writing quality was to be expected after a major assault on the brain like a stroke. It could also make proving authenticity tougher. Before forming an opinion she would need to take measurements and view the documents through her stereo microscope. Already, her mind had begun taking inventory of the writing style, the alignment, the master patterns.

"How old was Mr. Sorensen when he died?" she asked.

"Uh, he was seventy-three."

Claudia did a quick mental calculation. That meant Torg Sorensen was around twice Paige's age.

As if reading her mind, color flooded her client's face. "I know people think I'm just some gold digger who married an older man for his money, but it's not true! And I didn't forge his signature, either! I *loved* him."

Sensing his mistress' distress, Mikki the dog jumped up with a sharp yip. He pressed his front paws against her chest, licking her chin and doing a little cha-cha on her lap.

Bert Falkenberg frowned and cleared his throat, antsy again.

He doesn't know what to do with her.

"I know it must be upsetting to be accused," Claudia said in a neutral tone. "If I take this on, I'm going to need a list of his medications."

Paige frowned. "Why would you need that?"

"Some drugs affect handwriting, so I'd like to know what he was taking. I'll also want to see his medical records, so I'll know exactly what his physical condition was at the time he signed the will."

"He had a stroke, he—"

"Did he sign on his own, or was someone guiding his hand? Was he lying down or sitting up? Was he wearing corrective lenses? What kind of writing surface did he use? What time did he take his meds?" Claudia met Paige's bemused expression with a smile. "It's always important for me to know these things. But it's even more so in a case like this, where there's such a major change in the handwriting. I'll give you a list of my questions."

Paige's hand moved rhythmically over the little dog's fur, but her eyes were glued to the paper in Claudia's hand. "At first, he couldn't use his right hand at all. Then he started working with a physical therapist, and after they released him from the hospital we hired a private therapist. When was that, Bert?"

"Two-and-a-half weeks after the first stroke."

"He was pretty impatient and hard to deal with." Paige's lips twisted in a rueful smile. Her next words confirmed what Claudia had seen in Torg Sorensen's handwriting. "The truth is, he was *always* difficult, he—" She seemed to catch herself. "About a week after he came home from the hospital, he had me call his secretary over to the house. They were locked up in his room together all afternoon. That must be when he changed his will. It was a couple days later when the second stroke hit him and he went into a coma. He never came out of it."

Claudia noted that the will had been witnessed but not notarized, which she thought was surprising, given the size of the Sorensen estate. A mobile notary could have been called in. Why had that not been done?

Two witness signatures appeared under the name of Torg Sorensen, testator. Bert Falkenberg was one of them. He'd written a small, illegible signature that slanted to the left. His handwriting told Claudia that he would not be forthcoming unless there was something in it for him. Left-slanted writers were particularly hard to get to know. The illegibility added another layer of emotional distance and said that he guarded his emotions well.

The second witness signature was larger, more conventional. The name *Roberta Miller* was penned in the Palmer model common to older women who'd had religious school training, and was typical of many who worked in administrative jobs.

"Is Roberta Miller the secretary?" Claudia asked.

Paige confirmed that she was. The question was more out of curiosity than a need to know. Paige's attorney would question the witnesses, but unless they were accused of forging the signature on the will, Claudia would not need to interview them herself.

The rude bleat of a cell phone interrupted once again. This time it was Falkenberg who dug out his mobile phone and checked the screen. He sighed. "Annabelle again." Excusing himself, he hauled himself off the sofa and headed for the front door, answering the phone as he went.

"She's a new student at the Sorensen Academy," Paige said, answering Claudia's unspoken question. "She's having a hard time settling in."

"Oh, is it a residential school?"

"A few of the girls live on site. Annabelle's one of them. The trouble is, we're dealing with some bullying. The other girls are constantly picking on her because she's, well, a bit different from them. She doesn't even *try* to fit in."

"Different?"

Paige looked uncomfortable, as though she regretted opening that line of conversation. She leaned toward Claudia. "This is confidential, right?"

"Yes, of course."

"A couple of months ago, Annabelle tried to kill herself. She came to us right out of the hospital. That's why we can't ignore her phone calls. She's still pretty fragile."

The front door opened and Bert returned. "I'll talk to her when we get back," he said, lowering himself onto the sofa beside Paige.

"She's taken a liking to Bert," Paige added. "He's become kind of a father figure for some of the girls."

Claudia felt a stirring of interest about Annabelle, who had been so unhappy that she had attempted suicide, yet felt comfortable phoning this bear of a man. He did have that cuddly look. Maybe she saw him as a teddy bear, rather than a grizzly. A young girl might be drawn to that kind of man.

An image of her own father—loving, but ineffectual in the face of her mother's vitriol—flashed through her head. She turned to Bert. "What's your position at the school, Mr. Falkenberg?"

"I help Mrs. Sorensen with the business end of running the Academy. The administration of a private school is quite different from a public one."

"I'm sure it must be." Returning her attention to the case, Claudia indicated the file folders on the table. "To be quite frank, Mrs. Sorensen, this is not an easy case. The physiological effects of the stroke on your husband's handwriting complicate things. So, I'll do my examination and let you know whether I think I can help."

"But Bert *saw* him sign it, didn't you, Bert?"

"Yes, yes, that's right, I did."

Paige's body strained forward, something like desperation showing in her eyes. "You *have* to testify that his signature is genuine—that's what I'm paying you for!"

"No. What you're paying for is my objective opinion, and that's all I can promise you." Stacking the folders together in a neat pile, Claudia slid them back across the coffee table with an apologetic shrug. "I'm not your lawyer, Mrs. Sorensen, I'm an advocate of the court, and that means I deal with the truth, *whatever* it may be."

"But I'm *telling* you the truth—he signed the will."

For a long moment, no one spoke. Then the sudden roar of a leaf blower outside shattered the silence, startling them all. The sound rose and fell under the window, amplifying the tension in the room as the gardener walked the noisy machine up the pathway. The return to quiet when he switched it off was as jarring as the racket it'd made.

Bert Falkenberg snatched the file folders from the table and tossed them into his briefcase, giving Claudia an icy stare. "If you can't handle this case, maybe you can refer us to someone who can."

CHAPTER 2

Taken aback by his abrupt change in attitude, Claudia gave Falkenberg a quizzical look. "You're welcome to take your case to someone else. I'm not going to testify unless I can prove my opinion based on the evidence you've given me."

Falkenberg's cold glare relaxed into a grin and he extended his hand. "No hard feelings, Ms. Rose," he said, dropping the hand when he saw she was not going to take it. "I wanted to see if you're easily rattled."

"I have enough experience that I don't need to be tested, Mr. Falkenberg."

"The attorney representing Mrs. Sorensen's stepchildren is Frank Norris—ever run into him? He's quite the pit bull. We need someone who's going to be a strong witness. You'll do fine. Take your time and do whatever examining you need to."

Sighing, Paige scratched the little dog's head with her sculpted French acrylics. "Enough theatrics, Bert, give her the money."

He took an envelope from his briefcase and tossed it onto the table. "Here's your retainer agreement and a check. Stuart Parsons will call and schedule you to testify at the hearing next week—assuming you agree the signature is genuine, of course."

Of course.

Claudia watched them drive away, feeling unsettled. She considered the discrepancy between her impression of the Paige Sorensen she had spoken to on the phone and the Paige who had showed up for their appointment. Then she thought about Bert Falkenberg's prying eyes going over her living room with more than a passing interest. Neither felt quite right, and the *something* continued to niggle at her, just beyond consciousness.

She poured a fresh mug of her favorite Brazilian roast and took Paige's folders upstairs to her second floor office.

Land being at a premium in the beach community of Playa de la Reina, homes were built *up*, rather than out. When she had bought the house years ago after her divorce, Claudia demolished the walls between two small bedrooms to create a spacious, airy workspace that ran the length of the house.

She dropped into her chair behind the scarred old executive desk and tapped her way to YouTube. After finding a meditation she liked, she closed her eyes, hoping to get in touch with the sense of words left unspoken.

Breathe…one-two-three… Focus on the sounds coming from the stereo: water gurgling, wood flute, loons warbling. Four-five-six…vapor bowls humming.

But instead of decompressing, her brain continued to buzz with a jumble of unwelcome images. Just before Paige's appointment she had received an email letting her know that a client in whose case she had testified had lost. It was not the first time she'd had a client lose, but this one was different. She had taken the worst beating of her career on the witness stand.

The client, Boris Becket, had insisted on representing himself in his lawsuit against a large, powerful hospital—that was his first mistake.

The hospital had presented a consent form that gave them permission to perform a brain surgery that had left him permanently disabled. Pointing out that even a child could see it wasn't his signature, Becket had steadfastly ignored Claudia's appeals for him to hire an attorney. He had an excellent case—wasn't that enough?

No. It wasn't. And there was a reason for the saying, "a man who represents himself has a fool for a client."

Claudia arrived at court armed with exhibits to prove her points. She thought she was ready for anything.

Anything but the sleazy expert witness who testified on behalf of the hospital.

Becket had ignored her plea to obtain a witness list from the attorney representing the hospital—the second big mistake.

The opposing handwriting expert was a man named Andrew Nicholson.

In the small, highly specialized field of handwriting examination, Nicholson had earned himself a reputation for inflating his credentials like a helium-filled balloon. If she had known in advance that he was opposing her on this case, Claudia could have produced a raft of materials that would have impeached his credibility. But, blindsided by his unexpected appearance, and without a savvy attorney to protect her, she was left defenseless on the stand.

During his *voir dire*, where the witness explains his or her qualifications to the court, Nicholson had rattled off an astonishing number of professed accomplishments. Hell, he'd all but claimed to have analyzed *God's* handwriting. His assertions that he worked for the CIA and that he taught document examination at Stanford made Claudia sound like a rank amateur. She would have been impressed too, if she hadn't known what an inveterate phony Nicholson was.

In a previous case she had amassed proof of Nicholson's lies— an entire notebook full of proof. But that did her no good now. The notebook was back at her office and Boris Becket didn't have the skills and knowhow of a wily attorney to use them, even if the notebook had been in her briefcase.

She heaved a disappointed sigh. Losing on a level playing field based on the facts was one thing; combating the smoke and mirrors of an out-and-out liar was something else entirely. Her confidence in the legal system and in herself had taken a body blow. The last thing she wanted was to get back on the witness stand.

And that brought her thoughts back full circle to her afternoon visitors. Her gaze fell on the folders they had left with her. She thought about everything Paige Sorensen and Bert Falkenberg had said, the inflections with which they had spoken, and evaluated it all with professional detachment. You could not be swayed by a client's story. Sometimes they lied.

Had Paige Sorensen lied to her? It didn't matter if she had. The signatures themselves would tell Claudia what she needed to know.

Any extraneous information was irrelevant.

Cases involving attorneys tended to generate a lot of paperwork. Claudia took a red accordion file folder from the supply cabinet and printed out a label with the name *P. Sorensen*, adding QD on the corner of the tab to designate it a 'questioned document.'

Once everything was organized, she opened the folders and spread the documents out on the desk before her.

Okay, Torg, talk to me.

Over the next two hours, Claudia made a meticulous examination of every document Paige had left with her. She began by viewing them under the stereo microscope and taking digital photographs through the trinocular lens port. After she was satisfied with the shots she had taken, she uploaded the pictures onto her computer.

Andrew Nicholson wouldn't even know what button to push, she told herself with satisfaction as she launched the graphics editing program she used for courtroom exhibit prep. Pulling up the photos, she displayed them on-screen, then electronically cut Torg Sorensen's signature from each document and pasted them into a new file that she named *Comparison Chart*. The chart comprised a column of isolated signatures that would make it easy for her to compare each of the known signatures to the one on the will in question.

Next, she magnified each signature on-screen until the tiniest details were exposed, and made notes on differences and similarities. She measured the size of each writing zone and keyed the numbers into a spreadsheet. It was tedious, mind-numbing work, but in the event she was called to testify, the measurements would lay a foundation for her opinion.

Once the numbers were recorded, she ran a formula to find the standard deviation for each measurement. Finally, she measured the relative height of the capital letters, the alignment of the baseline, and space between the names, repeating the process of adding them to the spreadsheet.

Her back and shoulders were getting stiff. She stood and stretched, walked around the office, working out the kinks, ran downstairs to exchange the cold coffee for a cup of sweet mint tea.

The tea boosted her energy, and the break gave her a second wind. After completing her notes about idiosyncrasies in Torg's authentic signatures, she made a new copy of the questioned signature on the will and checked it for similar writing habits.

The next step was to use a tool in the graphics editor to make the questioned signature semi-transparent. Overlaying the transparent copy on each of the known signature standards allowed her to make a direct comparison. Even in cases where a forger was able to make a clever simulation of the pictorial elements of someone's name, the unconscious aspects of the signature could not be copied. It would take a highly skilled forgery to fool Claudia's trained eye, and highly skilled forgeries were rare.

When the phone rang, she welcomed the interruption.

"Claudia, hello! It's Stu Parsons. How're you doing?"

Her first thought was that Paige had called the attorney and asked him to put pressure on her. "Hey, Stu," she said, hiding her suspicions. "Thanks for referring Paige Sorensen. I'm working on her case right now."

"Isn't she a sweetheart?" His tone held genuine affection. "Her husband was a close friend of mine for many years. So, how's the case coming, anyway? I'm counting on you, you know—you're my star witness."

Claudia laughed, a little uneasy with his characterization after the Boris Becket fiasco. "Don't put the onus on me, Stuart. It is what it is. If I can prove her case, I will. No promises."

"I know you'll do a super job," he said. "You always do."

"Thanks for the vote of confidence. I'm glad you called; I've got a question for you. Have the Sorensen children retained their own expert yet?"

This was information Parsons would receive in Discovery—the part of the trial process where each attorney got access to information, documents, and evidence that the other side had accumulated, information that would help the attorney to zero in on the strengths and weaknesses of his or her case.

"Norris hasn't designated an expert," Parsons mused. "And the deadline is past. It's possible he's got someone waiting in the wings for rebuttal, though."

If that were the case, Norris would not have to name the witness until they came to the stand to testify. It could be a sneaky strategy that would prevent Parsons from deposing Norris' expert before the hearing. Not knowing who her opponent was, or whether there would even be one, left Claudia edgy.

They chatted for a few minutes longer, and she gave Stuart Parsons her preliminary findings, with a promise to email the final results to him later in the evening.

After they ended the call she began the next segment of her examination—a careful study of the writing impulse—the movement from each starting point of the pen, where she placed a red dot, to its stopping point, which got another red dot. A green dot went at every turning point and a blue one at every intersecting line. Then she compared the numbers and colors of dots on the questioned signature to the ones on the known signatures.

When she had finished, she printed out her exhibits. She had concluded that the signature on the will was genuine, and that meant she would be on the witness stand next week. The thought made her queasy. One thing she had learned from Boris Becket's case: if you can bamboozle the judge or jury with fancy pretend credentials, it's anybody's game. When it comes to the legal system, there is no sure thing.

The sound of a key in the lock downstairs brought Claudia to her feet. She stretched, surprised at how the shadows had lengthened while she worked. The pool of light from her desk lamp made scarcely a ripple in the dusky office. The computer clock told her that more than two hours had passed since the last time she had gotten out of her chair.

"Up here," she called, moving around the room to flip on some lights. She heard heavy footsteps on the stairs, and a moment later, Joel Jovanic entered the office loosening his tie, his suit coat bunched over his arm.

"Hey, I'm looking for a good handwriting expert."

Claudia started moving toward him. "What are the qualifications?"

A slow smile curved his lips. "Hmm, let's see—great body, long auburn hair, excellent kisser."

She walked into his space and grabbed a handful of his shirt. "C'mere, I'll give you a referral."

25

Fatigue had etched fine lines around his mouth and eyes, but his lips were warm against hers as they melded naturally together. She stroked her fingers along the dusting of stubble darkening his jaw. "Long day?"

"M'hm." He rested his head against her hair and didn't try to hide his yawn. "Starting around four this morning." A detective with LAPD, he was currently working sex crimes.

She slipped her arm through his and led him to the comfortable sofa in a far corner of the office. Her favorite place to rest and recharge her batteries. "A drink?"

"Not yet; I just want to zone out." Jovanic sank into the cushions and stretched his long legs in front of him. "Some people are unbelievably fucked up. Nothing the gas chamber wouldn't cure."

Claudia curled next to him and laid her head on his chest. "Oh, come on, I know there's a soft heart beating in there."

"Don't let that rumor get out, you'll ruin my reputation."

"Want to talk about it?"

"No, I want to forget about it. Tell me about your day instead."

"Oh, you know, the usual—young, beautiful widow inherits elderly husband's estate and the kids are pissed. They're claiming she forged the will."

"Trophy wife?"

"She says she was in love with him," Claudia said. "No, wait, she said she loved him—that's different, isn't it?"

Jovanic closed his eyes and leaned his head back. He gave another wide yawn, once again not bothering to cover it. "So, what happened to the old guy?"

"Massive stroke; he died."

"You sure about the stroke? You don't think the young and beautiful *Mrs.* Old Guy had anything to do with it?"

"You've been a cop too long." Claudia unbuttoned his shirt and slid her hand into the curly thatch of chest hair. "The signatures are consistent with brain damage from a stroke."

"You're positive she didn't put a pillow over his face and give him a little help over the edge?"

She withdrew her hand and gave him a gentle poke in the belly. "Not everyone has a suspicious nature like you, Columbo."

Jovanic reached down and grabbed her ankle. "Is that what

you want—Columbo?" In one quick move he had her on the floor and was straddling her, pinning her arms with his legs. "Gotcha! It's useless to struggle."

Lying on the carpet, she looked up at him with a sly smile. "So, who's struggling?"

He grinned and shifted his weight to release her arms. Tugging her tee shirt free of her jeans, he pulled it off over her head. She raised herself on her elbows and began unbuckling his belt. His eyes were closed, the rise and fall of his breathing accelerating as she worked his zipper. Then his hands were on her shoulders, pulling her up to meet his lips.

The kiss deepened. But the muted ring of his cell phone ruined the moment.

"Goddamn it." He groaned, straightening. He grabbed his coat from the arm of the sofa where he had tossed it and dug his phone out of the pocket. "Yeah? Jovanic."

Claudia rolled onto the sofa, keeping her disappointment to herself. She might as well be involved with a doctor, considering all the times Jovanic had to take calls when they were on the verge of making love.

Just a minute, a little voice in her head mocked. *What about your work?* A forensic conference, a TV interview about some high-profile case, and weekend plans get cancelled.

It had seemed like the ideal relationship a few months ago when they'd reached out to each other like castaways on a deserted island; two self-avowed workaholics, survivors of marriages that had been destroyed by their all-out devotion to work. Now history was repeating itself, and the relationship was taking a backseat to their careers.

Jovanic rose to his feet, the phone pressed to his ear with one hand, the other holding up his trousers. "Anyone else there yet? How's it looking?" And, "Okay, I'll be there in twenty."

He snapped the phone shut and began zipping his trousers, buckling his belt. "That was Alex. We have to blow out of here tonight. Something's developing in San Jose with that porn ring."

Alexandra Vega was Jovanic's new partner. His very charming, very sexy partner. Claudia handed him his tie and jacket and pulled her tee shirt on. "Do you know how long you'll be gone?"

"It's an extradition. The arrangements could take a while. Sorry, babe."

"Anything I can do to help?"

"Thanks." He pulled on the coat, fished out his wallet. "Here's my credit card. Can you get us on a flight tonight? I'll head over to my place and get packed."

"Sure. Need a ride to LAX?"

"Alex is picking me up. We'll leave her car at the airport."

So much for a romantic evening.

CHAPTER 3

Morning brought the marine layer: a damp blanket of cloud cover, a pronounced nip in the air. Mist drifted over the beachfront neighborhood like grey fleece and soaked into the wooden slats of the deck off the living room. Fall had barged in overnight.

Claudia threw on sweats and thick socks before opening the sliding door to the deck, which housed her version of a garden. She loved nature, but had never been much of a gardener. A few herbs in a Mexican clay pot were her consolation prize for the flowers that refused to grow. The greens looked good on the deck and she figured if she ever learned to cook something more complicated than mashed potatoes they would probably taste pretty good, too.

Trimming the dead leaves and watering the soil with her galvanized aluminum watering can gave her some time away from her desk, but as she worked, soaking the roots of the rosemary, basil, meadow rue, and the rest, working bonemeal into the soil of a struggling tomato plant, her mind was still busy with Torg Sorensen's signatures and his widow, Paige, whom she found enigmatic.

The sound of a car engine in the driveway made Claudia straighten and look over the balcony. As if her thoughts had conjured the woman, Paige Sorensen stepped out of a Mercedes. Not the vehicle Bert Falkenberg had driven the day before. Paige's version had a custom paint job the same blue as her eyes.

Claudia wiped her hands on the dishtowel tucked into her

waistband and waited as Paige exited the car alone. No little dog or Bert Falkenberg today. Despite the weather, Paige's long legs were bare, tanned and muscular in khaki shorts and backless high-heeled sandals. In a green silk camp shirt, her long hair drawn back in a ponytail, she looked ready for Club Med.

Paige came up the flagstone path to the house, waving at Claudia. "Hi there, can you spare a few minutes?"

Claudia hesitated. She didn't welcome clients who dropped in unannounced, and she felt at a distinct disadvantage in her gardening clothes and no makeup. Still, she was curious to see which version of Paige had come to visit—the innocent girl, the bereaved widow, or the self-possessed charmer.

"I wasn't expecting you," Claudia said, less than welcoming but not refusing the visit outright.

Ignoring the hint, Paige started up the staircase. "I was hoping for a chance to talk with you privately."

"How about making an appointment?"

"I promise not to stay long. *Please?*"

Claudia looked back her for a moment, then curiosity got the better of her. "Wait a second, I'll come around and unlock the door." She went inside and wiped her feet on the mat, giving herself a disapproving glance in the wall mirror beside the front door.

See what happens when you don't have a real *job? You don't get dressed for the day. Just because you work at home...* Firmly shutting off her mother's voice, Claudia mustered a smile. "Can I get you some coffee?"

"I'd love some," Paige said, following her into the kitchen. She slid onto a chair at the breakfast table while Claudia washed her hands at the sink. "I apologize for dropping in like this."

Claudia busied herself filling the Mr. Coffee with water as Paige plowed on. "I shouldn't have let Bert come with me yesterday. Honestly, he can be downright annoying. I know he's trying to protect me, but he thinks I don't know how to take care of myself."

Claudia took a container of Folgers from the freezer and measured coffee into the filter, thinking that it seemed an odd opening to the conversation.

"Protect you from what?" she asked, watching the amber liquid begin to drip into the carafe, perfuming the air with the smell of fresh coffee.

"My stepchildren." Paige gave a tight little laugh. "Isn't it dumb to call them that? They're all older than me. Anyway, they hate me. Bert says they'll fight to the death to get the estate away from me."

Moving through the routine of getting out mugs and spoons, Claudia wondered—not for the first time—about the role Bert Falkenberg played in Paige's life. Yesterday there had been moments when she'd caught him looking at Paige with desire in his eyes that guaranteed either he was more than just a business advisor, or hoped to be very soon.

Taking the sugar bowl from the pantry, she set it on the table. "It sounds like an awkward situation for everyone. What do you take in your coffee?"

"Nonfat milk?"

"Is nonfat half-and-half okay?"

Paige raised a perfectly penciled brow. "Nonfat *half-and-half?* You're kidding, right?"

"Nope. Made for those of us who like the taste of cream but can't afford the calories." Claudia opened the refrigerator and showed her the carton. "I sound like a TV commercial, don't I?"

Paige smiled. "I'll take some. Calories are not my friend, either."

"It must take a lot of work to stay in as good a shape as you look."

Paige pantomimed lifting weights. "I work out every morning. I have to stay alert to handle the girls."

"Speaking of the girls, how's that one doing? The one who kept calling you yesterday?"

"Annabelle. She'd got into a fight with her roommate; that's what all the calls were about. If someone doesn't see things her way, she has no problem getting physical with them." A note of frustration crept into Paige's voice. "Bert had a chat with her about it last night, but I don't think she's afraid of anything or anyone."

"She's afraid of *something*," Claudia reasoned. "You said she tried to kill herself."

Paige's expression softened. "Poor kid, she's had a lot to deal with. Her mother was killed in a car crash when she was six. Annabelle was in the car, but she was thrown clear."

Automatically, Claudia's heart went out to the girl who had suffered such a traumatic loss. "No wonder she has problems."

"It was big news at the time—I'm sure you saw it on TV. Her mother was Valerie Vale, the actress. Her father is Dominic Giordano."

"The movie producer?"

Paige nodded. "He's the head of Sunmark Studios."

"I do remember the story," Claudia said. It had been a fairytale wedding made for the media—the producer and the starlet. Claudia recalled all the hoopla that surrounded the event. The fairytale had turned tragic a few years later when Vale's car slammed through a guardrail high above Malibu and plunged into the ocean below, leaving behind a young child.

"Annabelle's had plenty of problems. She has trouble making friends and," Paige broke off. She looked down at her hands, appearing suddenly unsure of herself. "Um, Claudia, the reason I came here today—"

Claudia waited, figuring that Paige wanted to plead her case, to make sure she was going to offer the "right" opinion on the questioned signature. If that was it, she would shut her down, fast. In fact, she *had* decided in Paige's favor, but it had to be clear that her opinion was independent of any pressure.

"Yesterday, when I was here, you didn't let Bert push you around." Paige paused, then rushed on. "Well, I got the feeling you were someone I could trust."

"Yes?" Claudia responded cautiously. Paige might trust her, but at this point the feeling was far from mutual. "What is it you're concerned about?"

"It's just—I guess I'm like Annabelle. I don't have anyone I can to talk to either; no one."

"*You* have no friends? I'm not sure I believe that." Claudia got up and went to the refrigerator and filled the creamer jug, then leaned back against the kitchen counter, waiting for the coffee to brew and waiting for what might come next.

"Oh, I have plenty of *acquaintances*. The women at the country club *tolerate* me because I've got money, but they make it obvious I'm not one of them. It's like 'Pretty Woman,' remember that old movie? Julia Roberts gets all dressed up like a perfect ten in gorgeous clothes, but the women at the party make fun of her because she doesn't belong. Well, that's how I feel."

Paige made a wry face. "There's always plenty of men around with their tongues hanging out. But it's not the same as having a girlfriend to talk to and, well, I feel like *we* could be friends." It sounded like she was inviting Claudia to a play date.

Claudia had a policy that said mixing business with friendship was a bad idea, but something about the wistfulness she heard in the other woman's voice intrigued her. "I'm willing to listen," she said, still wary. "But I'm not a therapist."

"I need a *friend*," Paige repeated. "Not a therapist; someone who's not involved with the Sorensen family. Someone who doesn't have any vested interest in what happens with this—" she waved her hand. "This mess I'm in. Someone I can talk to because, basically, I'm scared."

Claudia swung around from the coffee maker, where she had been filling their cups.

"*Scared?* Of what?"

"Not *what. Who.* Torg's son Dane."

"Why? What's he done?"

"He hasn't actually *done* anything; it's just a feeling I have. It's the way he looks at me, it's downright *creepy*." She gazed straight into Claudia's eyes and spoke in a low voice. "I get the feeling he'd love to wrap those big hands around my throat and squeeze the life right out of me."

The dread in her voice prickled Claudia's spine. She couldn't help feeling uneasy, even though she'd never met Dane Sorensen. Taking the chair across from Paige, she wrapped her hands around her mug for the warmth. "You can understand him being upset about the will. You said his father left virtually everything to you."

"It's more than that—I can *feel* it, the way he hates me! He has a twin sister, too. Diana—the Wicked Witch of the West. It's weird; the two of them act more like a married couple than brother and sister. They even share a house."

Claudia sat quietly and waited. She knew the perfect Barbie doll had a less than perfect life, but clearly there was more to the story.

"Bert's right; Dane is dead set on taking the school away from me."

"What does his sister think of that?"

Paige snorted. "Diana thinks being twins gives them some

spooky supernatural link. He makes the decisions and she follows whatever he says."

Claudia wondered again about Paige's motives in showing up with these revelations. "Paige, it sounds like you've got a lot to deal with. But the family dynamics aren't going to affect my opinion on your husband's will."

Paige spread her hands in protest. "I'm not here about that! I *know* you don't need to hear the family dirt. I *know* it makes me look pitiful, but I'm all alone. Honestly, I need a friend."

"What about Mr. Falkenberg? You said he wanted to protect you."

"Not in that way," Paige said, then fell silent.

Claudia waited for her to clarify her comment, but she didn't. "So, you said they're out to get the school?"

"The Sorensen Academy," Paige said, nodding. "It's this enormous old mansion Torg's parents built back in the '20s. Then his father got into trouble in the Depression and went broke, so he turned the house into a school for rich girls. Torg inherited it and kept it going."

No wonder her stepchildren resented her, Claudia thought. Naturally, they would expect to inherit such a place and keep it in the family. But Paige's next words dispelled that happy notion.

"The land up there off Sunset is real hot property. Dane always expected to get his hands on it, and it turned out he already had plans to demolish the place as soon as his father died. He wants to tear it down and build luxury condos. Pretty cold, don't you think?

"He didn't even wait until his father was dead to get an architect and have the blueprints made up. Torg found out about it and went ballistic. The school meant a lot to him, but I think he was more hurt that Dane would do that to him."

"So it's all about money?"

"Dane owns a construction company and Diana sells real estate. They would make a bundle on both ends of the deal if he built those condos."

"Do you have any of his handwriting?" Claudia asked. As a handwriting analyst, she was always curious about personality and the way it revealed itself in the written word.

Paige's eyes widened. "Why?"

"Handwriting reveals what motivates people, and it can help you understand how to deal with them."

"Really? I'd love to know what makes those people tick. I'll see if I can dig some up."

"How did your husband find out what his son had planned?"

For the second time, Paige looked uncomfortable. She paused for a long moment. "Bert used to be Dane's right-hand man."

That could explain the condition of Bert Falkenberg's fingernails and his apparent discomfort with the high quality apparel he wore. Construction seemed to suit him better than an office job.

"Bert was really upset when he found out what Dane planned to do. He thought it was all wrong, that the house and the school should stay in the family. But since Dane was his boss, he couldn't just go and tell Torg about it." She fidgeted in her chair, swinging her leg back and forth like a kid. "He knew I would, though. Maybe I shouldn't have told him. Dane and Torg had this huge fight and then Torg had the stroke. They never spoke to each other again. I feel like it was my fault. If I'd kept my mouth shut, Torg might still be alive."

"Wow," Claudia said, at a loss for words. Then she got it. "Is that how Bert came to work for you?"

Paige nodded. "It got even uglier when Dane found out that Bert had betrayed him. He fired him, of course. I felt responsible, but with Torg so sick I couldn't do anything. Then he passed away." Defiance crept into her voice. "I couldn't handle everything all on my own, and Bert was out of a job, so it worked out well for both of us."

Claudia knew she should tell Paige to stop. If the Sorensen children's attorney asked in open court whether she had any knowledge of the family relationships, she would have to tell the truth. It might appear to be a conflict of interest.

What was it her grandmother used to say? *In for a penny, in for a pound.* At this point it wouldn't make all that much difference.

"Did Torg cut the children out of the will altogether?" she asked.

"Neil got a small trust fund. He's the youngest, and he's disabled, so Torg made sure he'd be taken care of. The twins got some family heirlooms they don't care about."

"Dane does sound like a problem," Claudia said. She sipped her coffee, trying to keep an open mind while Paige sat there looking sweet and pretty, perfectly turned out. But Paige's next words were neither sweet nor pretty.

"I hate the fucking bastard," she blurted. "*I hate him!*"

CHAPTER 4

On the morning of the Sorensen probate hearing Claudia allowed an hour for the seventeen mile drive to the L.A. Superior Courts building on Hill Street. MapQuest had optimistically promised a twenty-minute trip, but the five lanes of brake lights she encountered upon entering the Santa Monica Freeway told her that even an hour wouldn't cut it.

She popped a couple of Rolaids, forced herself to uncurl her knuckles from around the steering wheel, and navigated to the Rosa Parks Freeway, then the Harbor to the Hollywood.

Exiting at the Temple off-ramp, she made her way through the confusing maze of one-way streets to the Dorothy Chandler Pavilion across the street from the courthouse complex.

The Dorothy Chandler provided subterranean parking for those about to enter the hungry maw of the L.A. County legal system. On any other day, Claudia would have parked in an uncovered lot on Olive, south of First, and walked back to the courthouse, but the clock had run out ten minutes ago and she was late for her pre-hearing briefing with Stuart Parsons. It felt like a bad omen.

Turning the Jaguar into the garage she made a rapid circuit of the street level, her hopes of easy parking soon dashed. The roof seemed to press down on her, awakening an old fear of being trapped as she drove down the ramp into the cement bowels of the earth.

Level two, *Zip.* Three, *Zilch.*

On level four she spotted backup lights near the end of the next row over. Turning the corner she braked halfway down the row, leaving the driver plenty of room to back out.

From behind came the sudden sound of squealing tires turning too fast on the slick cement floor. Claudia instinctively hunched her shoulders and tightened her grip on the wheel, waiting for the impact.

A streak of silver filled her rearview mirror for an instant, then a small car roared past and slipped into the newly vacated space. Claudia stared at the vintage Aston Martin in disbelief, then anger, as a man in a tweed jacket climbed out of the car.

Tall, broad shouldered, his hair was a tawny mane that brushed his collar. A tie hung loose around his open-necked shirt. She lowered the window and leaned out.

"Hey, what the hell?"

The man took off at a jog toward the elevators, throwing a contemptuous grin over his shoulder. "Tough shit, babe. You snooze, you lose."

Still furious at the rude man, Claudia made a mad dash to join the long line of courthouse visitors waiting to get through security. Twenty or so people ahead, some idiot's pocket change set off the metal detector.

Goddamn it!

Had the hearing started yet? She was scheduled to be the first witness. She checked her watch—twenty minutes late. The judge would be pissed; the attorneys would be pissed. She could imagine Paige biting her expensive acrylics to the quick. She'd sent a text to Stuart Parsons, but he hadn't responded and she didn't know whether he'd gotten the message.

The line shuffled forward like slugs on the sidewalk, then it started to rain.

An omen? How about a prophecy of doom?

Still cursing the jerk who had stolen her parking space, Claudia blamed him for the water spots staining the tan leather of her briefcase, and for her lank hair. If she hadn't had to spend extra time looking for parking, she would have missed the rain.

She made it through the metal detector at 10:15.

Any reasonable person would understand that traffic snarls were beyond her control, Claudia assured herself, pressed behind a half-dozen other silent riders in the stale coffee-and-cigarettes-smelling elevator. She'd even left home early. She dabbed her hair with a tissue, wishing she'd taken the stairs; wishing she'd swallowed a tranquilizer; wishing this day were behind her.

Judge Harold Krieger glared right at her as she entered the courtroom twenty minutes late. At the counsel table on the Defendant side, Paige Sorensen and Stuart Parsons turned to look at her. Relief registered on both faces.

"Is this the witness we've been waiting for, counsel?" Judge Krieger inquired pointedly as she took a seat in the back row. No time to catch her breath.

"Yes, Your Honor. We'd like to call Claudia Rose."

With a deep inhale, Claudia gripped her briefcase and rose, the theater-style seat giving a loud *whup-whup.*

In the front row of the gallery a woman twisted around and fixed her with an angry scowl. Smoldering, hooded eyes in a broad, square face. This had to be Diana, one of the Sorensen twins. She was seated next to a wheelchair that was parked at the end of the row, and Claudia remembered Paige saying that Neil, the youngest Sorensen, was disabled.

Diana Sorensen jerked around to face the judge. Her black crepe jacket seemed to strain at the seams, as if her animosity bulged against her skin, struggling to break through her clothes. Her father's widow was the enemy, and by extension, so was the handwriting expert she had retained to represent her.

Claudia could feel the woman's gaze burning into her back as she maneuvered around the wheelchair. She pushed through the swinging gate that separated the gallery from the counsel table, her nerves twanging like an overstrung guitar.

The bailiff stood up and faced her. "Face the clerk and raise your right hand," he said after Claudia ascended the two steps to the witness stand.

She spelled out her name for the record and promised to tell the truth. Then she sat down and placed her briefcase on the table. She took out the exhibit book she'd made over the weekend for the judge and the attorneys, and arranged her notes in front of her, using the time to calm herself.

Inhale deeply through the nose. Hold for a count of six. Breathe out slowly through the mouth for a count of four. Ball the hands into tight fists until the tension travels all the way up to the shoulder muscles, then let go. In, two-three-four-five-six. Hold it. Out, two-three-four.

Claudia swung the microphone close to her mouth, waiting for Stuart Parsons to begin voir dire. Her eyes roamed around the courtroom, taking in the half-dozen spectators and the parties occupying the counsel table.

On the plaintiff's side, a man was whispering to his attorney. He looked up at her; with a shock, Claudia realized he was the jerk from the parking garage. The man in the Aston Martin was Dane Sorensen.

She stared at Dane, who stared boldly back. She doubted he even realized that she was the driver of the old white Jaguar whose space he had stolen.

The Sorensen twins' facial resemblance was strong, yet their coloring was quite different. Diana's face was pale, her hair straight and dyed jet black, giving her a Morticia Addams look. Dane was ruddy; his grey-flecked hair flew in all directions in untidy wisps, as if his comb had attracted static.

He looks tough. As if he grew up in a bad neighborhood, hanging out on street corners picking fights, not in a mansion off Sunset Boulevard. It was easy to see why Paige was afraid of him.

Claudia glanced at the occupant of the wheelchair. He had the face of an aesthete. Translucent skin, sad eyes trained on the back of Paige's head. Limp blond curls, forehead beaded with sweat. Despite the mild fall weather a blue and red plaid blanket covered his legs and he was bundled into a cable knit fisherman's sweater. His hands gripped a dark blue Dodgers cap in his lap.

Stuart Parsons rose and took a moment to fasten his coat. He was about seventy with sharp blue eyes and thick, sensual lips in a pudgy pink face. Dandruff flecked the lapels of his dark pinstripe suit and his shoes were scuffed, not spit-shined, as one might expect from a lawyer in the five-hundred dollar an hour range. But that was his personal courtroom theatrics, and Claudia knew from past experience that he was far sharper than he might appear to the casual observer.

Parsons smiled at her and nodded. "Good morning, Ms. Rose. Would you please begin by telling us your occupation?"

"I am a handwriting examiner."

"Thank you. And were you retained to examine some handwriting in the matter before the court today?"

"Yes, I was asked to compare known signatures of Torg Sorensen to the signature on a will that is being challenged."

"Ms. Rose, were you paid for your appearance in court today?"

"Yes."

"Were you paid to express any particular opinion in this matter?"

"My opinion is not for sale. I'm paid for my time and expertise."

"Okay, good. Now, let's talk about how you became a handwriting expert."

There was no jury to impress at this hearing. The judge alone would decide the outcome of the proceedings, and it was up to Parsons to show him why his expert was credible.

He walked Claudia through her qualifications. The list was long, and he was meticulous. They covered her education and training, publications and research, papers she had presented at conferences, and media appearances.

When he asked about awards she had received, the Sorensen's lawyer, Frank Norris, interrupted. "Your Honor, we'll stipulate that Ms. Rose is an expert. Let's get on with it."

Judge Krieger, already looking bored, nodded. "Fine, so stipulated."

Parsons had informed Claudia that the judge was retiring at the end of the month. Sorensen versus Sorensen would be one of the last cases he heard in his courtroom and it showed.

"Thank you, Your Honor," Parsons said. He strolled to the lectern and placed his notes on the book stand. "Ms. Rose, would you please tell us what a questioned document is, and explain to the Court your method of examining one."

Claudia turned and addressed the judge. "I'll be glad to. In this case, a questioned document means that the authenticity of a signature is in dispute." She went on to explain all the steps she had taken in her examination of Torg Sorensen's handwriting and the questioned signature.

Norris' pen flew furiously across a yellow legal pad as she spoke and Claudia wished she could see his handwriting. He stood six-three; even seated he was imposing in his sober grey suit. His dark hair was slicked back, a little too heavy on the gel.

Claudia had seen Norris in action before and knew he used a condescending style of cross-examination that made him a good candidate for prick of the month. She did her best to ignore him and not wonder what he was writing, or what it would mean for her. Lawyer jokes started buzzing in her head like a swarm of annoying gnats:

What's ten thousand lawyers at the bottom of the ocean? A good start.

What's the difference between a catfish and a lawyer? One's a bottom dwelling, scum sucking scavenger; the other's a fish.

She forced her attention back to Stuart Parsons, who had been searching his notes for something but was now asking her a question.

"How many of Mr. Sorensen's actual signatures did you examine?"

"A total of fifty-seven signatures, which were represented to me as genuine."

This was the easy part. She was beginning to relax, hitting her stride now. Reading through her notes, she described in detail the handwriting samples Paige had supplied for her examination.

"And what did you discover regarding the way Mr. Sorensen signed his name?"

This was her chance to give the judge a mini lesson in handwriting examination.

"No person signs his or her name exactly alike twice, so it's important to first establish a range of personal variation. In other words, we need to know how many different ways a writer forms his or her signatures by examining a large number of them. I did this with Mr. Sorensen's signatures and found that he maintained a high degree of consistency over a long period of time. Under microscopic examination, it was clear to me that even in the signatures made *after* his stroke, where there was tremendous deterioration in the writing, his personal writing characteristics remained largely the same."

After that, Parsons got down to the nitty-gritty, asking her to demonstrate her findings. Claudia handed the exhibit books to the bailiff who distributed them to the attorneys, their clients, and the judge. She had made a series of enlargements of the signatures, both the genuine ones and the questioned one on the will, illustrating the differences she had found with colored arrows and circles.

She did her damnedest to keep her explanation snappy and interesting, but about ten minutes into her testimony, Judge Krieger yawned pointedly, and she could hear his stomach grumbling from behind the bench. It was no surprise when five minutes later he suggested that Parsons wrap up his direct examination. Claudia had been on the stand for the better part of an hour.

The lawyer's bushy white brows drew together into a frown. "Well, okay, Your Honor. I do have one last thing, if I may." He paused for a long moment, glancing over his notes and then at Claudia before asking his question.

"Ms. Rose, did you reach a conclusion regarding Torg Sorensen's signature on the California Statutory Will?"

"Yes, I did," said Claudia, leaning into the microphone. "In my professional opinion, the signature on the will is consistent with the standards I used for comparison. I have no doubt that the signature is genuine."

CHAPTER 5

Anyone who said they enjoyed cross-examination is either a masochist or a liar.

Claudia watched Frank Norris push back his chair and approach the lectern. It was after the lunch break and the attorney for the Sorensen clan was about to do his best to make Claudia look stupid. It was her job not to help him. A herd of butterflies in elephant boots danced the tarantella in her stomach.

Someone had left a pitcher and a hermetically-sealed glass on the table in front of her, but she didn't touch them. She refused to let Norris see her sweat, although her mouth was as parched as the Mojave in August.

God, I hate this part.

She put on her game face and inhaled a calming breath, hoping she appeared more relaxed than she felt. Paige looked like she might jump out of her skin, and who could blame her—her financial future was riding on Judge Krieger's ruling. On Claudia's testimony.

No pressure.

Norris made a big production of gathering his notes, then strolled to the lectern as casually as if there were no place he would rather be. He glanced down at his legal pad, then at Claudia. For several long seconds he stood there looking at her, saying nothing.

Intimidation tactics.

"Ms. Rose," he said at last in a lazy drawl. "Earlier, we heard you testify about a *range of variation*. That's what you called it, am

I right?"

"Yes."

"Well, let me ask you, in all your *many years of experience*—would you say there is generally a group of people who have a tendency to write their signature virtually the same way on nearly every occasion?"

"Signatures are an individual matter. Some people write virtually the same every time, some don't."

"Well then, are there individuals, *in your experience*, who will write their signature remarkably different over a period of time?"

"Again, it depends on the individual. Some signatures have a greater range of variation than others."

What do lawyers use as contraceptives? Their personalities. If Norris's personality were bottled, the population explosion could be squashed in a month.

Frank Norris cleared his throat. "Well, would you say that older people—maybe people in their seventies, who learned to write at a particular time in history, write significantly the same way?"

Claudia knew at once where Norris was going. He was implying that a man of Torg Sorensen's age would stick to the way he had been taught in school because, back then, penmanship was a big deal. When Torg went to grade school, knuckle-rapping to produce perfect cursive was SOP. Nowadays, the ACLU would crawl all over any teacher who used a ruler on a kid's knuckles if their running ovals weren't up to par.

"I have to repeat, Mr. Norris, it's an individual matter that cannot be generalized."

He removed his eyeglasses and stared at her with a challenging expression. "Okay then. In looking at the fifty—what was it, fifty-seven documents?"

"Yes, fifty-seven."

"The fifty-seven documents; did you find *any* differences in the known documents?"

"As I testified this morning, there was a small range of variation between the known signatures—some minor differences."

"And in looking at the questioned document, was there a range of variation in the *alleged* signature of Torg Sorensen on the will?"

"There can't be a *range* of variation in one signature."

"Well, Ms. Rose, looking at the questioned signature, don't you think the 'T' in the name 'Torg' is quite different from the exemplars you examined?"

"There's a slight difference, but a difference in the way a capital letter is formed is far less important than the many *similarities*, including—"

It wasn't what Norris wanted to hear and he cut her off.

Parsons interrupted from his seat. "Objection, Your Honor. Counsel asked a question. He should allow the witness to respond."

Claudia waited for Judge Krieger to rule on the objection. He shuffled some papers and nodded at her. "Go on, Ms. Rose, you may finish your answer."

She decided to take advantage of the opportunity to give the judge another mini lesson in handwriting examination. "I was saying that there are far more important aspects of handwriting than just the way the capital letters look." On the bench, Judge Krieger leaned forward, paying attention now.

"The spacing, proportions and other more important *unconscious* factors, like letter and word impulse in the questioned signature, are virtually *identical* to the known signatures, even though the letter forms—like his capital 'T'—were affected by his physical condition due to the stroke."

Claudia saw it on Norris' face when he realized he had shot himself in the foot. Smart lawyers never ask a question to which they don't already have the answer. He frowned. "All right now, Ms. Rose. You received the California Statutory Will with the *alleged* signature of Mr. Sorensen—the questioned document—from where?"

"From my client, Mrs. Sorensen."

"And do you know where Mrs. Sorensen obtained it?"

"No."

"So, it's possible that Mrs. Sorensen could have signed it herself, isn't it?"

"Objection!" Stuart Parsons snapped. "There's no foundation for counsel to draw that conclusion."

Judge Krieger heaved a dramatic sigh. "Sustained." He removed his glasses and rubbed the bridge of his nose as if trying to hold on to his last thread of patience. "Grandstanding isn't called for, Mr.

Norris. There's no jury here, and if there were, you'd be in trouble."

"I'll withdraw the question." Norris' lip curled into a smirk. "Ms. Rose, isn't it true that you're not a *real* handwriting expert at all. You're *just* a graphologist, aren't you?"

Claudia waited for Parsons to object, but he was whispering to Paige and had failed to hear the attack. She was on her own.

"I've been accepted as a handwriting expert in more than fifty trials in superior, criminal and federal courts," she said, looking Norris directly in the eye. "Graphology is a specialty of handwriting examination concerned with behavioral profiling. It's a separate part of my practice from document examination, and I did not use graphology in forming my opinion in this case."

He showed an insincere flash of teeth. "I see. Tell us, have you had any law enforcement training? Or training in an accepted forensic document-examining laboratory?"

Despite the pleasure it would have given her to knock the shit-eating grin off his face, she kept her tone cool. "There is no state or federal requirement to train in a specific lab."

"Objection." That was Parsons, tuning in at last. "Your Honor, it's my recollection that Mr. Norris already stipulated to Ms. Rose's expertise. It's not fair for him to question it now."

Judge Krieger's hangdog features sharpened. "That's right, he did. Mr. Norris, do you have any *other* questions of this witness?"

"Yes, Your Honor, thank you. Ms. Rose, if you don't even know where your client obtained the document, how can you testify as to its authenticity?"

"I was given a series of signatures that were represented to me as undisputed to use for comparison to the questioned signature. As far as I know, no one has suggested that those signatures were not genuine. It was my job simply to compare the handwriting, not to identify where the documents came from." She used the authoritative tone she sometimes adopted when guest-lecturing a college class.

"I formed a preliminary opinion based on a photocopy, but later I visited the courthouse where the original will was filed, and looked at it under a portable microscope. I photographed it, then I redid my examination and found that it supported my earlier opinion."

"No further questions of this witness."

"Thank you, Ms. Rose, you may step down."

Claudia gathered her things and stepped off the dais, almost giddy with relief that Norris had let her off easy. His next words dispelled the notion that it was because she'd done such a bang-up job.

"Your Honor, at this time we would like to call a rebuttal witness to the stand."

"All right, Mr. Norris, who is your witness?"

"He's waiting outside in the hallway. I'd like to call Andrew Nicholson."

Andy Nicholson! Of all people.

Parsons grabbed Claudia's arm as she went to move past the counsel table. "Do you know him?"

It was a little late to ask. Without offering written proof that Andy was more or less impersonating an expert, Parsons' options were limited.

Angling her body so that her back was to the gallery, Claudia leaned close to Parsons' ear and cupped a hand around her mouth. "You can impeach him, but the materials are in my office. Can you ask for a recess?"

"Mr. Parsons?" The judge prodded.

"A moment please, Your Honor." Parsons spoke into Claudia's ear in a rapid whisper. "Krieger will never allow a recess. You'll have to coach me during this guy's testimony. That's the best we can do."

Parsons motioned to his paralegal, who gave up her chair at the table; Claudia slid into it.

"Your Honor," Norris whined, his hands spread in protest. "I'm going to object to this witness sitting at the counsel table. It's crowded enough here as it is."

Parsons half-stood, leaning on the table. "Judge, I ask leave of the court to allow this witness to assist me. We were not expecting this rebuttal witness. Ms. Rose is an expert. I'm *not* an expert in the field of handwriting analysis."

Judge Krieger rolled his eyes and spoke in a tone one might use on a four-year-old. "Everyone can move over. She can sit at the table. Mr. Norris, give counsel a copy of your expert's curriculum vitae and call the witness."

A tall, good-looking blond with more Scandinavian blood than his clients, gossip had it that Andy Nicholson would point the finger at his own mother for a big enough chunk of change. His less charitable colleagues whispered that Andy was sleeping his way to success with both genders.

He had dressed for court in a knockout Hugo Boss charcoal pinstripe suit and pale grey satin tie. Taking the chair Claudia had vacated, Andy crossed one knife-sharp pleated pants leg over the other and clasped his long, slender hands on the table in front of him.

He's trying to impress the judge, Claudia thought, cursing him for looking so relaxed.

"Mr. Nicholson," Frank Norris began, his tone respectful as it had not been when he questioned Claudia. "Would you please tell the Court about your background in the field of handwriting examination."

Andy threw a captivating smile at Judge Krieger. "I'd be delighted to, Mr. Norris. Okay, I learned handwriting analysis in Switzerland, and I've been doing this for about twenty-five years now. I teach document examination to the CIA and the FBI, and I've written several textbooks."

Listening to the same old lies he'd gotten away with for so many years, Claudia had to fight to contain her rising fury. It shouldn't have been personal, but it was.

"I have a Master's in Psychology, and I've been teaching at USC for about twenty years. Let's see, I've been a member of the American Society of Handwriting Examination for ten years. I'm board certified by them."

Scribbling on Stuart Parsons' notepad, Claudia shoved it at him.

He took a tour *of the FBI. No Master's. Taught graphology in adult ed ten years ago, not document exam.*

"In those twenty-five years, have you ever been called to testify in court?" Frank Norris asked.

"Oh yes, Mr. Norris, many times."

"About how many?"

"Oh, I don't know, hundreds! Maybe thousands."

"Offer this witness as an expert, Your Honor."

Judge Krieger nodded. "Any objection, Mr. Parsons?"

All Stuart Parsons could do was shrug. "I'd like to reserve the issue of Mr. Nicholson's qualifications, Judge."

The trouble was, Andy's supposed background *sounded* so good, he spoke with such confidence, that few attorneys thought to challenge him. With a judge like Krieger, who made it obvious that he would rather be on the golf course than the bench, he might be inclined to give Andy's testimony more credence than Claudia's. Unless Parsons could sweat Andy into admitting his lies, they were dead in the water.

Keeping one ear on Andy's testimony, Claudia took a legal pad from her briefcase and began scribbling a list of questions for Parsons to use in his cross-examination. Meanwhile, Norris was beginning his direct, asking Andy about the signatures he had examined.

"I examined *hundreds* of Mr. Sorensen's signatures. *None* of them matched the one on the will." He unrolled the exhibit he had brought with him to the stand: photocopied enlargements of a handful of signatures.

In a rambling fashion Andy explained his rationale for his opinion, concluding, "It was obvious to me that the signature on the will did *not* match the standards."

Despite the rambling and the lack of reasoning, he sounded convincing.

"Mr. Nicholson, do you find the questioned signature at all similar to the standards?"

"Well, yes, Mr. Norris, and I can understand how Ms. Rose might think it was written by the same person. But you could put the questioned signature next to any one of these other signatures, and they are also very similar, except none of them have exactly this kind of 'T', as I pointed out in my exhibits. Therefore, I declare that this signature is a forgery."

Only the judge can declare it a forgery, jackass.

Parsons bumped his foot against Claudia's under the table. "You've got smoke coming out of your ears," he whispered. "Relax, I'll take care of him."

Norris said he had no further questions and Stuart Parsons rose from the defendant's table. He buttoned his jacket, took Claudia's notepad to the lectern, and turned to face Andy. "Mr. Nicholson, have you taken any courses or workshops specifically related to your duties as a handwriting examiner?"

"Sure, I've taken lots of them."

"Specific to document examination?"

"Well, sure." His eyes darted down and to the left, a sign that he was lying.

"Objection," Norris said, using the same line that Parsons had earlier used on him. "Mr. Nicholson has already been accepted as an expert."

Before the judge could respond, Parsons interrupted. "Your Honor, since this witness didn't appear on the Plaintiff's witness list, I had no opportunity to depose him or check out his credentials ahead of time."

"All right, Mr. Parsons," Krieger said. "I'll give you some leeway, but move it along."

"Thank you, Your Honor. Mr. Nicholson, have you ever attended a conference given by the Scientific Association of Forensic Examiners?"

"I've been to Association of Industrial Security meetings."

"Is that a handwriting examination organization?"

"Many of the members use handwriting analysis."

"I remind you, Mr. Nicholson, you're under oath and you have to answer truthfully. I'm going to repeat my question: have you *ever* attended any conferences of the Scientific Association of Forensic Examiners?"

Andy fidgeted in his seat, knowing that Claudia attended the NADE conference and would be aware if he failed to tell the truth. "Uh—no."

"Have you attended any meetings where handwriting authentication was taught?"

"I've taught handwriting analysis at many meetings."

Parsons gave him a cold stare. "Answer the question. You are under oath, Mr. Nicholson. Have you ever attended any conferences or seminars where the examination of questioned documents for handwriting authentication was taught?"

Andy squirmed a little. "It's all part of the same—"

"Answer the question."

"But I was just—"

"You have to answer the question," Judge Krieger interjected, frowning at Nicholson over the tops of his glasses. He turned away and typed something into his laptop.

"Are you saying you have *not* attended any professional meetings or conferences solely for handwriting examiners and that are *not* related to graphology?"

"Well—"

"What scientific journals do you read that are specifically relevant to your job as a document examiner?"

"I, uh, there are lots of them."

Parsons reeled off the list of professional journals Claudia had noted for him, and got Andy to admit that he hadn't read any of them. She almost felt sorry for him. He would be lucky if he didn't face a charge of perjury.

"Mr. Nicholson, you've listed the American Society of Forensic Examination on your curriculum vitae and claim you've been a member for ten years. It's true, isn't it, that the ASFE has been in existence for less than five years?"

"That's—they…"

"It's also true, is it not, that you claim to have taken courses with the American Society of Forensic Examination?"

"I did take their courses."

"The fact is, Mr. Nicholson, you never did take any of their courses. Isn't that correct?"

"Of course I did."

"Isn't it true that you ordered their basic course, but returned it unopened and demanded a refund?"

Andy opened and closed his mouth a couple of times, resembling an unhappy trout snagged on a hook. He stared at Frank Norris, helpless. Norris stared back. Apparently this was all news to him.

That'll teach him for not checking out his expert, Claudia thought with some satisfaction. She had discovered for herself that every claim Andrew Nicholson made on his curriculum vitae was either grossly inflated or a fabrication. Yet, somehow, he had gotten away with it for years.

Judge Krieger gave Andy a dark look and ordered him to respond.

"Yes, but I—"

"Mr. Nicholson," Parsons was on a roll. "Did you happen to bring with you the 'hundreds of samples' of Mr. Sorensen's signature that you claim to have examined in this case?"

Andy looked abashed. "Counsel might have them."

"Have you listed anywhere all those *hundreds* of signatures in a report so it can be verified that you actually did examine 'hundreds' of them?"

Bright splotches of red appeared on Andy's cheeks and on his neck around his Adam's apple. "No, but I—"

Parsons spoke over him and Norris didn't bother to object. "So the handful of exemplars that you've produced for us today in your Exhibit, these are the ones that you've selected for his Honor to look at. Am I right?"

"Yes."

"Then we have no way of knowing that you did examine 'hundreds' of signatures because you only brought these few?"

With a disgusted glance at his witness, Norris found his voice. "Objection, Mr. Parsons is testifying."

"Is there a question in there somewhere for the witness, Mr. Parsons?" Krieger asked.

"Yes, your Honor. Mr. Nicholson, what method did you use to compare the signatures?"

"I put them under magnification and I eyeballed them."

"Did you take any measurements?"

"I didn't need—"

"Did you compare the signatures by laying one over the other?"

"With all my experience, I don't need to do that."

Parsons raised his eyebrows and made an 'O' of his mouth, pretending to be impressed. "Why, that's very clever of you, Mr. Nicholson. Other experts in your field feel they need to take measurements and do comparisons, but your testimony is that you do not?"

"Objection. No foundation."

"Overruled."

"What do you know about Mr. Torg Sorensen's physical condition at the time he signed the will?"

Norris half-rose. "Objection. It hasn't been determined that Mr.

Sorensen signed the will."

"Overruled. Answer the question."

From the corner of her eye Claudia noticed Paige on the other side of Parson's empty seat trying to get her attention. Turning her head, she caught the tiny smile on the corner of Paige's mouth, and gave a slight nod of acknowledgment.

"His physical condition?"

"Yes. Did you ask your client about any medical issues?"

"Uh…"

"How old was Mr. Sorensen when he passed away?"

"Uh…" Andy Nicholson glanced over at Dane Sorensen. It was easy to see him making a quick calculation in his head. "Around sixty, I believe."

"Seventy-three," Stuart Parsons said pleasantly. "Were you aware that Mr. Sorensen had suffered a series of strokes?"

Nicholson glared over at his client. "No, they never told me that."

"Did you ask?"

"I don't recall."

Parsons nodded as if the answer was what he had expected. He continued, relentless. "Are you familiar with the literature in your field? For example, *Scientific Examination of Questioned Documents* by Ordway Hilton, or *Questioned Documents* by Albert Osborne?"

"Of course I am," Andy said, cocky, now that he could answer a question without fudging. "I have both those books. In fact, I brought a list of all the handwriting books I own, if you'd care to see it."

"Does Ordway Hilton or Albert Osborne, or any other authority in your field suggest that the correct procedure is to 'eyeball a document' in order to make such an important conclusion, Mr. Nicholson?"

"Well—"

"You do accept Hilton and Osborne as authorities?"

Andy straightened his tie, looking uncomfortable. "Of course I do."

"Then how can you say you accept them as authorities if you don't know what they say on such an important matter?"

Andy struggled for an answer that wouldn't make him look like a fool. In the end, in a peeved tone, he said, "I can't be expected to know everything they say."

"No further questions of this witness."

CHAPTER 6

The judge adjourned the Sorensen hearing for the day at the afternoon break. Paige's team huddled in the hallway outside the courtroom.

Bert Falkenberg, waiting to be called as a witness, had been relegated to the hallway for most of the day. Shortly before the recess he had taken the stand to testify that he had watched Torg Sorensen sign his will. Claudia thought Stuart Parsons' direct went well. Norris had reserved cross-examination for later. Now Bert stood at Paige's side, looking distracted.

"How do you think it went today?" Paige asked her attorney, linking her arm through his.

Stuart Parsons gave his client a fond smile, giving her hand a fatherly pat. "Bert did fine, Claudia was superb, and we beat Nicholson to a pulp. Let's hope tomorrow goes as well. Now, I suggest you go and have a glass of wine, relax, and forget about the case for the rest of the day."

"Come with us?"

Parsons shook his head. "I have to get back to the office."

"How about you?" Paige asked, turning to Claudia. "Buy you a drink?"

"That's an offer I can't refuse," Claudia said. Even the check Bert Falkenberg had handed her a moment ago failed to neutralize the stress of testifying. She could as easily have stood in the truck lane of the freeway and waited for a semi to mow her down as face another cross-examination right now.

"See you later, Bert," Paige said, dismissing him. "Stuart will give you a ride back, won't you, Stu?"

The attorney leaned over to drop a kiss on her cheek. Bert offered a mocking salute and clicked his heels together like a Nazi general acknowledging his commanding officer.

As the two men and Parsons' paralegal made their way down the corridor toward the elevators, the door to the courtroom swung open and Diana Sorensen swept through. Andy Nicholson followed, holding the door for Dane, who was piloting his brother's wheelchair.

Catching sight of Claudia and Paige standing by the long windows overlooking the courthouse mall, Diana marched over to them and thrust her wide, angry face close to Paige's.

"You thieving bitch," she shouted. "You *won't* get away with this!"

All chatter in the hallway ceased as people seated outside the courtrooms turned to stare. Dane Sorensen braked the wheelchair, strode back and seized his twin's arm. "Don't waste your time on those goddamn bloodsuckers, Di. They're not worth the dynamite to blow 'em all to hell."

Bloodsuckers. Including Claudia in the cheap shot.

Diana made an angry huffing sound, but allowed herself to be led away, leaving a spate of insults in her wake. Neil Sorensen remained silent during the exchange, his face hidden beneath the bill of his baseball cap as Dane wheeled him away.

"Nice family," Claudia murmured.

Paige's cheeks were stained scarlet. "Yeah, nice like the Borgias."

Andy Nicholson, who had watched from the courtroom door, sauntered over to Claudia and leaned in close. "Don't expect to win," he said in a low voice, so that no one but she could detect the sneer.

She stared back at him with distaste. "Yeah? Why's that, hotshot?"

"Remember last time," he said. "I'll *always* kick your ass."

Claudia crooked her finger, beckoning him even closer. When he bent down, she whispered in his ear, "Andy, go fuck yourself."

He looked stunned for a moment, then his lips twisted into a cocky smirk and she turned away, annoyed with herself for giving in to her temper. She was supposed to be a professional, which meant she shouldn't have reacted to his goading.

"Let's take the stairs," she said to Paige. "I'm not sharing an elevator with him."

The Downtown Brewery was a generic kind of restaurant where lawyers hung out between court sessions—dark, lots of leather, the redolence of liquor. They settled into a couple of club chairs in the bar. Claudia ordered a screwdriver; Paige, Jack and Coke, neat.

"I can't stand that Norris guy," Paige said with a little shiver. "How could you sit there so calmly and let him go after you like that?"

Claudia laughed, unwilling to admit how uptight she'd been. "I pictured him naked, with a teeny weenie." Then she got serious. "I hope the judge saw through Nicholson's b.s."

"How does someone like that get to testify as an expert? He came off as a total phony."

"The sad truth is, Andy's been challenged before, but he's gotten away with inflating his credentials for years."

"But *how*?"

"There's no state or federal licensing of handwriting experts, which means there are no controls. If the opposing attorney doesn't check out his claims and bring written proof to the judge that he's perjured himself, or else get him to admit he's lied, like Stuart did today, an Andy Nicholson can keep on testifying and get away with it."

"But that's against the law."

Claudia's lips twisted into a cynical smile. "Yes, it is. And it happens all the time."

"That's downright frightening," Paige said, crossing her slim legs as a pair of good-looking suits passed close to their table. Although the movement was subtle, Claudia caught the slight motion of her skirt as it twitched upward a touch. One of the suits turned and gave her an appreciative second glance.

The waitress flew by, tossed a couple of cocktail napkins on the table and left their drinks. Paige raised her glass to Claudia. "You were awesome today," she said. "Thank you."

Claudia smiled and bumped Paige's glass with her own. "Let truth prevail."

Paige echoed her words and swallowed some of her drink. "I wish I could light up," she said. "I don't smoke very often, but this lawsuit is making me twitchy."

"Court can do that to you."

"I wish Torg had told me about what he was going to do. At least I would have been prepared."

"How long were you married?"

"We met three years ago in Clovis, up in the Central Valley. Ever hear of it?"

Claudia didn't mind admitting that she had not. The vodka felt like a silk scarf caressing her throat as she began to unwind.

Paige gave her a lopsided smile. "I didn't think you would. I grew up in a trailer park there. It was the kind of town where they rolled up the sidewalks at eight o'clock, and the trailer park was definitely on the wrong side of the tracks. It's different now that it merged with Fresno. They're both booming.

"Anyway, there I was, teaching kindergarten and going crazy from boredom. I wanted more out of life, you know what I mean? I thought I *deserved* more." She stared at the glass in her hand. "Be careful what you wish for."

"How did you and Torg meet?"

"He owned a truck dealership in town. Some of the dealers got together and decided to hold a beauty contest. To tell the truth, it was more of a wet tee shirt contest. They were looking to bring in some business. First prize was a thousand bucks and a trip to L.A. I'd have done just about anything to get away. So I entered."

"Don't tell me—you won."

"I sure did. Torg was one of the judges in the contest. So I won and I came to L.A. and he hosted the weekend. Took me to Spago, clubbing at the hot spots."

"I guess he must have been in good shape."

Paige nodded. "He took good care of himself. He was handsome, a real charmer—Hugh Grant type, you know, but older."

"Maybe more like *Cary* Grant."

"Oh yeah," Paige agreed. "Cary Grant. After a couple of dates he said he was in love with me, that he wanted me in his life. I was attracted to him, too, of course."

Watching her closely, Claudia wondered how much the attraction had to do with the size of Torg Sorensen's bank account and the prospect of a glamorous life in L.A. She'd handled her share of cases where an older man had been taken in by a younger woman.

But that wasn't fair. She didn't know Paige well enough to make that kind of value judgment. Setting her glass on the table, Claudia gave Paige her full attention as she continued her story.

"Torg could be so persuasive. One weekend, about a month after we started seeing each other, he took me to Las Vegas and we got married at the Bellagio. It was amazing—he couldn't do enough to please me. Expensive jewelry, beautiful clothes, the Mercedes. He took me to Europe. All I had to do was say I wanted something, and the next thing I knew, it was being delivered.

"It's just, he was so insecure about the age difference. He'd talk about how proud he was that I was with him, then he'd go nuts when men my age looked at me. Pretty soon it got so it felt like I was in prison. He made me account for every second we were apart. Every time I walked out the door he would start texting or calling me, wanting to know who I was with, what I was doing." She broke off and dabbed a tear that welled up and threatened to overflow. "I'll tell you one thing, Claudia: marry for money, and you can expect to earn every dime."

So Jovanic had been right when he called Paige a trophy wife. Did she realize what she had just admitted?

"Were his children opposed to the marriage from the beginning?"

"What do *you* think? They hated me before we even met. When Torg was around they'd pretend to be polite because they didn't want to piss him off, but behind his back they were horrible—spiteful, malicious. The twins, anyway. Neil was always different. That was before his accident."

"This is beginning to sound like a nighttime soap."

"Just wait, there's more. After a while, I got tired of being a lady of leisure, so I asked if I could go to work at the school. It's grade eight through twelve, but I have teacher training, so I thought maybe I could be an aide or something.

"So Torg turns around and makes me headmistress—the rules are different for private schools, so he could, even though I don't have a degree in education. That's when the shit hit the fan. Diana had the job for years."

"He took out his daughter and put you in? I'm sorry, Paige, but your husband had all the finesse of a buzz saw."

"It was all about control for Torg. He did it because he could, and he knew there was nothing Diana could do about it. She wasn't popular at the school, but still…"

"And the twins got written out of the will."

"That was a power play, too. By the time he died, none of them were on speaking terms."

Remembering her own reaction to Torg's handwriting, Paige's explanation made perfect sense to Claudia. Power and control were the chief motivating forces in his personality.

"So Diana hates you because she wants the school; Dane hates you because he wants the land. What about Neil?"

"Neil. Oh God, Neil. That's another story. He's had this *huge* crush on me from the beginning. Right after Torg and I got married, he started showing up at the house almost every morning after his father left for the office."

"He was coming on to you?"

Paige exaggerated an eye roll and nodded. "He was so cute, and he kept making up one pathetic excuse after another for coming over. I might be a small town girl, but I knew what he was after."

Claudia couldn't help wondering whether Paige had given in to Neil's sweet-talking, but that was one question she couldn't ask.

Paige's voice hushed to the level of *True Confessions*. "He started getting more and more pushy. I was terrified that Torg would find out and think I was encouraging him. But the more I said no, the worse it got. Neil got crazy. He threatened to tell Torg that *I* was trying to seduce *him*! Then he had this terrible accident. He was thrown from his horse and broke his back. The doctors say he'll never walk again. He's lucky he's not a quadriplegic."

"Not what *I* would call lucky," Claudia said. She picked up her drink and took a long swallow. "Jeez, Paige, I guess you weren't kidding about needing a friend."

They smiled at each other across the table and Paige looked cheered. "How would you like to come and take a tour of the school?"

Claudia found herself drawn in, fascinated by the Sorensen story. "I'd love to. How many students are there?"

"About fifty girls in the middle grades—thirteen- to fifteen-year-olds. Most of them are involved with the film industry. Either they're into acting or their parents are actors, producers, directors. Some are spoiled-rotten rich kids who cause problems and take up a lot of my time. Like Annabelle, the girl I told you about."

Claudia had an idea that had been fermenting since she'd heard Annabelle's story the week before, but she was unsure of how what she was about to suggest would be received.

She said, "I've done some work with kids who have emotional problems. There's a program called graphotherapy. It's a series of handwriting movement exercises done to a special kind of music. I wonder whether Annabelle would respond to it."

"I've never heard of it," Paige said. "How does it work?"

"The specific hand movements and the music literally help calm the brain so the person can function better. Kids who use it develop better self-discipline, which helps them feel better about themselves. It's not very well known, but it's being used successfully in schools around the world."

Paige began to look interested. "Tell me more."

"I would analyze Annabelle's handwriting to learn more about her current emotional state. Then I would tailor some of these handwriting movement exercises for her particular needs. It's easy. The exercises take a few minutes a day. I would check her progress weekly and make adjustments as we go. After a few weeks we expect changes to appear naturally in her handwriting and in her behavior."

"This is sounding interesting. How long is the program?"

"I'd say a minimum of three months."

"Damn, I was hoping for a magic bullet."

"Wouldn't that be nice," Claudia said. "How old is Annabelle?"

"Fourteen."

"Would you say her suicide attempt was serious, or more like a cry for help?"

"She snagged a bottle of daddy's Jose Cuervo from the wet bar in the middle of the night and snuck down to the beach—they live in Malibu. She polished off what was in the bottle, then broke it on a rock and cut her wrists. Lucky for her, a man walking his dog found her or she would have succeeded. She claims not to remember anything about it."

Claudia felt a rush of sympathy, the way she had when she had first heard Annabelle's story. "Poor kid. Did she lose much blood?"

Paige shook her head. "The booze did more damage than the cuts."

"What happened to her? Psych ward?"

"Uh, uh. Remember, this kid's old man is Dominic Giordano." Paige paused to down the rest of her drink. Some of the social polish seemed to have worn thin as the Jack Daniels diminished in her glass, and she was sounding more like the small town girl from Clovis than the wealthy Bel Air widow.

"He had the juice to keep Annabelle out of the hospital and the whole nasty mess out of the media," she said.

"That's a lot of juice."

"He's had his share of bad publicity. He doesn't need any more."

"Oh yes, those young actresses."

Paige looked uncomfortable. "We don't talk about that," she said primly. "He's a paying customer."

Claudia didn't need Paige to confirm the story. She remembered how the whispers of illicit drugs and underage sex had disappeared behind a rumored settlement with the girls' parents for 'an undisclosed sum.'

In Hollywood, where big payoffs buy silence, tales of Dominic Giordano's alleged indiscretions were relegated to cocktail party gossip in a finger snap. Other stories had surfaced that connected his Sunmark Studios to organized crime. Stories of money laundering that were never proven.

Now, with an advertising blitz for his biggest film ever saturating the media, it was no surprise that Giordano would want to keep his name off the front page, except in *Variety*. The girls with whom he was reputed to have been involved were about the same age as his daughter.

"Shades of Roman Polanski," Claudia murmured. "Do you know why Annabelle tried to kill herself?"

The waitress returned and Paige ordered another round over Claudia's protests. When it came to booze, she was no heavy hitter, and she was already feeling pleasantly buzzed.

Paige said, "She'd been getting into trouble for a long time; long before the suicide attempt."

"What kind of trouble?"

"Shoplifting, drugs, running away from home. Then there was her personal best—joyriding in stolen cars with very bad dudes. Where she picked *them* up—well, honey, let's not even go there."

"Arrests?"

"At least a couple, but remember, daddy has friends in high places. He makes the bad stuff go away." Paige swirled her drink around in the glass. "Not that I'm cynical or anything, but sometimes it's all about who you know."

"Or who you snow," Claudia said, thinking about Andy Nicholson. She nursed the screwdriver, barely wetting her lips on the high octane OJ. "So, there's no one at the school that Annabelle can relate to?"

"She's a tough little wench, keeps to herself. Besides Bert, there's only one person she's shown any real interest in. That's Cruz, our athletic coach. Of course, *all* the girls are in love with Cruz. Curly black hair, *amazing* eyes. And he's got that oh-so-romantic scar." She drew a line across her lips to illustrate. "He won't talk about how he got it, which makes him even more interesting."

Claudia laughed. "This guy's ego must be the size of Canada."

"He's one very cool dude, all right."

From the gleam in Paige's eyes and the sudden pink glow in her cheeks, Claudia couldn't help wondering about her own relationship with the athletic coach. But what about Bert Falkenberg, the business manager? And Neil Sorensen? Paige was beginning to look like a *very* merry widow.

"*All* the girls flirt with Cruz," Paige repeated. "But Annabelle— I've seen her staring at him when she thinks no one's watching. She does it all the time. Her eyes are glued to him."

"Does he notice?"

"He pays more attention to her than anyone else. He goes out of his way to talk to her. I have to admit, it bugs me."

"You must have done a background check on him?"

"Squeaky clean."

"Have you talked to him about it?"

"Not yet. I'm keeping an eye on it. It's not that I think there's anything going on. I just don't like it."

Claudia stirred her drink with her straw, blending it to lessen the impact of the alcohol that had sunk to the bottom. "Do you know of any sexual abuse in Annabelle's background?"

"No, but like I said, she hasn't opened up."

Annabelle Giordano was sounding more intriguing by the minute. Claudia started to speculate on what she might find in the girl's handwriting. The possibility that she might be able to help her through graphotherapy intrigued her. "Let's start by getting a sample of her handwriting."

Paige snapped her fingers. "I've got an idea. You could come and give a talk about handwriting analysis! It would be such a kick for the girls."

"I'll be glad to."

Paige's exuberance turned serious. "We'd better do it soon. If the judge rules against me, there won't *be* a school."

CHAPTER 7

The Sorensen Academy is a residential and day school for young women with special emotional needs that are not adequately served in the standard setting. Located in the hills above the UCLA campus, the Sorensen Academy has been known as an outstanding resource for combining education and emotional healing since 1968. Our program offers a desirable alternative to long-term hospitalization, as we keep the student body size small, allowing our girls the advantage of personalized attention in a homelike environment.

The front cover of the brochure displayed a glossy photograph of the old mansion that had long ago been converted to a private school for wealthy young women: climbing roses on cream-colored walls, twenty-five foot high entryway, a fountain burbling in the courtyard—all the charm of a fairytale castle.

A fairytale castle with the requisite goblins and ogres, Claudia thought, closing the brochure and returning it to the antique side table.

Paige's fear that she would lose her case to the Sorensen children had prompted her to schedule Claudia's talk to the student body the week after the hearing.

The last witness had left the stand, the lawyers submitted their evidence, and Judge Krieger took the case under advisement. Now all that remained was for him to notify counsel of his ruling.

Claudia waited in the lobby, reviewing the handwriting samples she'd chosen to present: Britney Spears, Selena, Taylor Swift, Michael

Jackson. Pop stars would grab the students' attention faster than Hillary Rodham Clinton or Michelle Obama, whose handwritings she would also show.

She got up and crossed the foyer to study a photo display that decorated one wall. Groups of students dating from the early days of the Sorensen Academy—girls dressed in World War II fashions. Hippie peaceniks of the sixties in empire dresses. Gen X'ers and sophisticated young women of the New Millennium with old eyes in baby faces, daring the photographer with defiance—captives of the camera, refusing to smile.

Claudia glanced through the foyer doors and saw that it was raining again. She was glad she had dressed warmly. Black wool jacket, dove grey cashmere turtleneck, long skirt and ankle boots— dressed up enough to command respect, but not so formal as to distance her from the girls. She had pinned her favorite prop on her lapel–a gold cloisonné fountain pen.

A door at the back of the building swung open and Paige ran in from the rain, laughing. The man following close behind her was laughing, too. When Paige saw her, she called out.

"Claudia! You are the *best*, showing up in this miserable weather. I was afraid you might cancel."

The man helped her out of her neon yellow slicker, his hands lingering on her shoulders. Paige took the dripping garment from him and hung it on a coat rack by the door. "This is Cruz Montenegro, our athletics director," she said over her shoulder. "Cruz, this is Claudia Rose."

Cruz was exactly as she had described him. Inky hair and indigo eyes. The faded line of a scar showed up against his tanned skin, slightly disfiguring the full lips, giving him an air of mystery. His nose was crooked enough to suggest it had been broken. Tanned biceps bulged from the sleeves of an athletic shirt with *Sorensen Academy* emblazoned in two-inch white letters across the front.

"Yo, Claudia," sounding like Sylvester Stallone. "Gladdameetya, gotta run." He stretched out his hand to give hers a quick pump, slowing but not stopping. Running up the staircase, leaving her a view of a firm butt with thigh muscles that made his shorts look too small. A Greek god, had Greek gods hailed from New Jersey.

"See what I mean?" Paige whispered, her brows forming a

question mark.

"Not bad, Paige. Not bad at all."

"Yeah, he's pretty popular around here." Paige dragged her gaze away from the receding figure of Cruz Montenegro and beckoned Claudia to follow her. "We're all hyped about your talk. Need any help?"

"I've got it covered, thanks. Lead on."

Claudia grabbed the handle of the luggage cart she had loaded with her notebook computer and LCD projector, and followed Paige along the passage toward a pair of double doors.

The high-pitched chatter of teenage girls intensified as Paige drew open the doors and they entered a room that seemed to have been designed as a grand dining hall, or perhaps a ballroom.

Claudia's eyes were drawn upward to vaulted ceilings decorated with frescos of plump cherubs that could have originated in a 17th century Italian palazzo. Several rows of folding chairs had been grouped around a lectern and screen. Around forty teenage girls in uniform navy skirts and white knit shirts sat and stood in knots, chatting with each other or on mobile phones.

Claudia set up her laptop and digital projector while Paige called for order. In her khaki jumpsuit with her hair worn loose, the principal looked young and carefree, not like a woman terrified that a court judgment would tear this place away from her.

"We're very lucky to have a special guest with us today," Paige began in the girlish voice that had struck Claudia in their first phone call. "Claudia Rose is a forensic handwriting expert and she's going to tell us what our handwriting says about us."

Claudia's eyes roamed over the assembled girls as she waited for their attention. Which one was Annabelle Giordano, the girl whose attempted suicide had landed her at boarding school? "How many of you know how to write?" she asked. All hands went up.

"You should consider yourselves lucky. Many schools don't teach handwriting anymore. It's a valuable skill that helps you to understand information better and to remember what you learn. And like Mrs. Sorensen said, it tells something about your personality."

She held up a blank sheet of paper. "This is a symbol of your environment. When you pick up your pen and begin to write, you leave a trail of ink on the paper that shows how you behave within your environment.

"Your handwriting reveals how you're feeling at the moment, whether you're happy or sad; confident or shy; optimistic or feeling down. It shows how you think, how much energy you have, and many other things that make up who you are."

Their faces were rapt as Claudia spoke, projecting the handwritings of the pop stars onto the screen, explaining how their handwriting mirrored their emotions and experiences, and how it would change as they developed over their lifetime.

She dictated a sentence for the students to write. In seconds their voices had swelled to a crescendo, rivaling the sound of paper being ripped from composition books. Then she instructed them to switch hands and write the sentence again.

The room filled with groans and giggles as they struggled with the assignment. Then, above the chatter, a young voice said loudly, "This sucks *ass*."

Silence fell like a stage curtain. Heads twisted to the back of the room where the challenger stood just inside the door.

Her face was a pale oval, dark brows knit in a scowl. Long black hair fell over her shoulders, blunt cut, the bangs touching her eyebrows. One sock had slipped down to her ankle. She didn't bother to straighten it.

Despite her provocative words, there was something fragile about her.

Claudia raised an eyebrow at the rude comment. "An interesting observation," she said when no one made a move to set the girl straight. "What makes you think it sucks?"

The girl lifted one shoulder. Calculated nonchalance. "It's just a bunch of marks on paper. It doesn't mean anything. This is so retarded."

Claudia looked back at her, unsmiling. "There was a point to the exercise. I wanted to demonstrate that we have a *natural* writing hand and an *unnatural* one. Sometimes, when an accident or illness causes a person to lose the ability to write with their natural hand, they have to learn to use their unnatural one."

She went to the laptop and clicked the mouse to project a sample written by a man who had become paralyzed by polio and now wrote holding a pen in his mouth.

"Would you be able to write this well, using your foot?" Claudia asked the audience. "Writing with your unnatural *hand* was difficult enough. But after he practiced for a few months, this man's writing became similar to the way he wrote before he was paralyzed. Any guesses why?" Her eyes scanned the audience. The girls were all staring at the screen. All but the girl at the back of the room, who gave a loud, contemptuous sigh and rolled her eyes.

Ignoring her behavior, Claudia continued to speak. "When someone passes you a note in class, how do you know who the note is from?" She waited for an answer, noting the renewed disdain on the face of the girl by the back door.

Several hands shot up and a girl in the front row called out, "Because you know their handwriting."

Claudia pointed at her. "Right. And you know their handwriting because it's unique to *that* person. Why? Because we all have different experiences, and we react to them differently, and the way we react is reflected in the way that we write. And that's because handwriting starts in the brain, not in the hand."

As she wrapped up her presentation, she couldn't help noticing that the girl at the back of the room ducked out before the enthusiastic applause died away.

"That was *awesome*," Paige said, still in girlish mode as the girls and their teachers filed out of the room. "But I have to apologize for Annabelle."

Claudia glanced up from powering down the laptop. "The girl with the snide remarks? I thought that might be her."

"We tend to ignore it when she does things like that."

"I noticed no one told her to sit down and button it."

"Our school psychologist, Doctor McConahay, says she does it to get attention, and when we react, it encourages her to do it all the more." Paige coiled the laptop's electrical cord, snapped a rubber band around it, and handed it to Claudia. "I don't agree, but *she's* got the psych degree, not me."

"It doesn't look to me as if Miss Annabelle is the type to be interested in graphotherapy."

"But she stayed for your whole talk. That's a good sign, isn't it?"

"Remains to be seen."

"Let's go up to my office. You can meet her and we'll see what she has to say for herself."

Paige asked the young woman at the reception desk to locate Annabelle. Her name tag said *Brenda*. Anorexic-thin, mousy brown hair and pasty skin. She looked out of place in a setting where tuition for one semester was higher than her annual salary.

Brenda said, "I saw her go outside. It stopped raining a while ago."

"Would you send someone to find her and bring her to my office," said Paige.

She took Claudia up the wide, sweeping staircase, stopping at a door about twenty feet along the landing. As she opened the door, Mikki, the Bichon Frisé sprang out of a basket next to the desk and danced over to his mistress, barking happiness.

Paige's office was more like a cozy sitting room, Claudia thought, taking in the old-fashioned love seat and overstuffed chairs. It looked like a place where a teenager with a problem to discuss might feel comfortable.

Paige stooped to ruffle the little dog's fur and mother him with baby talk. "How about some coffee?"

"Thanks, that would be great."

While she called down to the kitchen and ordered refreshments to be sent up, Claudia drifted to the window and looked out at the grounds below. As Brenda had said, the rain had let up, leaving miniature reflecting pools on the asphalt.

They were at the rear of the mansion and the windows overlooked a soccer field that must have once been a broad lawn. A path wound around the field, ending behind the goal post at a pocket-sized house nestled in a row of eucalyptus. From across the field, the windows sparkled in a sudden burst of sunshine.

"Is that house part of the school?" Claudia asked, as Paige replaced the phone on its base.

"The cottage?" She nodded. "We use it as a guest house. Cruz is staying there. Bert's not too happy about that. He'd like Cruz to live off-site, like him."

"Bert doesn't have his own cottage?"

"He used to be in that one, but when Cruz came on board a couple of months ago I moved him out. Bert needed more space for all his stuff, so I gave him an office over here, next to me, and he moved into an apartment on the Westside."

"Looks like Cruz had a visitor."

Annabelle Giordano had emerged from the cottage and started walking back toward the school. As she approached, Bert Falkenberg met her on the path. Claudia could see that the girl was talking rapidly, her face animated, unlike her earlier sour attitude.

Paige joined Claudia at the window. "Damn! I don't want her pestering Cruz."

"Will Bert bring her up here?"

"Uh huh, I expect Brenda cornered him for the job."

"At least Annabelle seems to like him."

"I guess you could say he's kind of a father image. His first wife took his two daughters out of state and he doesn't even know where they are. It makes him sad sometimes. I guess he's—what do they call it? Substituting?"

"Sublimating."

"That's it. He's *sublimating* his fatherly instincts by being kind of a counselor for the girls."

"How does Doctor McConahay feel about that?"

"Look, most of these girls have fathers who don't pay them much attention," Paige said, sounding defensive. "They can use a nice man to talk to. I know, because I grew up that way, too. Well, not that my father was rich like theirs, but he worked all the time to support my mom and me. Young girls *need* an older man to talk to."

An older man like Torg Sorensen?

"You put a lot of trust in Bert."

"Absolutely. He's like a favorite uncle around here."

Paige must have read Claudia's silence as disapproval. "I did speak to Doctor McConahay about *you*," she said. "She gave the go-ahead for Annabelle to do the handwriting exercise program with you."

There was a sharp rap on the door and Annabelle slouched in, having re-acquired her earlier sullen demeanor. Bert came after, followed by a heavyset middle-aged Hispanic woman wearing a pink and white maid's uniform and a big smile. She wheeled in a tea wagon with a silver coffee service and a plate of pirouette cookies.

"Thanks, Maria," Paige said, then turned to Annabelle with a stern expression that aged her.

"Annabelle, I think you have something to say to Ms. Rose after the way you behaved downstairs."

The girl's mouth dropped in disbelief. "For *what?* I didn't *do* anything."

"You know you *did*."

Annabelle narrowed her shoulders, stared at the carpet, and mumbled something unintelligible. Claudia would rather have let it go. She might deserve an apology, but forcing Annabelle into one would be counterproductive to her plans.

Paige raised her voice a notch. "Annabelle, you're going to have to speak up, I want to hear your apology."

Annabelle's eyes remained focused on her water stained running shoes. "*Sorry*," she said a little louder but still unrepentant.

Mikki pranced over and bumped her leg with a wet nose. She bent down to scratch his neck. He rewarded her by licking her leg. Unexpectedly, Annabelle giggled.

Paige said, "Annabelle, look at me. I want to know what you're sorry for."

The girl's chin jerked up, showing angry red splotches on her cheeks. She straightened her spine, four feet ten inches of defiance. "Chill *out*, I didn't fucking do anything."

Bert Falkenberg stepped up. To Paige's visible relief, he put a firm hand on Annabelle's shoulder, taking charge. "That's *enough*, Annabelle. Don't you ever cuss at Mrs. Sorensen."

"*Fine.* I apologize for having an opinion."

"Having an opinion isn't the problem," Claudia said, thinking it was time to add her two cents. "It was the way you expressed yourself that made you look bad in front of everyone."

Surprise flared on Annabelle's face, making her thoughts transparent: I *looked bad? I thought I was making* you *look bad!*

Very subtly, the balance of power had shifted. Claudia looked to Paige. "Maybe Annabelle and I could speak privately for a few minutes?"

It was Bert Falkenberg who spoke. "Anna, take Ms. Rose to your room, please." It was more an order than a suggestion and Claudia waited for another display of rebellion, but Annabelle merely sniffed her contempt for them all and headed for the door.

"What*ever.*"

CHAPTER 8

"Do all the girls live in?" Claudia asked for the sake of making conversation as they ascended to the third floor, where the residential students lived.

Annabelle walked a few feet ahead, scuffing her shoes on the carpet. She treated Claudia to the nonchalant one-shoulder lift. "Most of them live at home with their *loving* parents."

Dropped off in an endless line of high-end SUV mommy mobiles, no doubt, thought Claudia, taking note of the girl's sarcasm.

Annabelle's room was furnished in ultra-feminine Laura Ashley that seemed out of synch with her temperament. Twin beds with white iron bedsteads, puffy duvets with gingham trim; matching wallpaper, matching window treatments on dormer windows. Two study desks, each with a laptop computer that slammed the Victorian decor into the twenty-first century.

One of the beds was home to a menagerie of stuffed animals and Beanie Babies. An assortment of books and a boom box shared a shelf above.

Annabelle plopped onto the other bed, which had no decoration and looked desperately barren by comparison. Maybe at fourteen she considered herself too grown up for stuffed toys. Or maybe the attempt to end her own life had propelled her beyond the desire for childish comforts.

One item adorned Annabelle's nightstand, a framed photograph positioned away from the casual onlooker. Claudia angled herself so that she could see the picture—a small child with dark hair, around four or five years old, cuddled in the arms of a laughing beauty. Neither guessing that their time together would be so violently cut short.

When she caught Claudia looking at it, Annabelle grabbed the photo and turned it face down on the nightstand.

"Is that your mother?" Claudia asked, although she had already recognized the starlet, Valerie Vale.

"What do you care?"

Despite her defiant words, Annabelle's voice held a note of such melancholy that Claudia wanted to reach out and put her arms around her. But the girl's body language warned her to tread lightly.

"I do care."

Annabelle's lip curled in disdain. "Why should you? You don't even know me."

"Not yet, but maybe if you would show me your handwriting I could start to." Claudia drew a chair from the desk and sat down. "So, how about it? I'll tell you what it says about you, and who knows? *Maybe* you'll find out that handwriting analysis doesn't totally suck ass."

Annabelle shot her a quick glance from under her lashes, surprised that an adult would quote her own rude words back at her. "I bet Paige already told you everything about me." Defiantly using the headmistress' first name.

Claudia smiled. "I don't think Paige *knows* everything about you."

Annabelle went over to the window and threw it open. The sun had disappeared behind the clouds and a fine drizzle had started up again. She dipped her hand into her pocket and brought out a crumpled pack of Winston cigarettes, shook one loose and stuck it in her mouth. Without looking at her, she offered the pack to Claudia. "Smoke?"

This is a test.

"No thanks," said Claudia. "I don't smoke. And I'd rather you didn't while we're together."

Annabelle snorted. "You gonna rat me out?"

"You'd like that, wouldn't you? Give you an excuse to stay angry."

"I really don't give a fuck," Annabelle said, but she hesitated, jammed the cigarettes back into her pocket. The next dive into her pocket produced a piece of grape Bubblicious.

Annabelle unwrapped the bubblegum and popped it into her mouth. This girl had built a solid wall of defenses, but at least she wasn't going to force a showdown on this issue.

"So, are you gonna write something or not?" Claudia asked, relieved that she wasn't going to have to deal with a display of defiance.

The girl stared at her, chewing hard, daring her to complain about the gum. Her need to defy anyone she viewed as an authority figure was so transparent that Claudia almost smiled.

"How do I know you're not just guessing?"

"Hey kiddo, if you don't want to do it, it's fine with me. I don't have anything to prove." Claudia got up and started for the door.

Before she reached it, Annabelle spoke up. "Why *should* I do it?"

Claudia thought about that. "Is there anything in your life right now that's not working the way you'd like it to?"

The girl gave a rude snort. "What do *you* think?"

"I think there might be a thing or two you'd like to change."

"What's that got to do with how I write?"

"Your handwriting shows how you feel and how you deal with life. There might be ways to do some things better, but we won't know unless we check it out. It's up to you."

Annabelle mused on that for a moment, blowing her gum into a big pink eruption, then sucking it back into her mouth. "I still think it's crap. What do I have to write?"

"Let's start with a few lines about anything you like. I'd also like you to draw a tree, and a picture of your family doing something."

A hint of suspicion crept into the dark eyes. She was obviously bright, and she'd probably had enough of being put under a microscope by the shrinks in the hospital. A suicide attempt would have netted her a battery of psychological tests, even if her father *was* a big shot. Still, curiosity sparked there, too.

"I thought you were going to analyze my *handwriting*. Why do I have to draw all that stuff?"

Claudia took several sheets of blank paper and a pen from her briefcase and put them on the desk closest to Annabelle's bed. "Because your handwriting is still developing. The drawings give me some additional information." She reached back into the briefcase and took out a magnifying glass.

Annabelle slid off the bed and edged toward her. Not too close, but enough that Claudia could sense that she was interested.

Like a wild animal; curious, but afraid of human contact.

"Draw a tree?" the girl asked.

"M'hm."

"What kind?"

"Any kind you want."

The tree was part of a projective test that would show Claudia how Annabelle viewed herself, her family, and her attitude toward her life. Deliberately refraining from giving her any explicit instructions, Claudia left her the freedom to express herself uncensored in the drawing.

Annabelle pushed her laptop to one side and sat down at the desk. Picking up the pen Claudia had left there, she uncapped it and sat staring down at the paper, tapping the end of the pen against her teeth.

Claudia watched her pondering what to write and guessed that she was trying to figure out how to do it without revealing anything of herself.

"Just so you know," Claudia assured her, "our conversations are confidential. The one exception is if you told me that you planned to hurt yourself or someone else. Then I'd have to report it. But aside from that, anything else you say or write, or draw, is between you and me."

Annabelle turned her head and stared at her for a long moment, chewing deliberately. She blew an enormous sticky pink bubble, which expanded and thinned until it burst, splattering her nose and mouth. Wordlessly, she peeled the gum off her face and popped it back into her mouth. Then she began to write.

While Annabelle wrote, Claudia surveyed the room. No scuffed slippers peeping from under the bed, no notebook covers tattooed with teen idol names, as there were on her roommate's side. A half dozen textbooks in an untidy pile on her shelf. No *Teen People* or *Elle Girl* magazines. In fact, Claudia concluded, Annabelle's space looked like she had just packed up her belongings in preparation for moving out. Wishful thinking? Yet, Paige had told her that

Annabelle hated going home.

The girl's voice intruded on her thoughts. "I'm done." She thrust the papers at Claudia with a look that challenged, *Okay, I dare you.*

The first page was the handwriting sample. Small, printed writing hugged the left edge of the paper, leaving virtually no margin on that side, but an excessive margin on the right.

The words themselves were compressed, but wide rivers of space flowed between them. Without reading what Annabelle had written, Claudia held the page at arm's length for a moment, then turned it over and ran her fingers across the back.

"Why are you doing that?" Annabelle asked, forgetting to maintain her fortress of indifference.

"I'm checking to see how much you pressed the pen into the paper. You have very light pressure. That means you hold your feelings inside until you can't stand it anymore, then they sort of explode. See how your writing doesn't slant to the right or the left, but stays straight up and down? That's another sign that you work hard at controlling your emotions." She paused to give Annabelle time to digest the information and respond, but the girl was staring at her with something like disbelief.

Claudia held the magnifying glass close to the paper, showing Annabelle the enlarged strokes and the small hooks that appeared at the beginnings and endings of her words.

"You chose to print instead of writing in cursive," she continued. "Connections between letters are sort of like holding hands with other people. When you break the connections between the letters, which is what you have to do when you print, it's like cutting off emotional connections. The amount of space you leave between words shows how close you want to be to other people. You leave very wide spaces between your words, which makes me think that you're afraid to let anyone get too close."

Annabelle glared at her. "I'm not afraid of *anything!*"

That's what Paige had said.

"I'm sorry, bad choice of words. What I should have said was, you need a lot of space. Is that better?"

"Not really."

Claudia ignored the retort and turned to the second page. Annabelle had drawn a tree that was little more than a scrawny stump. About one-third up the trunk was a knothole filled with ink. A half-inch higher came another, smaller knothole. This one was an oval shape, not filled in.

The poor little tree had a few shriveled branches that stabbed the sky. There were no refreshing leaves, no roots that would indicate feelings of stability.

"This is a sad tree," Claudia said. "It looks like someone tried to cut it down."

Annabelle hunched her shoulders, protecting herself. "It's my tree, I can do what I want with it." Including trying to kill it—kill *herself* by cutting her wrists.

"You're absolutely right. Tell me about the knotholes in the trunk."

"I don't know. I just put them there. I thought you were gonna tell *me* about it."

"Okay, I'll tell you what it says to me. When you were about six or seven years old, you lost something or someone that you loved a lot, and you've never gotten over it. Then, when you were a little older, you had another big loss, but that one wasn't quite as devastating as the first one."

"How did you know that?" Annabelle demanded. "Who *told* you that?" The coal-colored eyes filled with tears. She pushed her fists against them, struggling to contain her emotions.

"No one told me," Claudia said, telling the truth. The realization that the first knothole in Annabelle's tree drawing had a direct correlation with the loss of her mother had not occurred until that moment. She still had no idea what the second one represented.

"Knotholes in a tree trunk are symbols of painful emotional wounds," she explained. "Where you place them tells *when* the event took place. The top of the tree trunk is the present, now, when you're fourteen years old. The bottom of the trunk represents when you were born. The first wound appears a little below the middle of the tree, so that would be when you were about six. The second one is a little higher, so I would say you were about nine or ten."

"Oh my God, I can't believe you know that." Annabelle wrapped her thin arms around herself. She spoke almost in a whisper. "Marisa."

"Who is Marisa?" Claudia asked, surprised to hear this

unfamiliar name, rather than a reference to her mother.

There was a long silence. Then Annabelle seemed to reach a decision. "She was my nanny. She took care of me after my mama…" Her voice got higher as she choked up and abruptly stopped speaking. She turned away and Claudia saw that her shoulders were shaking. When she spoke, her breath came out in harsh gasps.

"When I was ten, one day I came home from school and she was gone. Her room was empty." Her voice quavered. "She promised she would always stay with me, but she lied. *Everyone* lies."

"What happened? Why do you think she left?"

"*He* tried to make her have sex with him and she didn't want to."

The words sounded as obscene coming from Annabelle's lips as what they suggested.

"Who are you talking about?"

"*Dominic.*" She spat her father's name with utter contempt. "He said it was because she was stealing, but it's not true."

"How do you know this?"

"I saw them in the pool house. Marisa took me swimming and afterwards she went to change in the dressing room. I was supposed to go in the house, but I hid behind the planter. I was going to jump out and surprise her. Then *he* came outside.

"He pushed open the door. She yelled at him that she was in there, but he wouldn't leave. I went and peeked in. Her bathing suit top was off and he was groping her. She was crying and trying to push him away, but he wouldn't stop. It was totally gross and disgusting."

For all her attempts at worldliness, she was little more than a child after all. A child who had witnessed appalling behavior by her parent.

"What did you do?"

"I yelled at him to let her go and he jumped back. Marisa pushed him away and ran into the house. She ran right past me like I wasn't there."

"What did your father say?"

"He yelled at me to mind my own goddamn business and he started hitting me. I hate him!" Tears quivered on Annabelle's lashes. "Why couldn't she have called me, or at least sent me a birthday card or something? She just left me."

The self-centered worldview of the ten-year-old she had been.

Claudia didn't believe that the nanny had deliberately cut Annabelle out of her life after caring for her for four years. Had she threatened to expose Dominic Giordano?

How many calls and holiday cards to Annabelle might her father have diverted? Or had it been a condition of the nanny's termination not to contact his daughter, ever? Punishment for refusing his advances. Or part of a payoff? It would be easy for a man of Giordano's stature to intimidate his employee into not reporting an episode of sexual harassment. It seemed plausible to Claudia that it could have happened that way.

She thought of the caution her friend, Zebediah Gold, regularly gave her: don't let yourself get involved with your clients, especially the young ones. He should know; he was a semi-retired psychologist. But Claudia had never learned how to do that. How could she keep her distance when this prickly little person so clearly *needed* someone to be involved?

She picked up the drawing Annabelle had made in response to her instruction to "draw the family doing something."

The drawing suggested more than a little artistic talent. Two figures were depicted. Close to the left edge of the paper, reminiscent of where she had placed her handwriting, Annabelle had drawn a lone female figure, which represented herself. It didn't take an expert to interpret the feelings of futility in the closed eyes and sad, turned down mouth; the sense of helplessness in the lack of hands or feet. The black hair surrounded her and reached her feet, Rapunzel-like, affording some protection from the outside world.

Across the page on the right-hand side, a much larger, menacing male figure was engaged in an act that made Claudia catch her breath. Annabelle had drawn her father pushing a car over the edge of a cliff.

Depicted from behind, he faced away from the viewer, a shocking portrayal of the rejection Annabelle felt by Dominic Giordano, whom the drawing showed she believed had turned away from her, both symbolically and literally.

Abruptly, Annabelle grabbed the drawing from Claudia's hands and crushed it into a ball. "*I hate him,*" she said again, with a vehemence that prickled the hair on Claudia's arms. "I'm gonna get even with him. I *swear* I will."

CHAPTER 9

Paige handed over a mug of good coffee. "So, how'd it go?"

Claudia took a grateful sip. She felt emotionally drained after her meeting with Annabelle. "Better than I expected. She's agreed to try the graphotherapy program. I left her with some exercises to do."

"But what did she *tell* you?"

"It's a therapeutic relationship, Paige. She has to be able to trust me if she's going to confide in me. I can't give you details."

Paige's eyes narrowed. "You're kidding, right? Did she say anything about me? Did she talk about Cruz?"

"No, I'm not kidding, and don't ask me specific questions, because I won't answer them. It would interfere with the therapy if she found out."

"Who's gonna tell her?"

"No, Paige," Claudia said firmly. "I'm not going to share what she said to me."

What Claudia had said wasn't strictly true. Handwriting analysis was an unlicensed profession, so she was not legally bound to confidentiality laws the way a therapist would be. But Annabelle had begged her, "Don't tell anyone! Promise you won't tell anything I told you."

What was I supposed to do? Claudia asked herself.

So Paige was royally pissed, but couldn't very well refuse to let Annabelle work the program for a month's trial. If the combination of hand movements and therapeutic music was going to help unlock the logjam of emotions, some initial signs should have appeared by then in her handwriting. At that time, they would reassess the situation.

Claudia hurried out to the Jaguar. She had parked under a shedding jacaranda tree and the wet flowers made a purple mush under her feet. The wind-buffeted rain tore at her umbrella, and her sprint from the school's portico left her soaked to the skin. Shivering, she started up the car and turned on the heater.

The rain pelted the windshield in noisy sheets, mocking the wiper blades as she left the Sorensen Academy and turned onto Sunset. Any other day she would be admiring the mansions that lined the Boulevard. Today it was a challenge to see six feet in front of her. Worse, an overturned vehicle on the east side of the street kept the traffic moving at a snail's pace.

About a mile from home the skies began to clear, and as she crossed Lincoln onto Jefferson a double prism of color arced across the road ahead. The stunning beauty of it took her breath away. She started to reach for the cell phone. A rainbow that spectacular was meant to be shared.

Before she could dial, Jovanic's special ring tone sounded.

"Hey, where are you?" he asked without preliminaries.

"Almost home. I've been over at the Sorensen Academy, getting to know my new graphotherapy student–"

"I've been thinking about you," he interrupted.

"Oh, yeah? What were you thinking about?"

"How much I miss you."

Claudia's lips curved into a smile as she signaled left near the beach end of Jefferson and started driving up the hill. "So, tell me, Columbo, how much *do* you miss me?"

"Mmmm, enough."

She grinned. Jovanic was a little like Annabelle. Getting him to share his feelings was about as easy as stripping old wallpaper.

She said, "I miss you, too."

It was an understatement. Paige's case and other work had kept her busy, but over the past couple of weeks Jovanic had been out of town, his absence gnawed at her like a toothache. He was four hundred miles away—one hour by air, but it could have been another galaxy. Tony Bennett's signature song, *I Left My Heart in*

San Francisco, had taken on a whole new meaning.

"It's been pouring down here," she said. "How's your weather?"

Why am I talking about the weather when he's telling me he misses me?

"Raining like a monsoon," he said. "But right now, I'm looking at a very cool rainbow."

"Me, too. I wish you were here and we could look at it together."

His voice faded on the cell phone.

"Can you hear me? Damn signal's breaking up, I'm losing you. When are you coming home?"

"Real soon."

"I can't hear you. How soon?" She turned the corner of her street.

Her driveway came into view and there was Jovanic, standing outside the garage, his cell phone at his ear, wearing a goofy grin.

Suddenly, the rainbow looked even brighter and more beautiful.

CHAPTER 10

The week after her first meeting with Annabelle Giordano, Claudia returned to the Sorensen Academy. She wanted to check Annabelle's graphotherapy exercises early to correct any mistakes before they became ingrained.

Paige had requested to see her first. As Claudia approached Paige's office, angry voices from inside froze her hand mid-knock.

"And when we're through with you," shouted a woman's voice, "you won't have a pot to piss in!"

Paige's lower-voiced response was muted by the door and the sudden barking of her dog.

"Didn't your mother tell you eavesdropping is a no-no?" a husky male voice said, close to Claudia's ear. The spicy scent of cinnamon chewing gum hit her nose at the same instant.

She swung around to face Cruz Montenegro. "I'm *not* eavesdropping."

He grinned, splitting the light scar line that ran across his lips. "Hey, come on, *somebody's* gotta bust your chops."

She gave him a withering look. "Listen, dude, I don't need—"

A crash and the sound of glass breaking interrupted her retort. Cruz shoved past her and flung open the door. Over his shoulder, Claudia could see Paige and Diana Sorensen. They faced each other like snarling tigers. Paige's face was leached of color. Diana's complexion matched her cherry red suit.

Shattered crystal and a bouquet of roses littered the carpet.

Water spilled from the vase left a dark stain.

Mikki, the Bichon Frisé, hurled his pint-sized body at Diana's legs, growling and barking. Diana kicked out, doing her best to stomp the dog, which was doing its best to bite her.

"You crazy bitch," Paige cried, grabbing up her dog and holding it close. "Get the hell out of here!"

"This is *my* school! You're nothing but a gold digging—"

It happened in an instant, too fast for either Cruz or Claudia to react. A guttural sound came from Diana's throat as she lunged, grabbing at Paige's sweater, and shoved her with both hands.

Paige's arms wind-milled. She staggered backward and landed on her butt in the midst of the broken glass and roses. With a cry of pain she let go of the dog. Mikki ran to his basket, yelping, and cowered there, his little body trembling.

For a nanosecond no one moved. Then Cruz thrust Diana aside and lifted Paige to her feet as if she weighed nothing, asking her if she was okay.

She leaned into him, whimpering, shaking her head, *No*. Bright red blood ran between her fingers, streaking the front of her white angora sweater.

Diana, swinging around to leave, spotted Claudia in the doorway. Her eyes narrowed to slits. "This is *your* fault," she cried. "This is all your fault!"

Dumbfounded, Claudia stared at her. Knowing that nothing she said would improve the situation, she backed out onto the landing, allowing Diana Sorensen a wide berth. But the larger woman closed in on her and backed her up against the wooden banister. She was taller than Claudia by three inches and outweighed her by a good twenty pounds.

"You helped her steal our inheritance." Diana's hot breath blasted Claudia's face. "You crooked fake," she rasped. "You're a scammer, just like *she* is! How much did she pay you to lie for her?"

Then she made the mistake of jabbing Claudia with her finger.

Without stopping to think, Claudia grabbed the finger and bent it in a direction it was not intended to go. "Are you insane? Get the *hell* off me."

Diana's mouth opened in surprise. Her hand balled into a fist and she drew back her arm. In that instant, Claudia had enough time to wonder whether the railing would hold her when the blow landed, or if she would go tumbling over the side, the way they did in the movies.

But the blow never came.

A small, dark figure hurtling along the landing launched onto Diana's back. Diana staggered backward, trying to throw her off, but Annabelle had one skinny arm wrapped around her neck and clung like a demon. Her free hand seized a hank of Diana's coarse black hair and gave it a vicious yank.

"You little shit," Diana Sorensen bellowed like an enraged elephant. "Get her off me!" But Annabelle wrapped her fingers tighter and twisted.

"Annabelle, let go!"

Claudia's arms encircled the girl's waist as her mind raced to catch up with what was unfolding. Annabelle's body was as substantial as a bag of bones, but she was surprisingly strong, and refused to be dislodged.

Cruz came out of Paige's office, took in the scene and barked an order for Claudia to step aside. He grabbed Annabelle and hoisted her off Diana's back with ease. "You *stay* here," he said, setting her down.

She glared at him and opened her mouth with a retort, but seeing his expression, shut it again and backed up against the wall, rebuffing the protective arm Claudia offered.

Somewhere in the building, a buzzer sounded. Seconds later, classroom doors could be heard slamming open on the ground floor below. After-school voices filled the hallways. In a matter of moments, this ugly scene would be the object of dozens of curious stares.

Diana swung around on all of them, her eyes wild with fury.

Before she could attack again, Cruz grabbed her arms and held her. "Come on, Miz Sorensen, you don't wanna do this."

Paige came to the doorway, a wad of facial tissues pressed to her palm. Her voice was pitched near hysteria as she addressed her stepdaughter. "Get out of here *now*, Diana, or I'm calling the police."

Diana ripped out of Cruz's grasp. "Yes, why don't you call them?" She rubbed her neck, which bore the mark of Annabelle's hand, and sneered at Paige over Cruz's shoulder. "Even *you* aren't *that* stupid."

Paige spun on her heel and stalked back into her office, slamming the door behind her.

"You won't get away with this!" Diana shrieked after her. "I'll make sure you don't!" She brushed at her skirt with sharp, angry strokes, and straightened her jacket, trying to restore a shred of dignity.

Diana elbowed her way through the posse of gaping students lining the staircase, ignoring the raunchy cat calls that chased her and rushed out through the front doors.

Claudia bent to retrieve the composition book Annabelle had dropped in her sprint across the landing and handed it to her. "Thanks, kiddo, that took a lot of guts."

"He should have let me jack her up," Annabelle said, adopting an indifferent posture. But her breath came in quick pants on the residue of a waning adrenalin rush. She rubbed her arms where bits of shredded skin peeled away from the crisscrossing of scratches left from Diana's talon-like fingernails.

It must hurt like hell, Claudia thought. Then Cruz offered to take Annabelle to the school nurse and Claudia caught the secret smile that briefly touched her lips. Attacking Diana had certainly gotten Cruz' Montenegro's attention.

Paige was lying on the sofa in her office, getting ready to down a couple of Vicodin that Cruz brought in. Nobody asked where he'd got them.

"Diana was here because the judge's ruling came in." Paige swallowed the tablets and set down her glass of water, then wearily exchanged the bloody gauze on her palm for a new wad. "Guess who won the case?"

"So, the school is officially yours," Claudia said. With careful fingers she picked up a small shard of glass the maid had overlooked in cleaning up the mess, and dropped it into the wastebasket. "Congratulations. I think."

"There's something wrong with her—Diana. Can't you see they're both crazy, the twins?"

"I definitely wouldn't want to meet them in a dark alley."

Paige stared back at her with big eyes. "I'm going to have Bert get me a gun."

"Don't you think that's a little extreme?"

"You saw what she's capable of. I told you, I'm afraid of them. And now that I've *won*, God knows what they'll do to get back at me. Diana was right, I can't call the cops. The wrong kind of publicity would be death to the school."

Claudia regarded her with concern. "Losing is a big blow for them. They need some time to deal with it. A gun isn't the answer."

Paige's shoulders slumped and she looked at her injured hand. "What am I going to do about Annabelle? She was out of line, attacking Diana like that, even if the crazy bitch deserved it."

Claudia said, "She was defending me."

"You don't know Annabelle. She'll use any excuse to get into a fight."

"Ahh, I thought it was because she liked me." Then Claudia told Paige how pleased Annabelle had looked when Cruz offered to take her to the nurse.

Paige looked back at her through eyes that were already starting to droop from the medication. "I hope he's not going to be trouble."

CHAPTER 11

Paige called around eight, sounding punchy. "Hey, Claudia, my friend."

Claudia covered the bowl of vegetable soup she was eating and took the phone into the living room. "How's your hand?"

"Hellacious when the drugs wear off. Lucky there's more where those came from, huh?" She giggled and said something to somebody in the room. Back to Claudia. "Hey, Claudia, I got a big favor. Need your help."

Claudia's bullshit antenna went up and started quivering. "What's going on, Paige?"

"I don't know if you can tell, but I'm kinda out of it."

"Yeah, I could tell."

"So, I'm not up to staying on top of Annabelle this weekend. She needs someone watching her and—"

"And what?"

"I was thinking, she seems to have taken a real shine to you."

Claudia laughed. "Last week she said my lecture was crap."

"But she changed her mind." Paige's voice turned wheedling. "She started doing your handwriting program."

"Paige, you can't be serious? I'm not a *babysitting* service."

"But I'm gonna be spending the weekend in bed. There won't be anyone to watch her. She'll get herself into more trouble."

"So you'd send her off with a stranger?"

"You're not a stranger," Paige pressed. "You're a *friend*. And anyone can see she likes you, we both like you, and look what she did for you today with Diana."

"This morning you were angry with her for attacking Diana. Make up your mind, Paige, you can't have it both ways."

"I thought, since you'd taken such an interest in her…" Paige turned away from the phone again, covered the receiver, said something muffled. Claudia heard laughter, a deep male voice.

"Where are you, Paige?"

"Over at the cottage." More giggles. "My buddy Cruz is nursing me back to health."

"So who's minding the store?"

Paige seemed to think that was hilarious. When she sobered up, she said, "I thought maybe you could take her for the weekend."

"The *weekend?*"

"Oh, come on Claudia, it would be so good for her, and I'll pay you. Your regular rate, what you get for court."

"You're willing to spend a couple thousand dollars to get rid of her for the weekend?"

"Don't put it like that!" Paige sounded stung. "You know that's not what I meant."

"That's what it sounds like."

Paige ignored the jibe. "Getting away from school for a couple of days would help Annabelle so much."

"I got the picture—you want to play with Cruz and you need to hand off this responsibility."

The truth was, it wasn't a bad idea. Claudia's brother had made plans for a weekend fishing trip, and his daughter, who was the same age as Annabelle, would be staying at Claudia's house.

Paige pushed some more. "If you have any problems you can call me on my mobile phone. I'll send someone to pick her up right away."

"Don't you have someone there to supervise the kids who board?"

"Well, yes, but this is Annabelle—she's kind of high maintenance. I wouldn't leave her with just anyone."

"Oh, thanks, that's great," Claudia said, not sure whether to be flattered by Paige's vote of confidence. "My niece is going to be here. She's still kind of innocent and my brother is very protective.

If Monica got into any kind of trouble, he would never forgive me."
Claudia heard herself weakening and Paige moved in for the kill.

"The poor kid hasn't made any friends here at all. She and your niece might hit it off."

"What about her father?"

"He leaves this stuff up to me."

They batted it back and forth a few more times, but Claudia knew she had already lost.

The way Annabelle had rushed to her defense, there was no disputing it, whatever problems the girl might have, she had guts—hard-won guts, grown out of the too-early loss of her mother and the disappointment of a cold father who had emotionally abandoned her; a conspicuous lack of friends; and a headmistress foisting her off on a relative stranger. Claudia reckoned that a weekend wouldn't be such a big sacrifice.

After she hung up she mused for a while on the various faces of Paige Sorensen that she'd seen. Over the weeks since they'd met she had observed the wounded widow, the wronged stepmother, the lonely woman seeking a confidante. At Claudia's handwriting analysis presentation the charming schoolmistress, and with this request, came the face of what seemed to be an unconcerned caretaker who would put her own needs before those of her charge.

Claudia tucked away a mental note to analyze Paige's handwriting.

CHAPTER 12

Pale morning light seeped through the blinds, probing the shadows in Claudia's bedroom. Saturday. The sound of water running in the shower.

She squinted at the clock. Eight-twenty. She'd slept late, but Annabelle wasn't due until ten, Monica at ten-thirty. Plenty of time for a leisurely breakfast.

Jovanic emerged from the bathroom, a towel draped around his lean, muscular body. Being a cop meant he had to stay fit, and he worked at it with regular sessions at the gym. A little shiver of happiness ran through her.

He dropped the towel and crawled back into bed. He slid an arm around her and nuzzled her neck as she scooted against his body, which was cool from the shower. She felt him harden against her.

His hand stole up over her abdomen and cupped her breast. Claudia sighed with contentment and rolled onto her back in response. His hands, then his tongue explored the familiar peaks and valleys of her body, making her gasp. She let her mind go blank and gave herself up to the sheer pleasure of being in his arms.

Getting onto her knees, she urged him onto his back, stroking him, loving the way she could make him groan. It was these times when she was tempted to give in and make the commitment he had been pressing her for. Lost in the moment, Claudia realized that someone was ringing the doorbell.

"Aw shit!" Jovanic grumbled, rolling away from her and off

the bed. "Who the hell is that?" Grabbing the towel from the floor and wrapping it around his waist, he slid open the deck door and stepped out onto the balcony, leaned over to look. "There's a kid on the porch."

Claudia scrambled out of bed and into a pair of leggings she'd left draped over a chair the night before. "She's early."

The doorbell rang again, more insistently.

Jovanic closed the balcony door with an irritated snap. "There's a guy with her."

"Bert Falkenberg, I'd guess." With an apologetic shrug, Claudia pulled on a long tee shirt and hurried downstairs, hoping the scent of sex didn't cling too conspicuously.

Falkenberg was dressed in Levis and a western shirt, his wiry hair slicked back.

"I know we're early," he said, resting his hand on Annabelle's shoulder. "But she couldn't wait to get here. I hope you don't mind. She ate breakfast before we left."

Annabelle wore hip hugger jeans and a belly shirt that showed a lot of skin, including a ring-pierced navel. Her black hair was brushed to a high gloss and hung like a half-drawn curtain on either side of her face. Muttering a barely audible greeting, she slouched inside.

The big kid-sitting experiment.

Claudia showed them into the living room. Falkenberg's eyes darted around the room the way they had on the day he'd brought Paige to see her.

"Can I get you some coffee, Bert?"

He turned, realizing belatedly that she had asked him a question. "Thanks, but I have to get going."

"Where are you off to?" Claudia didn't care about his social life, but she was curious about Paige's. Considering the responsibility she was taking on, it irked her that she didn't know for sure whether Paige's weekend plans included Cruz or Bert, or someone else altogether.

"Palm Springs." He cupped his hand to his mouth as if about to share a dirty secret. "I play a little poker at Agua Caliente when

I get a chance."

"Win much?"

He gave a self-deprecating shrug, but Claudia didn't miss the pride behind it. "Let's say I win more than I lose," he said. "I prefer Vegas, but I don't have time this weekend."

"Going alone?" Claudia persisted, hoping for more details.

He shook his head. "I've got a lady friend who likes to go along."

"Oh. How's Paige doing?"

He looked away, focusing his gaze on the framed Lena Rivkin painting on the bookcase. "I haven't seen her today, but I'm sure she'll be fine. Diana's lucky she doesn't want to press charges for assault."

"Do you think the Sorensens are as dangerous as Paige believes?"

He gave her a knowing smile but did not answer and that made her wonder why.

To fill the awkward silence, Claudia got the remote control from the coffee table and handed it to her young guest.

"Annabelle, you can watch TV while I shower and get dressed. My niece will be here in a little while and we'll go do something fun."

Annabelle blew a big purple bubble, popped it. She plopped onto the sofa and Falkenberg dropped her backpack on the floor beside her. "Here's your stuff, Anna," he said.

The girl glanced up from clicking through the channels with an elaborately bored sigh. "Whatever."

He reached out to chuck her under the chin, but she jerked her head away. "Behave yourself for Ms. Rose, okay, young lady?"

Claudia saw him to the door, wondering with a little ripple of unease if she had gotten herself in too deep. Kids were not her specialty.

Upstairs, Jovanic was dressed in shorts, one foot up on a chair, lacing up his running shoe. Claudia came up from behind and wrapped her arms around him, leaned her cheek against his bare back. "We're always getting interrupted at the worst moments."

He grunted and straightened, threw a tee shirt over his shoulder and swatted her on the butt as they headed downstairs. "You mean the *best* moments, don't you?"

Annabelle's demeanor improved with Falkenberg's departure, and Claudia began to harbor a small hope that the weekend would be a success, that she could balance her attention between the two girls and Jovanic. But when she introduced Annabelle to Jovanic, he made no attempt to hide his annoyance at the terse response she gave him, and that small hope took a nosedive.

God. Is the entire weekend going to be like this?

"Bert made that up about me wanting to come over here early," Annabelle said when Jovanic had jogged down the street. "*He* was the one who couldn't wait to get away from the school."

"Why would he make it up?"

Shrug. "Paige pissed him off and he probably didn't want to look like a dork for bringing me so early."

"How do you know Paige pissed him off?"

"I heard them yelling." She made an innocent face. "I wasn't *trying* to listen. Bert wanted her to go with him, but she said she had other plans."

"So he put it on *you*?"

Annabelle gave another couldn't-care-less jerk of her shoulder and changed the subject. "Is your boyfriend a cop?"

"What makes you ask that?"

"I can *smell* it." She wrinkled her nose for emphasis. They were in the kitchen snapping cans of soda and awaiting the arrival of Pete and Monica.

Annabelle took the gum out of her mouth and drank from the can. "He *is*, isn't he?"

Exasperated, Claudia folded her arms and gave her the skinny eyes. "What if he is? Is that a problem for you, Annabelle?"

"He's your boyfriend, I'll cut him some slack."

"That's mighty big of you."

"No problem." Annabelle dipped her head, but she couldn't quite hide the smile that transformed her into a regular kid instead of a sullen brat.

Then her cell phone rang and the scowl fell back over her face. She crossed her arms in a defiant pose and stared at Claudia.

"Aren't you going to answer it?" Claudia asked.

"It's just my father."

"Then answer it, please."

With a big show of impatience, Annabelle dug the phone out of her pocket.

"What?" There was a pause while her father spoke, then she said with great indignation, "I did not!" Another pause. "That's all you care about. Well, I don't have your keys… No…"

She powered off the phone and stuffed it back into her pocket. "He's always blaming me for everything. I didn't take his stupid car keys." Her eyes blazed with resentment. "I wish…"

Her wish stayed on her lips, interrupted by the doorbell. Running feet sounded on the teak floor of the living room. A lanky girl dressed in denim overalls rushed into the kitchen, long hair flowing from beneath a floppy sunflower hat. A classic California Girl in the making.

The girl threw herself onto Claudia. "Aunty C!" Her voice was muffled in the hug. "I can't believe Daddy's letting me stay over! How cool is that? He never lets me go anywhere!" She did a quick pirouette. "Are you Annabelle? Hi, I'm Monica." Somehow, it all came out in one breath.

Annabelle stared at the girl bouncing around the kitchen as Monica prattled on. "Daddy's putting my stuff upstairs. Aunty C, if I showed you some handwriting, would you, like, tell me about that person?"

Claudia grinned at her. "Does this 'person' happen to be male?"

Monica blushed and giggled. "Well—"

"*Duh!*" Annabelle interrupted with a big eye roll. "What else?"

The two girls' eyes met, and Claudia was amazed to see something click. Annabelle, who hadn't made a single friend at the Sorensen Academy in the months she'd been there, had made an instant connection with Claudia's niece.

Maybe Paige wasn't so far off the mark. Getting away from school and meeting someone who knew nothing about her background—someone who was as opposite as she could be—would give Annabelle another chance.

When Claudia joined the men in the living room they were laughing

99

at something on the television. At six-two, Claudia's brother, Pete, matched Jovanic for height, but his build was slight. Today he looked more like a lumberjack than the computer techie he was. Strictly L.L. Bean in jeans, heavy work boots, and plaid flannel shirt flapping open over a dark tee. He wore his forty-three years well.

A stranger might not see it, but since his wife's death two years earlier, Pete's laughter never quite reached his eyes. Of course, Claudia was no stranger. She put her arms around him and squeezed. "All set?"

"Yes, ma'am. I'm gonna catch me some tuna *thiiis* big." He stretched his arms wide.

She laughed. "Sounds like a fishy story to me. Something to eat first?"

"No thanks, Sis, I want to get to San Diego and check out the boat." He turned to his daughter and wrapped his arms around her in a bear hug. "Do everything your Aunt Claudia says. Stay close to her when you go out. Don't go off by yourselves."

"Oh Daddy, stop worrying! We're going Christmas shopping."

Claudia glanced over at Annabelle, who had hung back and was watching with a guarded expression. The contrast between the two motherless girls was not lost on her—a doting daddy for one, a distant absentee father for the other.

Pete left, and Jovanic, who had returned from his run, followed shortly afterward. The girls went upstairs to unpack their overnight bags. Claudia went into her office to work on a handwriting analysis while they waited for her friend, Kelly Brennan. The four of them would head for the mall. It was still November, but the holiday season got more elastic every year.

About thirty minutes later there was a knock at the office door and Monica's blonde head poked around it. "Could you look at that handwriting now?" She came over to Claudia and stuck a sheet of lined notebook paper in front of her. "*Please?*"

Claudia stretched and pushed her chair away from the desk. "Sure, let's take a look at this guy."

Annabelle sidled in after her and gazed around the office with interest. "This is where you work?"

"This is it. Pull up a couple of chairs."

"Why did Joel leave?" Monica asked.

Claudia switched on some lamps while the girls settled themselves. "He had some stuff to do at his apartment. He'll be back later, after we get home from the mall." She unfolded the paper. "Okay, let's see what you've got."

It appeared to be a school essay.

"*Sports are worthless,*" it began. "*What's the point? They only cause pain and injury, shortening the life span of many athletes...*" It went on in the same vein for another dozen or so lines. The handwriting was tense, narrow and brittle, the pressure heavy on the paper. Claudia looked up at her niece with a frown of concern. "This isn't your boyfriend, is it?"

"No, it's for my friend. She thinks he's totally awesome— hardcore. She wants to know what you can tell about him."

Claudia hoped her niece was telling the truth. The handwriting reminded her too much of the two teenaged boys who had engineered the Columbine school massacre in the 1990's. They had murdered more than a dozen of their classmates before killing themselves.

"I get it that she thinks he's awesome, but this boy has some big problems. He's got a lot of anger inside him. Sometimes, when tension builds up, it can explode and hurt other people. It looks to me like his father is very strict, and the boy is feeling resentful."

"How can you tell that about his father?" Annabelle cut in.

"It's not one thing that tells me," said Claudia. "It's the total picture of the handwriting—the way it's laid out on the page, the way the letters look, the pressure. Lots of stuff." She gave her niece a serious look. "Monica, your friend should keep her distance. This boy has bigger problems than she can deal with."

A few minutes into the discussion, Annabelle ducked out, returning a moment later. "I have some handwriting I want you to tell me about, too," she said, handing over a small folded note card, the kind that comes with gifts and flowers.

Claudia opened it and eyed the block-printed message. It was well-developed, mature. Adult. No signature. Although she typically did not read the text of a handwriting she was analyzing until after the analysis was complete, she was curious to see what Annabelle had brought her.

"*Between the two holidays,*" she read to herself. "*Besos, besos,*

besos."

Kisses, kisses, kisses.

She glanced at Annabelle, hiding the stab of dismay she felt. "Who wrote this?"

"Someone I know."

"Where'd you get it, Annabelle?"

The girl glared at her, a sudden return of defiance, palpable in the set of her shoulders, the jut of her chin, the way she compressed her lips. "Are you gonna tell me about him or not?"

"First, I'd like to know what you're doing with this note. Was it written to you?"

"Just forget it." Annabelle snatched the card back and stalked out of the office. Claudia wasn't certain, but thought she heard her mutter, "*Bitch.*"

Monica stared after her new friend, looking appalled. "What's wrong with her?"

"Annabelle lost her mom when she was six years old," she explained. "She had a car accident, like your mom. But she's not close to her dad. I don't think he's around much, so she doesn't get a lot of attention. I guess that's why she acts that way."

Annabelle must be a real wake-up call for her sheltered niece, Claudia thought. Pete wouldn't thank her for that.

Claudia could see Monica's tender heart engage. Even as a child, she had always been protective of small creatures and underdogs.

"I'm gonna go talk to her," said Monica. "I'll make her feel better."

Claudia watched her go. *Jeez.* They hadn't even made it to the mall yet, and she was already worn out.

The shops had been holiday-ready since before Halloween, and consumers jammed the Westside Pavilion. Overhead, red neon outlined the arched roof of the mall. Reindeer and stars in the rafters, Christmas trees hung with every decoration known to man. Lights everywhere. *The Little Drummer Boy* 'parump-a-pum-pummed' from every speaker.

Despite the decorations, Claudia was not in a holiday frame of mind. Annabelle's mood had improved enough for her to offer a grudging apology for her earlier behavior. But she remained steadfast in her refusal to reveal where she had gotten the gift card or who had written the message in it.

They started at Planet Funk and went on to Hot Topic. Claudia began to feel ancient. She couldn't remember dressing so scantily or wearing such graphic tee shirts when she was Annabelle and Monica's age, and the music was way too loud. With an inward groan, she realized that she was echoing her mother. Kelly's suggestion of Victoria's Secret made her brighten. Maybe she would find something to improve Jovanic's mood.

Mistletoe and pink and white garlands adorned larger than life posters starring lingerie-clad models with impossibly perfect bodies in fur-trimmed Santa hats and shiny black patent leather, spike-heeled boots.

The girls headed for the Pink section while the two women browsed. Claudia picked a merry widow bustier from a rack and held it against her. "What do you think?"

Kelly shook her head. "Lose that feathery stuff around the top."

Claudia hung it back on the rack with regret. "It *is* kind of excessive, isn't it?"

"You need something to make him laugh."

"That's not exactly the response I was after, Kel."

"No, no, trust me, he's *way* too serious. It's that cop thing. You gotta lighten him up." Kelly pointed to a table piled with novelty stockings. "How about these?"

A pair of model legs stood on the table, displaying red silk thigh-highs. Embroidered in a holiday design in the lace at the top of one leg was *Merry Christmas.* On the other, *Happy New Year.*

"Like that old Mae West line," Kelly said cocking a hip and resting her fist on it.

"Which one? She had so many good lines."

"*My right leg is Christmas,*" Kelly quoted, imitating the sex goddess' sultry voice. "*My left leg is New Year's. Come see me between the holidays.*"

Claudia rolled her eyes. "Oh, jeez, that's pretty corny." She turned to another table, considering some black thong panties. "Just shows how—" She stopped mid-sentence. "Holy crap."

"What?"

A quick glance around made sure the girls were not within earshot. She told Kelly about the gift card Annabelle had showed her.

"It said, 'Between the two holidays. Besos, besos, besos.' Do you think–?"

Kelly raised her eyebrows. "Who's writing her shit like that?"

"She wouldn't say where she got it, but I'm pretty sure I *know*."

"So, don't keep me in suspense, grasshopper."

"One of the instructors at the Sorensen Academy. *Besos* is Spanish for kisses. He's Puerto Rican, *and* she's got a big crush on him."

"A frigging teacher? You've gotta be shittin' me. You have to report him. This is over the line, even for *me*."

"*If* he wrote it to her."

"What do you mean? You just said she got it from him."

"Paige Sorensen and this guy, Cruz, have a thing going on. She thinks he's hot, and I'm pretty sure they're together this weekend. Annabelle could have snagged it off Paige's desk."

"You know the guy?"

"We've met a couple of times." Claudia fluttered her lashes. "Soulful eyes you could fall into. Nice butt."

"So, introduce me."

"Forget it, it's complicated enough already. He doesn't need you hitting on him."

"Oh come on, I'm only up to ninety-seven. I'm falling behind."

"Jeez, Kelly, you're not still keeping score, are you?" For years, Kelly had been keeping a list of men she'd slept with. She was aiming for two hundred before she turned forty, which was a few short months away. "In this day and age? Are you fucking nuts?"

Kelly grinned. "No, honey, most of the guys I fuck these days are pretty sane."

Kelly dropped them back at Claudia's house late in the afternoon, loaded down with shopping bags. The girls were chattering to each other and giggling like lifelong friends.

Annabelle Giordano, normal kid. Go figure. It felt good to see her scowl replaced with a grin.

Jovanic was deep in a Lakers game. He greeted them absently.

"Why don't you girls go upstairs and try on your new duds?" Claudia suggested, hoping for a few minutes alone with him. They didn't wait to be asked twice. Moments later, the stereo was blasting from the spare bedroom.

Dumping her bags on the floor, Claudia selected the one with the Victoria's Secret stripes. Trying to compete with Kobe Bryant was a non-starter, so she waited for the break. When the commercials came on she folded back the tissue paper to give Jovanic a glimpse of its contents.

"Tomorrow night," she tempted, swaying her body suggestively in front of him.

He glanced in at the froth of black lace and leered at her. "How about tonight?"

She shook her head. "It'd be too weird with the girls in the next room. *Tomorrow*, I promise." She dropped onto the sofa beside him. "I think we covered every inch of that mall."

"Mmhm."

"Annabelle started to open up. First time I've seen her be—"

"I'm supposed to be impressed?" Jovanic interrupted with a scowl. "Can't you see she's playing you, Claudia?" He returned his gaze to the television. Kwame Brown scored and the crowd was on their feet, chanting. "Kids like her don't change this late in the game."

Claudia felt the hot flash of irritation burn up her neck and into her cheeks. "You think I'm so stupid I don't know if a fourteen-year-old is trying to manipulate me?"

"I didn't say you were stupid. You're just not used to dealing with juvenile delinquents."

She glanced behind them at the stairs. From the second floor the girls were singing along at the top of their voices as Missy Elliott rapped about how hot she was. The volume was high enough to drown out their conversation.

"She is *not* a juvenile delinquent. She's a kid who's been neglected and doesn't have anyone to care about her."

Jovanic got up and stretched. "Yeah, well, now she's got *you*, hasn't she, Mother Theresa? I'm going home."

"What the hell is wrong with you? What about the game?"

He made a sound of disgust and clicked off the television. "How am I supposed to watch the game with all that noise?"

"Joel, this isn't like you. Why are you so cranky?"

Jovanic shook his head and leveled a look at her. "Sometimes, Claudia, I get tired of playing second fiddle to your clients, your family, and now this–stray kid you bring home. You don't make time for us. This is a prime example—Paige asks you to take this girl for the weekend; you say sure, no problem. Same with Monica. You didn't ask my opinion. It never occurred to you that I might have wanted to do something alone with you this weekend."

"You never said anything about this weekend. Was there something you wanted to do?"

"It's a little late now, but yeah, I got tickets for Eddie Izzard's show at the Henry Ford Theater. Wanted to surprise you."

A sick feeling hit the pit of her stomach. Jovanic knew the popular British comedian was a favorite of hers. It couldn't have been easy to get the tickets.

"I'm sorry, Joel. I had no idea."

"That's what a surprise is, hon—no idea. Don't worry about it. I gave the tickets to Alex this morning." He picked up his windbreaker and slung it over his shoulder. "You know what you do, Claudia? You use other people to keep me from getting too close."

"That's so unfair. What about all the times your work gets in the way?"

"I'm not talking about work," he said, closing the front door behind him with a louder snap than he needed to.

Claudia stood there staring at the door.

"Shit! Shit! Shit!"

Upstairs, the music had ended and things were quiet. Claudia went into the kitchen thinking about what Jovanic had said and asking herself whether he was right about her pushing him away. She collected some Cokes from the fridge and a bag of chips from the pantry. As long as she was being criticized for having the girls over, she might as well make the most of it and take them a snack.

When she got to the second floor landing, an unmistakable smell hit her nose.

Marijuana. Dammit!

Paige Sorensen was probably hanging from a chandelier by her toes, having wild, satisfying sex with Cruz or one of her other admirers—maybe several of them—while she, Claudia, was stuck with a bratty pot-smoking adolescent and an irate boyfriend. Next time someone asked for a favor, she promised herself, she wouldn't cave in so fast.

Gritting her teeth, she rapped on the bathroom door. "Annabelle, you want to get me arrested?"

There was a brief pause, the sound of scuffling, whispering, then innocence. "I'm not doing anything."

"Open the door. *Now.*"

The toilet flushed and a long moment later the door opened. Annabelle and Monica stood there, looking guilty as sin.

CHAPTER 13

Annabelle slunk out of the bathroom, a pall of hemp-scented smoke clinging to her denim jacket like an invisible cloud. The straps of her backpack were looped over her wrist, dragging along the floor behind her. She slithered past Claudia and into the guest room, head down.

Hiding the bloodshot eyes, Claudia guessed bitterly.

Monica looked shamefaced. "I'm sorry, Aunty C," she whispered.

Claudia glared at her. "I can't believe this! Your father is going to *kill* me."

"I didn't smoke it, I swear I didn't." Monica's voice broke. "*Please* don't tell him. He'll never let me leave the house again!"

"You should have thought of that." Claudia raked her hand through her hair in frustration, afraid that Jovanic had been right. She raised her voice. "Annabelle, come back out here." And when she had rejoined them, "I can't have this going on here. Joel is a *cop*, for crying out loud."

"It was all my fault," Monica said quickly. "I asked Annabelle if she'd ever smoked pot. She wouldn't let me try it. I wanted to, but she said no."

"Listen, both of you. I'm happy to have you here, but you've got to follow the rules. Understand?"

Monica said, "Yes, Aunty C, I promise. Please don't tell on me, okay?"

From Annabelle, she got the shrug. "*Whatever.*"

"That's not good enough, Annabelle."

The girl swung around on her with a scowl. "How come everybody's always on my case? I didn't *do* anything wrong."

Claudia wanted to shake her.

After the pot-smoking episode, Claudia took a long, hard look at where she was going with Annabelle. The odor had lingered long enough for Jovanic to notice and go ballistic. She knew that his reaction would have been less heavy-handed if things had been better between them that weekend, but it was a pitched battle to talk him out of turning the girl over to the juvenile authorities.

In the final analysis, she concluded that what Annabelle needed most was consistency and an adult she could trust. Jovanic's feelings were important to her, but he would have to find a way to deal with her desire to help the girl. Having settled that in her mind, and figuring she could hold it over the girls in case either of them got out of hand, she decided not to report the incident to Paige or Pete.

For the next couple of weeks Annabelle was subdued and kept her nose clean at school. She and Claudia spoke over the phone several times and she dutifully faxed her graphotherapy worksheets twice a week.

Arriving at the Sorensen Academy for Annabelle's in-person graphotherapy session, Claudia found the lobby redolent with the scent of fresh pine from an enormous Douglas fir decorated as a Victorian Christmas tree.

She paused to enjoy the red velvet bows and pearl satin ribbons, the glittering stars and silver garlands draped over the boughs. Natural green branches showed from beneath the ornaments, making her glad the majestic tree hadn't been flocked with fake snow. Red-and-white striped candy canes, gingerbread men and painted glass ornaments sent her back to her childhood at Granny Arlene's house, before life became complicated.

Gift boxes were stacked around the base of the tree, some imprinted with the names of Beverly Hills department stores. *The gift-wrap alone must have cost more than anything I bought during the shopping trip with the girls and Kelly.*

"They're for homeless children," said Brenda, the receptionist, noticing her stare. "Mrs. Sorensen asked all the students and the staff to pitch in. She's taking the gifts to a homeless shelter in Santa Monica on Christmas Day with Mr. Falkenberg and Mr. Montenegro."

Claudia couldn't help being impressed. She had begun to think that all of Paige's interests were self-involved. "I'll run over to the mall after I leave here, and drop something off," she said.

A big smile transformed Brenda's plain face. "That would be awesome, Ms. Rose. Those poor little kids need all the holiday spirit they can get." She reached for the ringing phone as she asked, "You're here to see Annabelle?"

Claudia nodded. "Is she ready for me?"

"Yes, but Mrs. Sorensen wanted to see you first. She's in her office."

Claudia hurried upstairs, wondering about the reason for the summons. There had been no contact from Paige since Annabelle's visit. Maybe she was ready to say 'thank you.'

"They're at it again," said Paige as Claudia walked into her office. "The twins." She pointed to her desk, where a sheet of paper lay atop the blotter.

Claudia dropped into the guest chair. From her vantage point she could see the numbered lines running down the left side of the paper and guessed that it was a legal filing or pleading.

"What this time?"

"They've filed a lawsuit for 'undue influence!' We won the forgery case, but now this! They're claiming I *forced* Torg to sign the will." Paige yanked open her desk drawer and withdrew an envelope, extracted a sheet of notepaper and brandished it at Claudia. "I got this in yesterday's mail. I want to know what you can tell me about the person who wrote it."

The handwriting on the heavy cream-colored notepaper had a wild, uncontrolled rhythm. Thick black ink covered the page. Overly embellished loops, tangled lines, large, extravagant capital letters. The writer had left no margins at all on any of the four sides.

Claudia gestured at Paige with the notepaper. "Male or female?"

"Can't you tell it's a woman?"

"No, you can't conclusively tell gender or age from handwriting. What it does show is whether the writer's personality traits are more masculine or more feminine, and the emotional maturity level compared to chronological age."

She waved the paper. "This is not a girly girl. This is more of a masculine energy who takes over absolutely everything in her environment. See how she starts writing on the extreme left edge of the paper and doesn't stop until she gets to the edge of the right side? She bends the writing down on the right edge to cram in what she wants to say. That means you're forced to either twist your neck or turn the paper if you want to read it. Then she starts the next line so close to the last one that she writes over the tops of the loops on the line before."

"So, what does it *mean?*" Paige asked, clicking her fingernails on the desk in a jittery way that made Claudia want to grab her hand and stop it.

"She crowds people in an effort to control them. She stands too close when you're having a conversation. She doesn't know when it's time to leave."

"Diana sent it. That sounds like her all right." Paige turned her left hand over and stared at her palm, which was still healing from the cut she had suffered in Diana's attack. "I can't believe the crazy bitch is threatening me again. Hasn't she done enough?" She took the letter back from Claudia. "Did you *read* it?"

Claudia shook her head. "I don't have to read it to understand the personality."

"Okay, then listen to this." Paige began reading in a tone that dripped sarcasm:

"Stepmommy Dearest. You killed our father and stole our inheritance. I'm going to prove it and, when I do, I promise you'll pay in spades for what you've put us through."

"She's accusing you of killing your husband?"

"Wait," Paige said, looking grim. "You haven't

heard the best part." She took a deep breath and continued reading:

> "*We know what you've been up to. Don't think you're going to get away with it. You made our father's life a living hell, parading your boy toys in front of his face. Better watch your back—you might find a knife in it.*"

Claudia reached out her hand and Paige returned the letter to her. Studying the handwriting again, she tried to assess how much real danger the implied threat might pose. Her eyes rested on "boy toys," and she wondered whether Diana's brother, Neil, was included in the taunt.

She could feel Paige watching her, waiting for some kind of reaction. She asked, "What are you going to do about this?"

"What the hell *can* I do?"

"Get a restraining order against her."

Paige gave a harsh laugh. "A restraining order? How would *that* help?"

"A written threat is an arrestable offense. You have to show this to the police, Paige."

"I don't want to have her *arrested!*"

Claudia recalled the jolt of fear she had felt in the face of Diana's rage. "Why not? She's made a threat."

"I don't want the police," Paige said. "I don't want her going public with these accusations. Jesus, Claudia, would you send your daughter to a school where the headmistress has been accused of having affairs and killing her elderly husband? The accusations alone would be enough to destroy me."

Refolding the letter, Claudia laid it on top of the court papers on Paige's desk. A knot of schoolgirls passed the office door, chattering loudly. They called out greetings to Paige, who replied in a sunny voice, making it seem that all was right in her world.

Once the students were out of earshot, she dropped the Pollyanna act and repeated, "I'm *not* going to the police with this. I just want to know what you think of her handwriting. How dangerous is she?"

Claudia chewed on her lower lip, considering. It wasn't an easy question to answer.

"What you need to understand is, handwriting can't predict behavior, but it shows potential. She may or may not act on it, depending on circumstances. This is the sort of person who doesn't plan ahead, she acts on impulse. What disturbs me is she has this need to control everyone and everything, but she lacks self-control. I doubt she meant she would literally stab you in the back, but, Paige—why take chances?"

"I told you, the bad publicity!"

"Listen," Claudia said. "The guy I'm seeing is a detective. I could talk to him for you, get some advice."

But Paige was adamant. "No! They're going to find out I'm tougher than they think. They can't control me with their threats. I'll call their bluff."

"Not so long ago you were so afraid of these people you talked about getting a gun. Now you've got an actual threat and you're not going to do anything?"

A noise at the door made Claudia turn her head.

Neil Sorensen wheeled into the room, his wheelchair whisper-soft on the carpeting.

What's he doing here?

She hadn't seen him since the day of Paige's hearing, nor had Paige mentioned him since the time she'd come to Claudia's house, claiming to be seeking a confidante. Claudia shot a glance at Paige to gauge her reaction.

Paige's face cleared and her smile could have lit the Christmas tree in the lobby. "Hi there, sweetie," she said. She rose from her desk and went over to him, the bitter animosity she had expressed toward Neil's siblings evaporating as if Claudia had imagined it.

She bent down and kissed his cheek. Neil's hand reached up and grabbed hers. He turned it over and touched her injured palm to his lips. Maneuvering his chair around the furniture, he stopped a few feet from where Claudia sat on the sofa, watching them.

"Ms. Rose," he said, offering his hand, which was speckled with a whitish substance—paint or plaster by the look of it. He wore a gray sweatshirt stained with a similar material, and khaki cargo pants. "I haven't had the pleasure, at least, not formally. I'm Neil Sorensen."

113

His skin felt dry and cool as he took her hand. She had expected weakness, what she got was a firm grasp and the upper body strength of someone who worked out.

"Nice to meet you," Claudia said, wondering how she was supposed to react to Torg Sorensen's youngest offspring. Didn't he view her as the enemy the way his older siblings did? He wasn't looking at her with the same antagonism. His gaze appeared open and direct, curious. Out of the shadow of his brother and sister he seemed far more alive than she remembered from that day in court.

Oblivious to Claudia's discomfort, Paige sat next to her on the sofa so that her face was on a level with Neil's. "What's up, hon?"

He swiveled his chair in her direction. "I seem to have picked a bad time. I wanted to talk to you about Annabelle."

"Let me guess, she's causing problems again."

Neil's gaze shifted toward Claudia, and Paige said, "She's been working with Annabelle—some handwriting therapy, supposed to improve her behavior."

He tilted his head, the thin lips pursing. "Interesting. It does seem like she's been a little calmer. But you still need to do something about her, Paige. She's flat out refusing to do the assignments the way I want them."

"What do you want me to do, Neil, lock her in her room?"

Claudia's gaze bounced between them like a spectator at a tennis match. Paige noticed her puzzlement and smiled. "Oh, I forgot, you didn't know, Claudia. Neil's the art instructor here at the school."

CHAPTER 14

Claudia left the office wondering why Paige had never mentioned that Neil Sorensen worked at the Academy. It seemed an important piece of information to have left out. She had spilled her guts about the rest of the family, and even talked about Neil coming on to her.

With this latest revelation, Paige's claims to need a friend rang hollow. Maybe what she needed was an audience.

Wondering what other information Paige might have withheld, Claudia was fuming by the time she hit the lobby. She would work Annabelle through her graphotherapy program, she decided, and then walk away from the Sorensen Academy and the melodrama that seemed to cling to Paige like Velcro.

The end of the day. Study Hall in session meant silence at the Sorensen Academy.

When Claudia opened the door to the near-empty classroom where the graphotherapy sessions were held, her ears were greeted by the sound of a rhythmic *thud-squeak, thud-squeak*.

Alone in the room, Annabelle was hunched over her desk in a corner, a small shadow in her black sweater and black Levis. The sound was coming from her sneakers as she lifted her feet a few inches then dropped them, scuffing the polished wood floor.

Thud-squeak. Thud-squeak. Thud-squeak.

"Hey, kiddo," Claudia said.

No response. The shoulders stayed hunched. The sneakers continued to rise and fall.

Thud-squeak. Thud-squeak. Thud-squeak.

"Annabelle?" Claudia reached out and put a gentle hand on the girl's shoulder, only to have the shoulder wrenched away. "What's wrong?"

"I don't want to do this anymore." The mumble was barely audible. "It's not making any difference."

"Funny you should say that. I heard from your art teacher that he's pleased with your improvement."

"He's lying. My life still sucks."

Claudia sat down at the desk next to her. "Did something happen?"

Without looking up, Annabelle gave her head a fierce shake. "Just go away. Leave me alone."

"I came across town to see you. Why don't we talk about it?"

Another sharp shake of the head. "No!" Her voice broke on a half-sob and she muttered a few words that included 'slut.'

"Who are you talking about?" Claudia asked.

"Leave me *alone*."

"Sorry, kiddo, that's not an option."

Silence.

"Annabelle, please look at me."

The girl turned toward her and shot her an angry glare. "*What?*"

With her face turned into the light, Claudia understood why she wanted to avoid scrutiny: the makings of a black eye and a swollen lower lip, a scratch across her cheek. The dark eyes sparked with rage and pain.

"Annabelle! What happened?"

Annabelle turned toward the wall, her back rigid with tension. "Don't worry about it."

The girl was pricklier than a porcupine.

Claudia wasn't sure what she should do next, so she kept going. "I'm your friend, remember? Please let me help."

Annabelle twisted back around to face her with narrowed eyes and pinched lips. "You *said* those exercises would work, but they didn't. They didn't do *anything*. It's the same as it always was."

"It's not magic, Annabelle. Things don't change overnight. But *some* things are better, aren't they? We had a good time at the—"

"Leave me the *fuck* alone!"

Enough is enough.

Claudia got to her feet. "Call me if you change your mind."

Later, Claudia was in the kitchen of her friend, Zebediah Gold, drinking tea and relating what she knew about Annabelle Giordano.

"Sounds like a very troubled child," Zebediah said. He squeezed a large dollop of honey into his cup, then wiped the lip of the honey bear bottle with a damp paper towel and set it back on the table. "Somebody had better do something fast, or life is going to rise up and give Miss Annabelle a smack in the chops."

"Jeez, Zeb, why don't you have a little tea with your honey? I doubt she's had any real therapy, except what she got in the hospital after her suicide attempt. The graphotherapy she's doing with me isn't enough on its own."

"She needs long-term help after what she's been through," Zebediah said. He started ticking off items on his fingers. "Less than ideal home, she witnesses her mother's death. Beloved nanny disappears without a word. A child would perceive that as a rejection, even though she might understand from a logical point of view what happened. The father is neglectful. That's a form of abuse with a capital 'A.' So, what have I forgotten?"

"She's been in trouble with the law for shoplifting and joyriding with some punks who stole a car." Claudia shook her head, frustrated and disappointed. "We had one incident, on that weekend she stayed over, but overall, things seemed to go well. I thought—" She broke off and nibbled at an oatmeal cookie Zebediah pushed in front of her.

"You thought what? That your magic touch would affect an overnight cure of a condition that's taken eight years to develop?"

"Okay, I know it was dumb."

Zebediah's face creased into a smile that made him look a lot like Clint Eastwood. "Darling, you're anything but dumb and you do have a magic touch, but don't set the bar so high. And don't kid yourself. You *have* made a positive contribution. You put enough faith in the child to take her into your home and expose your niece to her. Unless she's unredeemable—and you wouldn't have done that if you thought she was—she's made a connection with you. It takes time. You've let her know you're there for her, even when she's behaving badly. Don't forget how she came to your defense when that Sorensen daughter attacked you."

"You just reminded me," said Claudia, and proceeded to tell him about the letter Paige had received from her stepdaughter with its implicit threat. "Don't you think Paige ought to tell the police in case Diana is the lunatic she appears to be?"

He rubbed his beard the way he sometimes did when he wanted to buy time. After thinking about it, he said, "The police tend not to take things like that seriously unless there's a long history of violence."

"She pushed Paige down and injured her. And If Annabelle hadn't jumped in, I might have gone right over that railing. That's pretty violent."

"But it sounds like Paige has her mind made up," Zebediah said. "There's not a lot you can do about that, and she's right about the bad publicity involving the police and what it would bring. But you *can* continue to be supportive of the child."

Claudia thought of Annabelle, sitting at the desk in the empty classroom. The dejection in the way she had hugged her sweater around her slight frame, her head turned to the wall, had torn at Claudia's heart.

"I went back to talk to Paige but she wasn't in her office. Maybe I shouldn't have left the kid alone."

"After the way she spoke to you, it was the best thing to do. Walking out let her know that her behavior wasn't okay. The way to teach someone not to treat you badly is by not putting up with it."

"I'm not so sure, Zeb." Claudia got up and poured more hot water over her tea bag. She veered onto another unanswered question. "I'm thinking Paige and Neil Sorensen must have been getting it on. Don't you think it was strange that she never told me he works at the school?"

"Sweetie, from what you've said, the entire Sorensen clan is pretty strange. How many times have you heard me advise against getting personally involved with clients?"

She made a goofy face but didn't answer. Truth was, she'd lost count.

The telephone was ringing as she unlocked the door. Dropping the grocery bags she was carrying onto the kitchen counter, Claudia snatched up the receiver. The caller ID display read *Sorensen Academy.*

"Hi, Claudia." *Paige.* "Brenda said you left early. What's going on?"

"Annabelle wasn't in the mood to work. I looked for you, but you weren't around."

Paige gave a little laugh that almost qualified as a giggle. "Neil was showing me some er, artwork, then Cruz came along and—those two guys can't stand each other. Neil's jealous for obvious reasons, and Cruz, well, that's another story. They're so funny to watch."

Claudia couldn't see the humor, but she kept her thoughts to herself.

"So, what happened that you left early?" Paige asked when she didn't respond.

"What happened to Annabelle? How did she get beaten up? I couldn't get her to talk."

There was a long silence and Claudia could almost feel Paige waffling on how to respond. "Don't you think you owe me an explanation?" she pressed. "You talked me into bringing her into my home, introducing her to my niece. If there's a problem—"

"Okay, okay," Paige interrupted. "It's not that kind of problem." She lowered her voice. "Hang on. Let me close the door." The phone clattered to the desk and moments later Claudia heard the click of the office door, then Paige was back.

"This is another one of those potential PR nightmares, so don't repeat what I'm going to tell you, okay?"

"Fine. What is it?"

"Annabelle tried to beat down her roommate, Britney Levine. She went for the girl's throat."

Claudia groaned inwardly. She wasn't shocked, or even surprised by Paige's revelation. Her work made her all-too-familiar with the many sides of human nature and she was more than a little jaded.

But she liked Annabelle, prickles and all, and she cared what happened to her. What Paige had told her didn't bode well for the girl's future.

"Why would she do that?" she asked.

Paige said, "Bert and I went out to dinner last night. Here we are, in the middle of the best prime rib in town, when I get a call from the night monitor. It seems Britney and a couple of the other residential girls had been making fun of Annabelle for the way she's always mooning after Cruz.

"According to one of the girls, quote: 'Britney tapped Annabelle on the back and Annabelle lost it,' unquote. She grabbed Britney by the throat and wouldn't let go. Britney's got the bruises to prove it. Then the other girls jumped in and started pounding Annabelle. That's when the night monitor heard the commotion and broke it up."

So Annabelle hadn't *started* the trouble, Claudia realized with some relief, even though it made little difference to the end result that she had been defending herself. Tucking the phone under her chin, she began unpacking the groceries and putting them away. "Throttling your roommate is serious. What's going to happen to Annabelle?"

"I had to call all the parents, of course," Paige said. "As you can guess, the Levines were furious, threatened to withdraw Britney from the school. That really made my day. Annabelle's lucky I didn't expel her."

"Why didn't you?"

"When I spoke with Dominic—her father—he said that if I would give her one more chance, he'd handle the Levines. I think they know each other. Ted Levine is in the Industry, too."

"Annabelle's father intervened?"

"Yeah. And whatever he said worked. The Levines called back *apologizing*! They said it turned out to be a misunderstanding between the girls; they'd make sure Britney behaved better." Paige gave a small huff. "I'd like to know what Dominic promised them to make them change their attitude that way."

"Maybe he made them an offer they couldn't refuse," Claudia said.

"Oh, that's funny, Claudia," Paige said, sounding less than

amused. "Christmas recess started today, thank god. When the residential girls come back, Britney will have been moved to another room. Annabelle can have their old room to herself."

"Solitary confinement?"

"That's what she wants. That's what she's going to get."

"So, Annabelle's gone home for Christmas?"

"No, she's the only one who's staying here. Her father's in Switzerland for the holiday. He asked me to keep her until next Tuesday, when he gets back."

With Christmas two days away, Dominic Giordano couldn't be bothered to make it home in time to spend the holiday with his daughter? Maybe Annabelle was better off at school.

Jovanic would be working over the long weekend and Claudia was flying to her parents' home in Seattle tonight, along with Pete and Monica. She toyed with the idea of asking to take Annabelle with them, but if Pete saw that black eye he would freak.

"What will she do for the holiday?" she asked Paige.

"She'll be with me. Her father sent money and I had Brenda pick her up a nice gift. Believe it or not, I'm cooking Christmas dinner. Cruz will be here, too, and you know that's all she cares about—Cruz."

Claudia unloaded cartons of yogurt and salad greens into the refrigerator, listening to Paige complain about Annabelle and how she wasn't sure it was worth the tuition money to put up with all the crap that came with it. But she had a feeling Paige was saying what she thought was expected. Dominic Giordano's influence would buy a whole lot of crap.

Without Jovanic, and with her mind on Annabelle's situation, Claudia did her best to fake some Christmas spirit, but her mother picked up on her mood and needled her about it the entire weekend. As usual, her father tried to defend her, and as usual it made things worse. Even Monica was relieved when they left for Sea-Tac Airport. Arriving home late Monday evening felt wonderful.

Claudia lay in bed, listening to the soft rumble of Jovanic's snores in the pre-dawn chill of Tuesday morning, the day Annabelle was due to go home and finish out the winter recess.

She thought back on her own fourteenth Christmas. Memories as bitter as bile, not worth revisiting. But that didn't stop them from pouring back: her parents fighting, her mother threatening divorce, not caring that Claudia and Pete could hear. That year, Claudia had rebelled; flunked her favorite subjects, fought with her best friends…wished she were dead.

She wondered how Annabelle had weathered the holidays.

Jovanic stirred, turned and spooned against her, mumbling something into her hair. She didn't know what he said, but she murmured an assent and scooted closer.

Annabelle and her problems ebbed to the far recesses of her mind.

But not for long.

CHAPTER 15

"Claudia!" Jovanic yelled from the kitchen, where he had been making coffee. "Come down here, hurry."

Claudia came out of the bathroom and onto the landing dressed in a long tee shirt, a mascara brush in her hand. "What did you say?"

"Sorensen Academy—something's happened there. It's on the news."

Something in his voice sent her running downstairs without asking for details.

Jovanic stood in front of the television dressed in dark slacks, a light blue dress shirt and darker blue tie, ready to leave for his shift. Claudia planted herself next to him and stared at the words, *Breaking News*, on the television screen, struggling to pick up the thread of the report.

Across the bottom of the screen, the crawl identified the reporter as Michelle Gillette.

"...this year's Laci Peterson case?" she was saying.

The camera pulled back, the shot widening to include Sorensen Academy's front lawn. The life-size Santa in his reindeer-drawn sleigh looked slightly ludicrous in the California sunshine.

Claudia's hand crept to her face, covering her mouth, which had dropped open as the impossible words continued to pour from Gillette's lips. "...apparently missing since Christmas Day."

Gillette turned to her right and the camera panned to include Bert Falkenberg, whose name and title were superimposed over his black Lacoste polo shirt. His ordinarily ruddy face was pale and drawn.

"I'm here with a representative from the school," Gillette said, pushing the microphone at him. "Mr. Norbert Falkenberg. Sir, what can you tell us about the situation?"

Claudia glanced wordlessly at Joel, then back at the television. *Omigod, what happened?*

Bert's grim expression sent a shiver of premonition through her. The muscles in his face were tight, but when he spoke his voice wobbled. "Our headmistress, Mrs. Paige Sorensen, has not been seen since Christmas Eve. The school is closed for the holidays, of course, so no one realized she was missing until today."

Annabelle didn't go home. What about Annabelle?

"When Mrs. Sorensen failed to show up for a scheduled meeting this morning and we were unable to reach her by phone, her rooms were searched, and when it became clear that she hadn't been around for several days, the police were called."

"How do you know that Mrs. Sorensen didn't just go away for the holiday?" Gillette asked.

"The housekeeper found Mrs. Sorensen's dog alone in her apartment at the school. He had no food or water, and well, frankly, he'd made quite a mess. Mrs. Sorensen would never have willingly left him in that condition." Bert fixed his gaze on the camera. "Her purse was in her apartment, but her car is missing. If anyone has any information on her whereabouts, please call the Beverly Hills Police Department immediately."

"Has Mrs. Sorensen ever gone missing before, sir?"

"Of course not."

"Isn't it true that her husband recently passed away?"

"Why, yes, a few months ago."

"Was Mrs. Sorensen depressed?"

"She was in good spirits when I last saw her."

Gillette paused for a moment, holding up a finger while she listened to the invisible voice speaking through her earpiece. She nodded, then plowed on. "Is it true that a student at the school is also missing?"

Oh, my God.

Bert's smile looked phony. "I'm not at liberty to reveal any further information."

"Will an Amber Alert be activated?"

The earlier hint of fear now came at Claudia with wrecking ball force. An Amber Alert would be issued only in the event of the kidnapping of a minor.

She thought of the newspaper stories she had read a few months back; stories about Dominic Giordano, Annabelle's father, and his reputed ties to organized crime. She couldn't help wondering whether there was any connection.

On-screen, Bert shook his head. "I'm sure there's no reason for such an action."

"Mr. Falkenberg, sir, I've been told that there were rumors of bad blood between Mrs. Sorensen and the missing student? Can you confirm that?"

"That's ridiculous. *You* said there was a missing student, *I didn't*. In any case, Mrs. Sorensen gets along very well with *all* the students."

"Our sources tell us there was a disagreement between them a few days ago."

"I'm not going to comment any further."

Gillette leaned on him like a prosecuting attorney grilling a witness. "Is it true the student has a juvenile record?"

He threw up his hands, waved her away. "You'll have to excuse me. I've been out of town and I don't have any additional information for you at this time."

"But do you believe there's a connection between the two disappearances? Mr. Falkenberg? Mr. Falkenberg?"

Bert Falkenberg made an abrupt about-face and headed for the front door of the school, trailed by a pack of question-shouting reporters and their cameramen.

Arranging her face into an appropriately serious expression, Michelle Gillette turned back to the camera and addressed her anchorman in the studio.

"Well, Paul, as you just heard, Mr. Falkenberg has refused to confirm it, but we do have a report from a reliable source that there is indeed a missing student and that she is the daughter of Sunmark Studios head, Dominic Giordano. As you know, Mr. Giordano has been…"

Jovanic muted the volume on the TV, cutting the reporter off.

Claudia dropped onto the sofa and stared up at him, a sick feeling welling up. "Annabelle," she whispered. "She's the only student who didn't go home for the holiday. Dominic Giordano is her father. What if the *mob* took her as a way of getting at him? Joel, you have to find out what's going on. What if—"

"Hold on, babe," Jovanic interrupted. "Is it true about the bad feelings between Mrs. Sorensen and the girl?"

"When I last talked to Paige she was planning on Annabelle spending Christmas with her. I don't think she was thrilled, but she didn't make a big thing about it." Claudia rubbed her face with her hands, smearing the mascara she'd just applied, leaving black smudges under her eyes. "I can't believe this. Where could they be? Burt's right, Paige would *never* leave her dog. Poor little Mikki, he must have been starving."

Jovanic grabbed his coat from the rack by the front door. "I'll see what I can find out," he said, and came back to kiss her. "Just hold tight until we get the facts. They'll show up with a good story."

Claudia knew it was his way of trying to comfort her. "If only!" she said.

She saw him out to the Jeep, watched him drive away, then went inside and poured herself a mug of high-test coffee, needing the caffeine kick. She sat at the kitchen table, struggling to stay calm and logical, trying to cheer herself. Maybe Paige had taken Annabelle on an impulse trip to Disneyland or something. With Paige, anything was possible. But what about Mikki?

Claudia glanced at the phone and promptly rejected the idea of calling the school. If Brenda was there, which seemed doubtful, the switchboard would be clogged with reporters looking for a juicy story, parents wanting to know what was going on.

The kind of publicity Paige had so wanted to avoid.

She thought of the threatening letter from Diana. Paige had been adamant about not showing it to the police, but the situation had changed in a drastic way. When Jovanic called, she would tell him about it and ask what he recommended.

She glanced over at the phone again, startled half out of her wits when it rang.

CHAPTER 16

Monica, her voice pitched higher than usual, talking fast.

"Aunty C, did you see the news? I was getting ready for school and daddy had the TV on and—she's going to be in a whole bunch of trouble, isn't she?"

"Whoa, kiddo, slow down. What do you mean?"

"*Annabelle!* She did something bad, didn't she? She's such a dork!"

"Monica, please slow down and tell me what you're talking about."

"She called me really, really late the other night, on Christmas Eve. She was majorly upset about that lady, the one who's missing—her principal?"

"Upset about Paige?"

"Yeah, Paige. Annabelle said she was a skanky slut and she said she was gonna get even with her."

"Get even with her about what? Did she tell you?"

"Well—" Monica hesitated. "I promised not to tell."

"Monnie, I know you don't want to snitch out a friend, but right now nobody knows where she is, or where Paige is, or if something's happened to them."

The long silence told Claudia that her niece was pained at having to break her new friend's confidence. "Sweetie, at this point, *anything* might help."

Monica gave a long, giving-up sigh. "She's—well, she's been

telling me about this guy she thinks is totally cool. Remember that handwriting she brought to show you, but she didn't want to say who he was? Aunty, he's really *old*. He *works* at her school."

A guy in his thirties would seem ancient to Monica. But maybe not to Annabelle.

She's looking for a father substitute.

"It was Christmas Eve when she called you?"

"Uh huh. She was s'posed to be in bed, but she snuck out and went to this guy's house 'cause she had a Christmas present for him. He lives on the school grounds, so it wasn't like she had to go anywhere far. She knocked on the door, but it was unlocked and she went in. It was raining and she wanted to put the present inside and leave, but then she saw her principal was there, and the guy, and they were—well, they were—" Monica faltered.

"They were what? Monica, you *have* to tell me."

"The bedroom door was open and Annabelle could see them. They—they didn't have any clothes on and they were in bed together."

Oh, no!

"Okay, I got it. What did she do?"

"Paige was yelling. At first, Annabelle thought he was hurting her, but then she could tell she liked it, what he was doing. She ran back outside."

"Did Paige see Annabelle?"

"No. She said there was loud music, so they didn't hear her. Aunty C, she was really freaked. She kept saying the F-word and she kept saying that she was gonna get that skanky slut, so when I saw the TV this morning—"

Just like Annabelle had said she was going to get her father for the time she had found him groping her nanny. *History repeating itself.*

Was it just talk by a wounded child? Or was Monica right, and Annabelle had *'done something really bad'*?

After promising her niece that she would handle it, Claudia went upstairs to the file cabinet and pulled Annabelle's file. If the girl was dangerous, there should be warning signs in her handwriting. Could she have missed something?

Annabelle's pain was there, staring her in the face, but potential for violence? No.

When she couldn't settle down to work, Claudia got in the Jag and drove to Bel Air. The police were gone but the media was camped out across the street from the school. The private security guard posted at the closed gates of the Sorensen Academy couldn't have been less interested in hearing why Claudia might want to enter the property.

His brown uniform and shaved head gave him the look of a Nazi storm trooper and attitude to boot. He leaned down and rested his elbow on the car door so that his face was level with hers. Judging from his pastrami and sauerkraut breath, Claudia guessed lunch at Canter's Deli in nearby Westwood. The Reuben was one of their specialties.

"No one gets inside unless their name's on my list," the rent-a-cop said. "*No* one, get it? That's my orders."

Claudia kept her tone pleasant. "If you'd call Mr. Falkenberg, he'll vouch for me."

"He's not in charge."

"Well, who is?"

"Listen, lady, all you hafta know is *your* name ain't on the list. If you got something to say about the missing person thing, go see the cops. Nobody inside gives a shit about anything else today. Now, you just back up your Jag-u-ar and hit the road."

"But—"

The rent-a-cop straightened and folded his arms across his chest to let her know that the conversation was over. His attitude didn't impress Claudia, but the nine millimeter Beretta on his hip did, and when he casually moved his hand to the butt of his gun, she shifted into reverse. Getting into a pissing contest with some testosterone-driven asshole was not on today's agenda.

She flicked a look in the rearview mirror before backing up. A late-model black Corvette shot up the driveway behind her and slammed to a halt, blocking her exit.

Cruz Montenegro jumped out and ran up to the Jag, waving the guard away. "Claudia, thank god you're here, I gotta talk to you." His eyes were bloodshot, the skin below them mottled and saggy.

"Fine with me, but this jerk won't let me in."

"I'll take care of him."

Claudia watched Cruz stride over to the disgruntled rent-a-cop, shoulders squared, chin jutting. Macho.

The conversation lasted all of thirty seconds. She couldn't hear what was said, but whatever it was, Cruz convinced the guard to move aside.

Michelle Gillette, the reporter Claudia had seen on the news, chose that moment to run across the street and start up the hill to the gate, calling out, asking for an interview.

Cruz spun on her and faced her down. "Get the fuck away from me," he snarled.

Gillette recoiled, looking scared. Without another word, she turned tail and hurried back to the safety of her news van.

Cruz jumped into the 'Vette and burned rubber backing up. He drove alongside the Jag and touched a remote control on the visor. The gates swung open and he drove in, beckoning Claudia to follow.

Her first time inside the guesthouse. It was a no-brainer to figure out that Cruz' hand hadn't decorated the place. Too frou-frou for Paige, too. Who, then? The first Mrs. Sorensen? Diana Sorensen, perhaps? Judging from her clothing, Diana's taste was too severe to have selected the old-fashioned pink-toned chintz upholstery and drapes, and the carpet with its cabbage roses. Chrome and leather seemed more her style.

The place was more than neat, it was immaculate. Spit-shined. Windows spotless even after all the rain, the furniture polished to a gloss you could see your face in. Not so much as a *TV Guide* on the coffee table. The house could have passed a Marine D.I. inspection.

"Brewski? Coke? Water?" Cruz asked.

"I'll take a beer, thanks." Claudia followed him into a kitchen as spick-and-span as the front part of the cottage and smelling of Pine cleaner.

Too much Pine cleaner.

Could all this cleaning be an attempt to hide something incriminating? Claudia scoffed at herself. *Too many episodes of Forensic Files.* "You're a better housekeeper than I am," she said to Cruz.

He glanced around as if seeing the place for the first time.

"Leftover from the Corps." He grabbed two bottles of Dos Equis from the apartment-size refrigerator and opened both, handing one to Claudia.

They moved back to the living area and Cruz plunked down in one of the overstuffed easy chairs, gesturing Claudia to the other.

She regarded the shadows under his eyes, and said, "You look like hell."

Cruz took a coaster from the coffee table and tossed it to her. "How would *you* look if you were grilled all night by the cops?"

"Like hell." Claudia set the coaster on the side table beside her chair and stood her bottle on it. She looked him in the eye and held his gaze. "Cruz, what's going on?"

Cruz released a loud, unhappy breath. "Damned if I know, Claudia, but I got this bad feeling the cops think I do." He ran a hand through his already tousled hair. It looked oily, like it was overdue for a shampoo.

Raising the bottle to his lips he took a long swallow, then squeezed the Dos Equis bottle between his knees and stared at it. Picked it up and drank some more, set it on the coffee table. He seemed antsy and Claudia waited in silence, giving him the space he seemed to need.

"They kept hammering at me. Same questions, over and over, a hundred different ways. Man, Claudia, you can't think I would never do anything to hurt Paige?"

Claudia drank some beer and set the bottle back on the coaster. "What makes you think she's hurt?"

He shot her a derisive look. "What do you think? She just left with Annabelle and forgot to say anything? Where would they go? And don't forget the dog. Like she'd leave that freakin' little rat with no food?"

Claudia shook her head. "Cruz, don't you have *any* idea where they might have gone?"

"Hey, like I told the cops—I got nothing to hide. If I knew where they were, I'd be the first one to drag their asses back here and make them explain themselves."

His eyes went to the windows, where the branch of a windblown tree was scratching at the pane. "Paige was with me on Christmas Eve. She sent Annabelle to bed and she came over about eleven. We had a few drinks, a few laughs; ended up in bed. I fell asleep. That's pretty much all there was to it. The cops wanted to know what time she left here. How the hell would I know? I wake up at seven the next morning, she's gone. I sure as hell don't know anything about the kid. I figured Paige went home early."

Claudia looked at him and saw a mixture of emotions on his face, the strongest of which seemed to be fear. That gave her pause. She said, "Here's a little surprise for you, Cruz: 'the kid' didn't go to bed. She was right here and she saw you and Paige going at it."

The languid blue eyes popped wide. "The fuck you talking about?"

"Somebody forgot to lock the front door. She dropped by with a Christmas gift for you, not knowing Paige was here, and she came inside. Whatever she saw, it was enough to upset her, big time."

"Aw, *fuck.*" Cruz smacked his palms against his forehead. "Fuck…*Fuck!* She called you?"

"No, she called my niece. They're friends."

"Goddammit! Paige and I—dammit—the kid—" Cruz leaned forward, elbows on knees, the Dos Equis bottle dangling from his hand. He shook his head. "Man, that's so fucked *up.*"

Claudia's gaze shifted, caught on the neatly made bed, visible through the open bedroom door. Annabelle would have had a clear view of what was going on in there from almost any vantage point in this small room. She drank some beer and wondered why Cruz had been so keen to talk to her.

Annabelle had called Monica after she'd seen them in bed, which was some time after eleven pm. What had she done after that? Impulse control was not her strong point. After the fight with her classmates, then finding Paige in a sexual encounter with Cruz, what might Annabelle have felt driven to do?

Cruz interrupted her thoughts. "There's something I have to show you." He drained his bottle and got up, returned to the kitchen and got seconds.

While he was out there Claudia heard him open a drawer. He returned and handed her a yellow Post-it note on which a few words were written in red ink.

Later–AnnaB–trouble

It was Paige's handwriting, yet not her *normal* handwriting. The words were scrawled and lacked the motor control of her usual style, which emphasized the appearance of the writing.

"Where did you get this?" Claudia asked.

"I found it on my nightstand after I got up Sunday morning," Cruz said. "Annabelle must have called while I was asleep."

Claudia dug in her purse for the small magnifying glass she carried with her in a toolkit. Holding it close to the paper, she checked the edges of the strokes and found them fuzzy. From the state of the handwriting she knew Cruz had grossly underestimated the amount of alcohol Paige had ingested. "How much was she drinking?"

He was noncommittal. "Couple glasses of wine. We both got pretty faded."

"So, when you say a couple, what do you really mean? Three? Four? Ten?"

"Shit, I don't know. I think…" his eyes went up as he searched his brain. "We drank our way through two bottles, maybe three."

"How about drugs?" Claudia caught his calculating expression and suspected he was trying to think up a lie. "You'd better tell me the truth, Cruz. This is some serious shit."

"Okay, we smoked a little weed, did a little E." He stopped, looking abashed. "See, Paige wants it rough, but she needs a little help loosening up."

Too much information, Claudia thought with distaste. But it was important, so she pressed him. "How rough, Cruz?"

"Hey, I don't *hurt* her, you know?" The protest was too quick. She stared him down until he glanced away, shifting in his seat. "It's just, well, she likes to be tied up. She likes that necktie thing."

"Necktie?" Claudia thought for a moment. "Are you talking about autoerotic asphyxiation?"

Oh hell, did Annabelle see that?

"Is that what it's called? Huh. Well, this isn't "auto," you know? It's dangerous if you do it by yourself. Even with a partner, you gotta be careful—time it just right—cut off the oxygen at just the right moment, then let up before—it makes a super intense climax. God, when she comes like that—" His face had become flushed, his eyes bright. He was getting turned on talking about it.

"That's what you were doing on Christmas Eve?" Claudia

interrupted, dashing cold water on his fantasy. "I'd think the police would find that interesting."

Cruz was out of his chair like a rocket. He loomed over her, his big, strong-looking hands gripping the arms of her chair. His eyes were impenetrable, but the rage in them made Claudia's breath catch in her throat.

CHAPTER 17

"Our sex life has nothin' to do with her going missing, you got that? I dunno why I told you that. The fuck is the matter with me?"

"Take it easy, Cruz. I—"

"*Dammit*, I wish I could remember what happened. I never even heard the phone ring." Cruz flung himself back in his armchair and pointed to the Post-it in Claudia's hand. "That note says 'trouble' and 'Annabelle.' That's a bad combination. The kid…"

"I know she's had her problems," Claudia said, trying to get her heart rate back to normal. "But I can't see Annabelle seriously hurting anyone, if that's what you're getting at." He'd felt so threatening standing over her and she hadn't been sure of what he was going to do. With that anger flashing in his eyes, he'd looked capable of just about anything.

"Well, *I* wouldn't hurt Paige, either," he snapped.

Claudia waved the Post-it at him like a tiny yellow flag. "Why are you showing this to me, instead of the police?"

"If I show it to the cops, they're gonna think *I* wrote it to give myself an alibi. You're an expert. I figure you tell 'em it's her handwriting, not mine, they'll believe you."

"An alibi for what?"

"For whatever. Paige is gone, the kid's gone—they're looking at *me!* Christ, it's a goddamn nightmare! I need them to believe it's her handwriting so they'll know she was okay when she left here."

"Don't you think the police are going to call this withholding evidence?" Claudia put the Post-it in her purse without waiting for his response. "I don't see her driving anywhere without getting pulled over, in the condition she was in when she wrote this, especially on Christmas Eve. You know the cops are all over the place, looking for drunk drivers."

"Then someone else drove her car."

"Who?"

"Who the hell knows?" Cruz's brows came together. He covered his eyes with his hands, wearily shaking his head. "I hate to think it, but Annabelle might have set Paige up. If she was as upset as you say she was, maybe she called her old gangster buddies."

Claudia stared at him in disbelief. "Come on, Cruz, you can't be serious."

He blew out a breath, shook his head. "I don't like it, believe me. You got any other ideas?"

"No, but I don't believe that one for a minute. She's the type to blow off steam by yelling, not planning to set someone up. When she jumped Diana Sorensen it was spur of the moment, an impulse.

"Now, look, about this note. If you want me to be able to identify Paige as the writer and rule you out, I'll need some of your handwriting for comparison."

"Yeah, sure, anything. What do you want me to write?"

She asked for his email address and promised to email him a form and instructions when she returned to her office.

He wrote his address on the back of one of her business cards. Claudia stared at the block printing, which she realized she had seen before. "Cruz, did you happen to write a gift card a few weeks ago and sign it, *Besos, besos, besos?*"

Now it was his turn to stare. "How'd you know about that?"

"Annabelle had it. I don't suppose you gave it to her?"

"You're kidding me, right? It was with some flowers I brought Paige."

She had been correct in assuming that Annabelle had snagged the card from Paige's office.

Claudia's cell phone vibrated on her belt. Jovanic.

Cruz rose from his chair and went to the bathroom while she took the call. Jovanic was running to catch a plane. Developments in his Bay Area case. He didn't have anything new to report on

Annabelle or Paige. They said goodbye.

As Claudia heard the toilet flush and the bathroom door open her cell phone buzzed a second time. The display read *Sorensen Ac.*

"Claudia," Bert Falkenberg said. "What are you doing over there? I can see your car from my office."

"I came in hopes of seeing you, but the guard wouldn't let me through. Cruz happened to show up at the right moment and got me in."

"Goddamn it, they have no right!" He sounded harried and angry. "I need a word with you before you leave."

Her heart was in her throat. "Has there been some news?"

"No, no, nothing like that. When can you be here?"

"Five minutes," she said, clicking off. To Cruz, she said, "Bert wants to see me."

Cruz' lips twisted into a sneer, distorting his scar. "You'd better watch out for ol' Bert. Did you know he used to work for Sorensen Construction?"

"Yes, Paige told me what happened. She hired him after her husband died. He lost his job because he didn't like Dane's plans for the school."

Cruz gave a snort of derision. "If you buy that, I got some oceanfront property in the Mojave to sell you."

"What are you talking about?"

"Bert's nuts about Paige. I think Dane planted him over here to spy on her."

"Are you saying Dane Sorensen and Bert have something to do with Paige's disappearance?"

"Hey, what do I know? I'm just a boy from the Bronx. Forget I mentioned it."

"Do you have any evidence?"

"Right now, I want the cops looking at *anyone* but me."

Claudia collected her purse and went to the door. "Since you brought it up—you *were* the last one to see her. You ought to get yourself a good lawyer."

After the obsessive neatness of Cruz's guest cottage, entering Bert Falkenberg's office for the first time was akin to walking into a giant rat's nest—assuming rats made a habit of surrounding themselves with piles of paper.

Claudia glanced around, looking for a space to sit, not finding one. Had there been an earthquake she hadn't heard about? Stacks of file folders and financial statements littered the desk, the credenza behind it, the guest chairs. Tax codes and a heap of *Wall Street Journals* plunked next to trade magazines targeting private school administrators and CFO's. The current copy of *Gaming News* sat atop one stack, looking out of place.

Bert caught her eye on that one. "Can't help it, I love to gamble. My big vice." He gathered up a bundle of file folders from one of the chairs and dumped it onto the floor, clearing a place for her, then edged around behind his desk and sat in the oversized executive chair. "I don't suppose you've heard from Paige?"

"Why would *I*?"

He smoothed a hand over his thick mass of hair, but wiry strays stuck up. His beard seemed to have become even grayer since the last time Claudia had seen him.

"Paige always seemed to have a tough time making friends with other gals, but she liked you right from the get-go. So I thought maybe, wherever she is—"

"You think she's gone somewhere of her own volition? Somewhere she *could* call me?"

"Lord Almighty, I have to hope so." His eyes turned toward the ceiling and he seemed to be calling on the Deity. "It's so strange, the two of them going off like that and leaving no word."

"They have to be together somewhere."

"Exactly, and I'd like to know where."

"How's her dog?"

"Mikki? He's moping around, missing her."

"I don't believe she'd leave him with no food, do you? It seems pretty obvious they didn't leave of their own free will, so what happened to them?" Claudia thought about Cruz' insinuation that Dane and Bert had conspired together to spy on Paige. Could he have been serious, or was he trying to divert suspicion from himself?

Bert spread his hands. "I wish I knew."

Claudia said, "Cruz was with the police all night. Have they talked to you yet?"

"Of course they have, but I was in Vegas over the holiday, I have nothing to contribute. They can get a lot more out of Cruz than me." Bitterness crept into his voice. "Maybe if she'd come with me, instead of him—" He let the rest of the sentence hang.

"How is Annabelle's father taking it?"

"Mr. Giordano insists on keeping this whole mess as low profile as possible. Which, as a matter of fact, is the reason I wanted to see you." He steepled his fingertips on the desk and brought them to his lips. When he spoke, he seemed to be searching for the right words.

"Uh, Mr. Giordano is—shall we say, mindful of all the truly dreadful possibilities presented by the current situation. Of course, Annabelle's prior history is, er, shall we say, less than satisfactory? Mr. Giordano feels that excessive media attention would not be in the girl's best interest."

"How is he going to manage that? It's already all over the media."

Bert nodded agreement. "True, some of it got leaked. If I hadn't been out of town at the time I would have made sure that didn't happen. But the barn door's closed now, and I want to make sure it stays that way."

"Who do you suppose leaked it?"

His expression darkened. "The Sorensens have a spy on the staff, I'm sure of it. Neil would be too obvious, and he's loyal to Paige, anyway. Maybe Brenda Rodriguez, the receptionist, but I don't have any proof. At least, not yet."

Claudia thought about it. She wasn't so sure Bert was correct about Brenda, but after Diana's behavior, it was easy to believe that Torg Sorensen's daughter would turn the situation to her advantage.

She was also considering the possibility that the Sorensen twins had somehow engineered the disappearances. She would have to let the police know about the threatening letter Diana had sent Paige.

Then the other part of what Bert had said struck her. "Wait a minute. Are you saying that Annabelle's father believes she's involved, not a victim? That she somehow *kidnapped* Paige?" Cruz had suggested the same.

"You can't think a fourteen-year-old girl—a *small* girl at that—could have subdued an adult—an *authority figure*, and keep her hidden for what, three days now? A *kid kidnapper*?"

"She may be small, but our Miss Annabelle is not so innocent," Bert said. "You probably know she's spent time in Juvenile Detention, and you can bet she learned plenty of bad habits there. Of course, she had to have had accomplices."

"But what would be her motive to do something so extreme?" Even as she asked the question, Claudia thought about what she had learned from Monica—Annabelle was jealous and angry about Paige's liaison with Cruz. Bert didn't know about that conversation and Claudia didn't tell him. Nonetheless, he came up with the right answer.

"Revenge," he said. "Annabelle's always trying to get Cruz to notice her. She's almighty pissed because he only has eyes for Paige."

Whether she wanted to believe it or not, Claudia had to recognize the possibilities in what Bert was saying. Looking at it objectively left her depressed.

"You don't believe she would *hurt* Paige, do you?"

Leaning back in his chair, Bert put his boot up on the edge of the desk. "We don't know what that girl's capable of now, do we?"

"You've got your mind made up about this."

"What are the alternatives?" Bert gave her a slick smile. "Don't look so down, Claudia. Even if it's true, nothing much will happen to her. She'll end up at some high-priced boot camp." He picked up a pen from the desk and began doodling dollar signs on a notepad. "I *would* like us to be clear on one thing—if you hear anything from *either* of them, you're to let me know first. In the meantime, I need your assurance that you aren't going to discuss the situation with anyone. We've gotta keep that barn door shut."

Claudia opened her mouth to respond, but Bert's office door suddenly flew open. Dane Sorensen filled the doorway with his bulk. Claudia knew then who was giving the orders to the guard at the front gate.

"What the hell is *she* doing here?" he demanded of Bert, refusing to look at Claudia.

"She's here at my invitation." Bert stood up as he spoke, and moved around the desk. Claudia stood, too. "This *is* still my office," Bert said.

Dane threw him an unpleasant little smile. "Not for long. I'm having papers drawn up right now to have your sorry ass thrown out of here."

"Why? Don't you expect Paige to come back?" Claudia heard the words fly out of her mouth before she could stop them.

Dane took a half-step toward her. Bert, who didn't appear to be intimidated by his former employer, made a protective move in front of her.

"She's got no business on this property," Dane said, his jaw tight. "This is my family's property and her presence is unwelcome."

Bert gave him a cool stare. "Correction. This is *Paige's* property, and until there's some word from or about her, *I'm* in charge in her absence. So don't go throwing your weight around just yet, Dane."

Dane's upper lip curled into a sneer. "I might say the same thing to you, you double-dealing prick. You figured to get the girl *and* the money. Well, things don't always work out the way they're planned, bucko." He strode away, leaving his presence bristling in the air as intensely as if he continued to fill the door frame.

Claudia felt a sudden strong urge to put distance between herself and the school and its atmosphere of menace. She took a step toward the door. "Bert, I'm outta here."

Bert reached out to put a restraining hand on her arm. "You *will* let me know if you hear from either of them, won't you?"

She looked down at his hand and made a movement that took her far enough away that he would have had to use force to maintain the contact. "I hope the same of you."

Bert's eyes narrowed. "Whatever game little Miss Annabelle is playing, it can't last much longer. If you try to protect her, you'll end up wishing you'd stayed out of it."

CHAPTER 18

That evening, Claudia hiked down to Cowboys, the neighborhood bar and grill at the bottom of the hill by her house, walking off the bad taste left by Bert's implied threat. She had arranged to meet Kelly and Zebediah there. Kelly was a family law attorney and despite her zany attitude, she often had good insights to offer on difficult cases. Zebediah added his expertise as a forensic psychologist.

The women ordered the house special: a burger smothered in green peppers, grilled onions and Swiss cheese that the menu named after the cowboy, 'William S. Hart,' and a batch of home fries big enough to feed a family of four. Zebediah, who was a vegetarian, ordered pasta primavera.

"You two are a couple of barbarians," he said, showing an expression of mock distaste. "How can you sleep after eating all that artery-clogging grease?"

Claudia took a swig from her bottle of Bud Light. "Joel's gone back up north so I'm sleeping alone. It doesn't matter what I eat."

Kelly deliberately rested her breasts on the table. She'd had them augmented a few years earlier, and they were full and perky. "You and your evil vegetarian ways," she said to Zebediah. "You know you're secretly salivating for a piece of *meat*."

He took the bait as she knew he would. "Oh yeah, baby." He gave her an exaggerated leer. "I'm *Kellyvating. Carne caliente*, yum yum."

Claudia looked at them both and rolled her eyes. After spending the day worrying about Paige and Annabelle, being able to relax and listen to her two closest friends' silly bantering made her feel almost normal.

Kelly put on a saintly face and folded her hands demurely. "Okay, Miz Priss, I'll make Zebby behave, I promise."

"Who's going to make *you* behave?" Claudia asked. "Could we talk about Paige and Annabelle's handwritings? I want to see if either of you pick up on anything I might have missed."

Zebediah grinned. "What about ol' buddy Bert's confidentiality admonition?"

"Screw Bert Falkenberg and the horse he rode in on." Claudia picked up the manila envelope she had placed on the empty chair next to hers. She removed the handwriting samples from the envelope and turned Paige's sample so they both could see it. "Paige is my client, not Bert. I'll do anything I can to help her, and if that means discussing it with you two, he ought to be glad he's getting three good heads for the price of none."

The handwriting sample was one that Paige had written specifically for analysis, prepared according to a set of instructions Claudia had given her: *Write a letter in ink on a full size sheet of unlined paper. Write a whole page, don't copy it from somewhere else and don't write poetry or lyrics. Include a signature.*

Kelly took it and looked it over. The carefully written script was filled with small, tasteful flourishes of Paige's own invention. "Oh my, she's a 'good girl' all the way, isn't she."

Kelly had sat in on classes that Claudia taught. She was referring to the school-model writing style, which often indicated someone who had a bottomless craving for affection, attention, and approval from men.

"Good girls need a daddy to please," Zebediah added. "You can bet your sweet ass she didn't have an adequate father, which means she'd look for fathering in relationships as an adult. From what you've told us, Paige found a daddy in Torg. Unfortunately, those kinds of parental replacements tend not to work out so well."

"You're right about that," Claudia agreed. "She told me Torg was very possessive after they got married." She drank her beer and listened to her friends confirm her own opinions about Paige's handwriting. Her analysis had covered all the bases.

A sharp gust of wind blew through the open patio doors and

wrapped around her ankles, making her shiver. Or maybe it was her fear for Annabelle's and Paige's safety that raised the gooseflesh on her arms.

Kelly wanted to know if Paige had given Torg anything to be jealous about.

Claudia shrugged. "According to her, she was a straight arrow. But, Torg's younger son, Neil, is in love with her. And Cruz, well, I don't know whether that's love or plain old lust. Then there's Bert—he's still an unknown in the equation, though there's definitely *some* kind of tension between them. I told you she gave him the job at Sorensen Academy after her husband died, didn't I?"

Zebediah arced a shaggy brow. "From construction company to ritzy girl's school. Interesting career segue."

"I don't know whether she was telling the truth about being faithful to Torg," Claudia said. "She's a big flirt, but it's not a crime to be attractive to men."

"You bet your bootie it's not," Kelly agreed emphatically. "But the *rub*, if you'll pardon the pun, is when she meets someone who's unwilling to be seduced by her flirting—someone who demands more realistic interaction."

"Annabelle evidently decided not to be seduced." Claudia removed the girl's handwriting sample from the envelope, along with the pictures she had drawn. "She tolerated Paige until she saw her in bed with Cruz."

Pointing at the handwriting, she said, "The pressure is too light. She keeps her emotions inside until she's ready to blow."

"And blow she did," Zebediah added. "According to what Monica told you."

Kelly took Annabelle's drawing from his hands and pointed to the figure of the man pushing the car over a cliff. "My God, look at this! Is this what she thinks happened?"

Claudia chewed on her lower lip. "All I know for sure is, she's angry with her father. What do you think, Zeb?"

But before he could offer an opinion, Claudia's cell phone rang with the music from *La Traviata*. "That's Pete's ring."

She answered the call, her eyes widening as she listened. "Oh shit…uh huh…uh huh…I know, I'm sorry…I *said* I'm sorry…have you called the cops yet?"

She moved the phone away from her ear and Pete's angry voice could be heard, yelling profanities. Then there was silence. Claudia closed the phone looking troubled. "He hung up on me."

Kelly, who had known Pete for most of her life, gave a low whistle. "Wow, he's *really* pissed. What happened?"

"Monica got a phone call from Annabelle."

"So, she's okay, thank god. Where is she?"

"Monica couldn't understand her, said she was hysterical."

"What about Paige?" Zebediah asked.

"I don't know. When Pete realized who it was, he grabbed the phone from Monica, but Annabelle hung up."

Claudia stared at her food without seeing it. She had conjured an image of Annabelle trying to make contact with the one friend she had—Monica—desperately seeking help with whatever mess she was in. Something pretty bad, she speculated, to cause the usually stoic girl to become hysterical. She pushed away her plate, her appetite evaporating.

"What about Caller ID?" Zebediah asked, voicing the question Claudia was asking herself.

"You heard Pete, I couldn't ask him anything. He's *livid* that Monica got involved."

Kelly shook the bottle of ketchup and squeezed a dab onto her plate. "The police can capture the number she called from, can't they?" she asked, dipping a home fry into the red sauce and popping it into her mouth.

The ketchup looked like blood and made Claudia feel sick. "I don't know. At least she's alive."

CHAPTER 19

Zebediah forked a chunk of yellow squash into his mouth and spoke around it. "I'd like to know what caused the hysterics."

"Maybe they had an accident and they're stranded somewhere," Claudia said, with hope in her voice. "You know, you hear stories—someone drives off a mountain road and aren't found for days."

"That would be the biggest irony," Kelly said. "Seeing as that's what happened to her mother."

Zebediah put his hand over hers and squeezed. "Claudia," he said gently. "If it were an accident, she wouldn't have any reason to hang up on Pete. You'd better either call the police or her father."

"I don't have her father's number," Claudia said. "Someone in his position, it's got to be unlisted."

"Joel could get it for you," Kelly said.

"Joel's on his way to San Francisco."

"One of your PI clients, then?"

Claudia glared at her, resisting the idea of calling Dominic Giordano, although she knew her friends were right and he had to be told. She rose from her chair and stuck a couple of bills under the salt shaker. "See you guys later. I'm going to call someone who can *really* help."

Jacob Barash was an Israeli security specialist living in L.A. Barash consulted Claudia when his high-profile clients received letters from stalkers. Sometimes the letters held threats, but more often than not, they fell into the 'rabid fan' category. Her analysis of their handwritings helped him to assess the potential danger to his clients.

Barash answered her call to his cell phone and promised he would do his best to get Giordano's number for her. She put up a carafe of coffee, but before it finished brewing, he was back with Dominic Giordano's home telephone number.

"How'd you do that so fast?" Claudia asked in amazement.

He chuckled. "Claudia, if I told you that, I'd be out of business."

She copied the information he gave her onto the pad she kept by the phone. "Thanks, Jacob, I owe you one."

"No problem. I owe *you* plenty. In fact, I owe it to you to tell you that it's not a good idea for you to get mixed up with this guy. I don't know what your business is with him, but from what I hear, he's involved with some pretty unsavory people."

"This is not a social call, Jacob. Believe me, I wouldn't be asking if it weren't important."

"Suit yourself, Claudia, but trust me, you should steer clear of him."

"I appreciate the concern. I'll be careful."

Claudia hung up the phone and stared at the number she had written on her message pad, thinking about what Jacob had just told her. He was right, she did not want to get involved with Dominic Giordano. Nothing she had heard about him made her feel good.

She thought of the news reports that linked him with organized crime, and she wondered again whether his rumored associates might have any bearing on the disappearances of Annabelle and Paige. That frightened her more than any other scenario she had considered.

What kind of reception would she get from the girl's father? She didn't expect warm and fuzzy, but hopefully, he would at least be happy to know his daughter was alive.

She picked up the phone and dialed, got a maid with Spanish-accented English who informed her that Mr. Giordano was out and not expected to return until late in the evening.

Claudia explained the urgent nature of her call and left a message for him to return her call as soon as possible.

Suddenly ravenous, she opened the Styrofoam box she had brought home from Cowboys and dug into the burger. She hadn't given any thought to food all day, so that even the reconstituted rubber that had started out as melted Swiss was sheer bliss. The sheer pleasure of food hitting her stomach made her moan.

She was swallowing the last bite when the phone rang again. *Private Caller.*

"Ms. Claudia Rose?" A man's voice, slight accent, similar to the maid she had spoken to earlier. "Please stand by for Mr. Dominic Giordano."

There was a click, then hold music. Had the caller been anyone else, she would have rung off without waiting. But for Annabelle's sake, she waited. It was a full five minutes before she heard another click and a curt voice in her ear: "So, what's the story?"

"Mr. Giordano?"

"You got something to tell me about my daughter? Or is there some other reason you're interrupting my conference call?" He sounded like Tony Soprano.

"I've been working privately with Annabelle at the Sorensen Academy for a few weeks," Claudia said. "She's also spent a weekend at my home, and made friends with my niece, who's the same age." She paused, giving him a chance to respond, but he said nothing, so she continued, "Your daughter telephoned my niece about an hour ago, extremely upset. She didn't give her location, nor whether Mrs. Sorensen was with her, but I was sure you'd want to know she called. I haven't told the police yet."

"Where do you live, Ms. Rose?"

"Playa de la Reina, why?"

"Give Juan the address, and hold off on the police." Another click, then the first man was back on the line, asking for directions. He said they were coming from the studios in Culver City—at this hour, a ten minute drive.

Giordano's brusque manner had put her on the defensive, but Claudia was curious to meet Annabelle's father. She gave Juan her address then went to brush her hair and freshen her makeup.

She changed from jeans into black linen slacks and a pullover sweater. Darkened her lashes, added a touch of blush; a spritz of perfume to heighten her confidence. It felt as though she were getting ready for an audience with a monarch. Given Giordano's position at Sunmark Studios, she supposed, in a way, that's what he was.

When the doorbell rang, she felt ready to meet the man who, according to his daughter, had sexually harassed her nanny then dismissed her; the man suspected of inappropriate behavior with young girls on his movie set.

A chauffeur in formal livery stood on the porch. Broad across the chest, thick black hair slicked back, Hispanic.

He introduced himself as 'Mr. G's driver.' When he reached up to lean against the door jamb his hand touched the top of the door. He could have been a bouncer at some nightclub. Beneath his coat Claudia detected the slight bulge of a holster, which made her nervous. *Bodyguard.*

"You should bring a jacket," he suggested. "It's kinda cool outside."

Over his shoulder she saw a long black limousine parked at the curb. "Why doesn't he come up?" she asked.

The chauffeur gave a slight 'after you' bow. "Mr. Giordano would prefer it if you would come out to the car, Miss." He didn't say it, but the implication wasn't lost on her: *what Mr. Giordano wants, Mr. Giordano gets.*

Making her go to him gave Giordano the upper hand and a chance to check her out as she came down the stairs.

It wasn't the chauffeur's fault that his boss was a control freak. Claudia grabbed the jacket she'd tossed over the back of a chair on returning home from Cowboys.

"Don't worry, Juan," she said, closing the door behind her. "I'll behave myself."

He gave her a grin, letting her know he got it.

Juan opened the limo's back door and Claudia leaned inside. The man reclining against the plush leather seats beckoned her to join him, reinforcing the perception of royalty.

Even seated he looked tall, rangy. Unusual for a man of Italian descent. Long, slender legs encased in fabric that clung as if it had been sewn on him. He wore a fine camel blazer and black turtleneck, Mark Nason loafers. Skin that had seen too many hours in the tanning booth; a shock of fastidiously groomed salt and pepper hair, mostly grey on the sides, neatly trimmed goatee and moustache. Eyes with too few smile lines at the corners.

"Dominic Giordano," he said, offering a less than enthusiastic handshake.

Not very impressive for a man of his stature, she decided. It left her feeling awkward about her own firm grip. Claudia climbed in and settled next to him.

"Why are we here, Mr. Giordano?"

He appraised her with a bold once-over. "I wanted to get a look at you."

"Okay, you've looked. Now what?"

His lips stretched into a smile. "Spunk. I like that in a woman. So, tell me what you know about my daughter's latest stunt."

It wasn't as though she had formed a picture of him as a doting daddy, but his words and his tone grated. No wonder Annabelle had problems.

Claudia summarized her last meeting with his daughter, her subsequent conversation with Paige, and ended on a rerun of Pete's latest news.

Giordano's face remained impassive as she spoke, but the manicured fingers tapping on his knee made her wonder.

When she fell silent, he said, "You've been conned, Ms. Rose. You haven't known my daughter long enough to learn her tricks. She's got a real talent for manipulating the system."

"Oh, I thought that was *you*," Claudia retorted, then wished she had bitten her tongue. "I shouldn't have said that," she said stiffly. "I don't know you."

Giordano stared straight ahead so she couldn't see his expression, but his lips were pursed and his tone was icy. "That's right, you don't, so keep your smartass opinions to yourself."

"Fine. What I care about is Annabelle's safety and Paige's, too. Why did you ask me not to call the police? Don't you think *something* needs to be done about this?"

He gave her a bored look. "You don't think I have my own people working on it?"

I should have guessed, she realized as the penny dropped. No wonder Jacob had been so speedy getting back to her. People like Dominic Giordano retained people like Jacob Barash as their own private police force. She wondered whether Jacob had laughed to himself as he recited Giordano's phone number to her.

Giordano smiled unexpectedly, showing what might pass for appeal if you were looking for a job in the movies and the casting couch was your one option.

"Claudia," he said, leaning toward her in a way that put him too far into her space. "Okay if I call you Claudia? Look, honey, I want to find her as much as you do—more—she's my kid, right? You and me, we're not enemies. We gotta work together on this. For Annabelle's sake, okay?"

His words impressed her as hollow. She was getting a strong vibe that his concern had more to do with avoiding negative publicity than Annabelle's welfare. She inched away from him on the seat until the arm rest pressed into her back. "You think Annabelle's to blame for whatever's happened, don't you?"

He brushed a piece of invisible lint from his jacket. "You know her history, am I right? I figure, any minute there's gonna be a ransom note or a phone call. It's a scam—those hoodlums she hangs with, they're in it with her, I guarantee it."

"You seriously believe she had Paige kidnapped?"

He frowned at her like she was a dull child who needed something simple explained. "*You* figure it out."

"If it were true, why wait so long to make a demand? And why would she call my niece in hysterics?"

"Fuck if I know, but this whole thing has Annabelle written all over it."

Claudia did not want to believe him, but he was right about one thing—she had known his daughter for a relatively short time, and Annabelle's record was not exactly unblemished. Yet, what she did know—and what she had seen in the girl's handwriting—made it hard for her to believe what he was suggesting.

Under her skin, it didn't feel right.

She reached for the door handle. "Good night, Mr. Giordano."

CHAPTER 20

By the time Friday rolled around Claudia's eyes felt as though she had rubbed grit into them. A couple of nights as she lay awake she considered sleeping pills, rejecting that option in case Annabelle called her and she wouldn't be able to wake up properly. Each time she thought that, a hateful little voice in her head would whisper, *not a chance*, which kept her awake longer.

The Tuesday evening conversation she'd had in Dominic Giordano's Hummer kept coming back to her. Giordano seemed so certain of Annabelle's involvement in whatever had happened to Paige. How could a father be so callous?

Or was he simply being realistic?

The rain started up again, painting a dank, colorless world outside her windows. The ocean was an unrelenting gray blanket. Even the tomato plants in the container garden on the porch had succumbed to so much moisture. Examining her puffy eyes in the bathroom mirror, Claudia felt as waterlogged as the poor vegetables; she couldn't stop crying. Something about Annabelle had touched her to her core and wouldn't let go.

Sitting in the house thinking about it was making her crazy. She grabbed her keys and hurried down to the garage.

The media had decamped. Claudia parked on the street and walked up the driveway to the school. Since the students had gone home for the holidays, she wasn't sure anyone would be on site to let her in, but a maid she recognized opened the massive front door to her knock. Behind the maid, a radio played Salsa music at ear-splitting volume.

"Nobody here but Senor Neil," the maid said, raising her voice over the carnival beat as she ushered Claudia in from the rain. "Senor Bert, he go to gambling." She carried a wet mop and there was a bucket on the parquet floor, with white industrial towels laid out, making a path to the sweeping staircase.

Waste of time in this weather, Claudia thought, stepping inside and wiping her high-heeled boots on the mat.

With its lights off and dried pine needles littering the floor, the expired Christmas tree looked as sad as Claudia felt. The gifts that had been intended for the children at the homeless shelter were still piled around its base. Paige and Annabelle had gone missing before Christmas Day dawned, so the delivery never took place.

The maid saw her looking at the packages, the gift-wrapped baby doll that Claudia herself had dropped off on the afternoon of Christmas Eve, the last time she had been here. The last time anyone had seen Annabelle.

"Still waiting to hear from Senora Paige," the maid said, her pleasant face lined with worry. "I no think she comin' back."

"Don't say that!" Claudia exclaimed, not wanting to acknowledge that even this woman, whose livelihood depended on her employment at the Sorensen Academy, had already given up hope.

The maid nodded, taking in her swollen eyes, and patted her arm. "Is okay. Be okay." She indicated the presents. "Senor Dane and Senora Diana, they come today to take to shelter."

"That's good," Claudia said, glad that the children would still receive the gifts, even though she resented the Sorensen twins horning in on Paige's generosity. "I'm going up to Annabelle's room," she said. "I won't be long."

"Sure, sure, Senora. You go this way." The maid pointed her mop at the towels, then turned away and resumed swabbing the floor to the Latin beat.

Claudia mounted the elegant staircase pursuing the nagging sensation that had urged her to drive across town on this soggy afternoon. A vibe that if she could sit in Annabelle's room for a few minutes she would be able to feel what the girl had been feeling before she disappeared, that she might be able to make some sense of what had happened. She knew she wouldn't have any peace until she tried.

The stairs to the third floor were located at the opposite end of the second floor landing. Upstairs, the sound of the radio was muted by plush carpeting. She felt very alone in the shadowy hallway.

The maid had said the Sorensen twins were coming to pick up the toys. With Bert out of town and not there to stand up for her, as he had the last time she faced off with Dane Sorensen, Claudia would do her best to avoid crossing their path.

Nearing Paige's office, she slowed her steps, startled by the aroma of cannabis.

Annabelle?

The ropey weed scent wafting into the hallway was a big *fuck-you* to the yellow crime scene tape that clung in curling plastic ribbons to one side of the lintel. Claudia hesitated, her hand on the doorknob, listening.

The distant sound of Tito Puente playing a mambo in the downstairs lobby reached her ears. Silence from inside Paige's office, and the slight scent of smoke curling under the door. Her heart was thumping double-time as she turned the handle and pushed it open.

For an instant she thought she was seeing a ghost standing at the window. But a ghost would have been transparent. Neil Sorensen's body was as substantial as her own. The unlit room, the rain clouds in the sky outside, and the grey sweatshirt and pants he wore created the wraithlike effect.

His wheelchair stood empty across the room.

"Hello, Claudia," he said, turning toward her, a piece of folded black satin pressed to his cheek. His long face was pallid, the almost bloodless lips stretched into a sardonic smile. "I'm not psychic, I saw your reflection in the glass."

"You can walk," Claudia said feeling stupid in the shock of seeing him on his feet. As she came further into the room, she could see that he was leaning on a cane.

"Been working at it for months," he said. "I wanted Paige to see me the way I was when we first met."

"Wanted?" Past tense, as if he didn't expect to show Paige the

154

results of his efforts.

The joint Claudia smelled in the hallway lay atop the soil in a Chinese evergreen. Neil picked it up and took a toke, then lowered himself to the sofa, unfolding the lace-trimmed chemise in his hand and smoothing it across his knees. There was something spooky about the way he stroked it as if it were a living thing.

"What do *you* think?" Neil asked in a low voice, looking up at her.

What *did* she think? A series of images flitted through her mind: he could walk; Paige had said he was jealous of Cruz; he had that cane.

"Where's Paige, Neil? Where's Annabelle?"

He sat there staring at her with empty eyes, stroking that piece of black satin. He had nothing to give her. Shaken, Claudia turned around and left.

The crime scene tape across the door to Annabelle's room was intact. Claudia peeled away one side and opened the door. After what she had witnessed in Paige's office, she did not think anything could shock her. The room was as she'd seen it last, except for smudges of fingerprint dust on several surfaces, and the laptop computer had been removed from the study desk.

Closing the door behind her she sat down on Annabelle's bed and shut her eyes. She took several deep breaths, intending to relax her body and empty her mind; to absorb the energy of the room. Maybe on some level she would be able to connect with Annabelle.

But Neil's weirdness and deception about his ability to walk kept intruding and she found herself unable to focus her thoughts. After ten minutes, she gave up trying.

Where are they? Where are they? The question kept circling in an endless loop in her head with no answers. Frustrated, she looked around the room and her eyes fell on the red notebook where Annabelle kept her graphotherapy exercises.

Claudia reached for it and began thumbing through the pages. The two of them had not been working together for very long—a few weeks—but positive changes were already evident in Annabelle's handwriting. The exercises she'd been doing to music were simple but effective—some formations looked like rows of brackets lying on their sides and were intended to level out the stormy right side of the brain. Other calming forms looked like propellers.

After doing each page of exercises, Annabelle would write a page of affirmations: *I release any feelings of anger and blame. I know I can create any reality I want.*

She had chosen these affirmations for herself after studying a long list Claudia offered her. Now she was gone and—Claudia jumped up at the sound of voices in the hallway—one she recognized. The very last person she wanted to run into—Diana Sorensen. And Diana was coming her way.

Without stopping to think, Claudia ducked into the bathroom and pulled the door almost shut behind her. She stepped into the old fashioned tub and closed the curtain around her just as Diana entered Annabelle's room, her tone sharpening. "Somebody's been in this room."

A man's voice spoke, tantalizingly familiar, but not enough for Claudia to identify.

"Fuck the cops and their tape, just get the stuff and I'm out of here."

"You're in an awfully big hurry, aren't you?" Diana sounded almost coy, which was strikingly out of character for the distaff Sorensen twin. "You never used to be in such a hurry."

The man responded roughly. "Jesus Christ, Diana, give it a rest. I'm trying to figure a way to get us out of this mess and you're—"

"It might be a mess, but at least I don't have Paige to contend with, now."

"Thanks to my daughter. Now shut up and get the shit together."

"I don't like you raising your voice at me."

"I'm gonna do more than raise my voice if you don't shut up."

"Stop it, Dom."

Claudia heard what sounded like a slap and then Diana was crying, "Don't, Dominic! Don't!" Another slap, and she was crying harder. "I never thought you would treat me this way."

"Why don't you listen to me, you stupid cunt?" Dominic Giordano shouted. "I don't need you in my face, putting pressure on me. Get off my fucking back."

Claudia held her breath, terrified that one of them would come into the bathroom. Peeping around the edge of the shower curtain she could see a sliver of the room through the hinged side of the door. Enough to show Diana lying across Annabelle's bed on her back, Giordano standing over her with a raised fist.

Oh shit, Claudia thought. *What do I do now?*

Giordano spared her from having to come up with an answer. Making a loud sound of disgust, he strode out of the room, leaving Diana blubbering.

"Damn him," Diana hissed to the empty room. "Goddamn him! I'll ruin him."

CHAPTER 21

Once Diana Sorensen had pulled herself together and left Annabelle's room, Claudia waited ten minutes before dashing downstairs and back to her car. She didn't know what the overheard conversation meant, but after her encounter with Neil, then witnessing Giordano's brutal treatment of Diana, all she wanted to do was get as far away from them all as possible.

The story of Paige's and Annabelle's disappearance soon faded from the media. Reporters went on to cover New Year's Eve celebrations and the latest heinous news where a different kind of disappearance grabbed the headlines: the trafficking of small children for the sex trade—a juicier topic for the networks to report on than a missing adult and teen.

Nearly a week had passed since Annabelle's last phone call to Monica. A week during which Claudia analyzed handwritings for clients, lectured at a Rotary Club luncheon, prepared her testimony for an upcoming court case. And all the while, running through everything she did, a current of hope, fear, and dread.

Jovanic was still in the Bay Area, which made the first New Year's Eve of their relationship a cheerless occasion. They wished each other Happy New Year, clinking champagne glasses against the phone while in the background on television, the ball dropped in Times Square.

Later, as Claudia waited for sleep, Annabelle's face floated through her mind, then her restless dreams, as vividly as if the girl's spirit had left her body and come to remind Claudia not to forget her.

As if I could.

New Year's morning brought brilliant blue skies and a return of warm weather. Claudia sorted clothes to launder with one eye on reruns of the morning's Rose Parade. Kelly dropped in around noon, making a blatant attempt to divert her attention from her missing friends.

"Come with me to Victoria's Secret," she cajoled. "They're having their year-end sale. I got a gift card for Christmas that's burning a hole in my pocket."

"No thanks, I'll pass." Claudia slung a sage colored towel at the pile of darks. Missed. After one more too-short night fraught with nightmares, Kelly's invitation held all the appeal of a bowl of cold oatmeal.

"Come *on*, Claud, you need to get out, take your mind off it."

"You don't need me to help you buy slutty lingerie for your flavor-of-the-month guy," Claudia snapped, her tone sharper than she had intended.

Kelly grabbed a pair of jeans out of her hands. "It wouldn't hurt you to buy something slutty yourself."

"We just *went* to Victoria's Secret. I just *bought* something slutty. I don't need any more sluttiness."

"Well, I do. So, how long are you going sit around moping? What if they *never* come back?"

Kelly's blunt words were like poison darts that hit the bull's-eye. Claudia sucked in a deep breath and blew it out on a long sigh. She rubbed her hands over her face. "It's on my mind all the time."

Kelly put her arms around her and gave her a hug, then a little shove. "Go take a shower and get dressed. We're going to the mall."

Most Sunday mornings, the streets in West Los Angeles are virtually deserted, abandoned by weekday workers sleeping in, or perusing the Sunday comics over their eggs and bacon. They wait until the sun hits mid-heaven and burns off the marine layer to venture out.

But this was New Year's Day and residents of the West Side conspired to flood Olympic Boulevard with traffic. The Westside

Pavilion parking lot was crawling with bargain hunters and packs of teens hanging out.

As they drove through the parking lot Claudia scanned the crowds. She couldn't help herself. More than once her heart clenched at the sight of a small-framed girl with long dark hair, wearing Tommy Hilfiger tie-dye or "distressed" Mudd jeans, walking arm-in-arm with a girlfriend. But in her gut, she knew better. Annabelle didn't have girlfriends to hang out with on New Year's Day, except Monica, and Monica was definitely not walking with her at the Westside Pavilion.

"What the hell is the matter with these people?" Kelly griped, turning the Mustang into an aisle they had cruised five minutes earlier, where bus-sized SUVs had forced themselves into spaces marked Compact. "It's like trying to squeeze a four-hundred pound chick into size eight pants."

"Use the valet parking," Claudia pleaded. "Hot young guys, right up your alley."

"I'm not paying a valet to park my car so I can go shopping. Even if they *are* hotties."

"*I'll* pay the valet. We're driving in circles."

"Look, someone's leaving." Kelly hit the accelerator and raced to the end of the aisle, but a Suburban turned in front of them and beat her to the empty space. She laid on the horn with her fist. "Dickhead!"

"Road rage," Claudia cautioned. "Lunatics carry guns around here." Then she remembered how Dane Sorensen had beat her out of a parking space at the courthouse. Her mind started to drift—were the Sorensens involved in Paige's and Annabelle's disappearance?

She had told the police about Diana Sorensen's letter to Paige. The detective in charge assured her they would check it out, but she had the feeling that was the last she would hear of it.

Kelly's angry voice brought her back. "I fucking *hate* rude people!" She revved the engine and left a patch of tire behind on the asphalt as they ploughed out of the Pico Boulevard exit. "I'm parking on one of the side streets."

Claudia grabbed the panic handle. "Forget it, Kel. All the streets around here have restricted parking."

Kelly shot her a look of determination. "We're *going* to find a place." She swung right at Overland and began cruising the residential blocks surrounding the mall, hanging a right at Manning, then again at Blythe.

Permit Parking Only signs were posted at close intervals on every block in the area—the City's attempt to appease residents who resented the shoppers clogging the streets in front of their homes.

They crossed Pico and traveled north, then east, and back south, passing a mishmash of architecture: miniature adobes next to three-story apartment buildings and picturesque chateaus that could have illustrated a book of children's nursery rhymes. Every dwelling was at least fifty years old, many older. Some showed it more than others.

"We're a mile from the damn mall," Claudia grumbled, although she knew in reality, the Westside Pavilion was an easy couple of blocks away. Leaning back against the headrest, she closed her eyes. "Let's call it off. I'm not in the mood."

"There has to be a place we can park," Kelly insisted, turning a corner. She pulled over to the curb to allow a larger vehicle to pass on the other side. The streets were so narrow they might have been designed to accommodate a horse and buggy. "Think positive. Ask the Universe to provide."

Claudia stared out at the neighborhood. The houses on this block looked older, smaller, shabbier than the ones closer to the mall, squatting next to each other in a claustrophobic fashion that felt somehow sinister.

"I don't think the Universe wants us to park here," she said.

Kelly snickered. "You aren't afraid, are you? Don't worry, I've been taking kickboxing lessons."

"*Kick*boxing? Jesus, Kel, I thought I knew you."

"I'm always fascinated by people who draw their conclusions based upon the limitations of their knowledge," Kelly said primly. "You can't expect me to be Miss Manners all the time."

"Miss *Manners?*" Claudia couldn't imagine any description less fitting for Kelly Brennan. She started to make a retort when she saw something that made her stomach lurch. "Kelly, wait, stop! Back up, back up!"

Kelly hit the brakes, testing their shoulder straps. "What's wrong?"

"Paige's car." Claudia jerked a thumb behind them. She turned and craned her neck. "In that driveway back there. The blue Mercedes, swear to god, that's her car."

Kelly moved the gear shifter into reverse and backed up until they were even with the driveway of the house Claudia indicated. She leaned down to stare past her friend and through the window. "What makes you think that's Paige's? There's a million Mercedes around here."

"How many cars have you seen that color?" Claudia asked slowly, asking herself whether she might be wrong. Certain that she was not.

The house where the car was parked was a one story dingy white clapboard; a 1920s bungalow that hadn't seen a fresh coat of paint since Ronald Reagan left the governor's office. Cracked grey trim flanked the curtainless front windows.

A hand-lettered sign in the overgrown front yard announced that the house was for sale by owner. In this area, even in its present condition, the house would command close to a million. Claudia recognized the telephone prefix as a South Orange County number seventy-five miles from their present location. The house had a distinctly unoccupied air. At that distance, 'Owner' must not visit very often.

Close to the garage was the Mercedes 500SL that matched Paige's eyes, its front end parked carelessly. The front passenger tire was partly on the concrete drive and partly on the grass median between the house and its neighbor.

"You really think that's her car?" Kelly said.

"Look—it has a Sorensen Academy bumper sticker."

"Holy shit. What's she doing here?" Kelly backed the Mustang up another few feet. She nosed into the driveway and braked to a stop behind the Mercedes and killed the engine. They sat there, looking at each other.

"I wonder if they're inside," said Claudia into the silence.

"You don't think Annabelle's holding her hostage in there, do you?"

It sounded ridiculous when Kelly said it that way.

"At this point, I don't know *what* to think."

"Let's call the cops."

"Yeah, okay—no, wait a minute, not yet."

Telling Kelly to wait in the car, she got out of the Mustang and approached the driver's door of the Mercedes.

A film of rain-streaked grime and cats' paw prints covered the trunk, roof, and hood of the vehicle. Claudia thought back to the last day it had rained. Wednesday, four days ago. She guessed that the car had not been moved in at least as many days.

Leaning close to the windshield, she shaded her eyes with her hand and looked in at the empty front seat, then moved to the rear door. The tint impeded her view, but she could see enough to determine that the back seat was also empty.

To her right, a screen door banged, startling her out of her wits.

An elderly man shambled into the front yard of the house next door. He wore a torn undershirt that stretched over a distended belly and his trousers were rolled up, revealing knobby knees and ghostly white legs.

With arthritic effort, he bent to pick up a garden hose, managing to keep his eyes on Claudia. "Hey, whaddya want over there?" he yelled as he began watering the lawn.

Claudia walked around the older model white Saturn parked in his driveway. Its crumpled front fender was beginning to show signs of rust.

"Hi, good morning, sir," Claudia said. "Can I speak with you for a moment?"

As she approached, she could see the white stubble peppering his jaw, the red spider veins radiating across the broad nose and cheeks. He squinted at her through cloudy eyes. "We don't need no *Watchtowers*," he said. "Happy New Year."

The gnarled old hands squeezed the hose trigger harder, directing the flow of water inches from her feet.

Claudia jumped back as the backsplash hit her jeans. "Oh, no, no, I'm not selling anything."

"Well, what is it? No one lives over there." His eyes were narrowed against the sunshine.

"The sign says the house is for sale."

"I got no key. Call the number on the sign, you wanna see it."

"I was wondering about the car in the driveway," Claudia said. "Do you know how long it's been parked there?"

"Why's that yer business?"

"My friend's car was stolen. I think that might be it."

"Now, why would a stolen car be settin' over there?" the old man snapped, and Claudia could see that he was determined not to give an inch in the courtesy department.

"Maybe the thieves were joyriding and left it there?" she suggested, with a sudden painfully clear recollection of Paige telling her of Annabelle's history of joyriding with her gangbanger companions.

The old man's eyes drifted to the house and he yelled as loud as a yodeler, "Lainie! C'mon out here."

The screen door opened and a rail-thin woman in flowered stretch pants came onto the porch, a cigarette between nicotine-stained fingers. She had thick red hair pulled into a ponytail, stray tendrils curling around her face. Younger than the old man by a good thirty years, she would have been prettier without the thousand tiny smoker's lines that puckered her mouth.

"What is it, Pop? The Reverend's on."

"She won't go to church," the old man said, looking skyward and speaking to no one in particular. "But ever' Sunday, she's got the Reverend Schuler on the damn television. *Reeeligiously.*" He finished a phlegmy cackle at his own joke, then jerked his head at Claudia. "This gal wants t' know about the car that's parked over at Lambert's. How long's it been settin' there?"

Leaning against the wooden porch railing, the woman he called Lainie appraised Claudia, suspicion in every sinewy muscle. Before answering, she tapped a shower of ashes into the bushes below, while her father squawked a futile protest.

Behind her, the screen door opened a few inches and two white-blonde heads appeared around it, about three feet above the ground. A boy and a girl, around five years old. They crept onto the porch, holding hands. The boy said something that sounded like, "*Ya chotzu damoy.*"

A foreign language? If it was, it was a language Claudia couldn't identify.

"Whadyouthinkyou'redoing?" Lainie screeched, whipping around and pointing a finger at them. "Get back in the house and shut that door right now!" The two children scurried back inside, but not before Claudia caught their frightened stares.

She wondered whether she ought to call someone about them. There was something poignant in the way they clung to each other that roused her suspicions about the way they were being treated. "Cute kids," she said, "Are they yours?"

Lainie turned back to her as if nothing had happened. Maybe nothing had. "I'm babysitting," she said. "What is it you want?"

Claudia repeated her story about the car. From the corner of her eye, she saw the old man turn off the hose and move out of sight, returning a moment later with a pair of electric hedge trimmers.

"Well, let's see now," Lainie shouted above the sudden clatter as he switched on the clippers. "I'm not sure I noticed.... *Hey, Pop!* Would you wait a minute?" Another drag on the cigarette, another cascade of ash into the shrubbery. "Lemme think. Wasn't there on trash day. Nope, I would of seen it when I brought in the bins on Thursday. That's right, it must've been over the weekend. Friday night. Yeah, Friday night, 'cause it was there yesterday."

Even at a distance of ten feet Claudia could smell the stale smoke clinging to the woman's clothing. "So, you're pretty sure it was Friday?" she asked.

"Nothin' *pretty* about it. It wasn't there Thursday night."

"You're absolutely sure?" Claudia asked, thinking of the rain on Wednesday. "It's very important."

The woman glared at her. "You calling me a liar or are you saying I'm stupid?"

Claudia put up her hands, "Okay, okay. Never mind."

The old man laid his clippers on the grass and limped up onto the porch. "You and that foul habit," he snarled, pointing at his daughter's cigarette. "It can't be doing my bushes any good, now can it?"

Lainie turned and went back inside the house, slamming the door shut behind her.

"She's lying," Claudia said after walking back over to Kelly's Mustang. "That car has been here over a week."

"Why would she lie?"

"How should I know? She wanted to get rid of me?"

Kelly said, "Tuesday is when they were reported missing."

Claudia nodded. "But they were last seen on Christmas Eve, which is a week ago yesterday."

"Time to call the cops," Kelly said.

Claudia started walking away. "I'm going to look around. You coming?"

"No way, grasshopper. And neither should you. Let's call the cops, *now*."

"We *will* call the cops, as soon as we see if either of them is here."

"For crying out loud, Claud, you're not still trying to save Annabelle's hide, are you? She's a lost cause!"

Claudia shot her a look of disgust. "I'll be right back."

She mounted the front porch and stepped onto worn outdoor carpet. She pressed her face against the dirty window glass and peered into the two empty rooms whose windows faced the street.

To the left of the front door was the living room, its carpet littered with bits of paper trash. Someone had left a wrinkled heap of mustard-colored draperies on the floor next to an open Yellow Pages. She could see a room divider, beyond which was the kitchen. To the right, a small empty bedroom.

"What would they be doing at a place like this?" Kelly said when Claudia returned to the Mustang. "Talk about a fixer upper."

Claudia dropped into the passenger seat. "Okay, let's call the cops." She got out her cell phone and dialed 911. "Shit, it's a recording!"

Recent news stories had complained about real emergencies going unanswered due to the glut of unnecessary 911 calls. She handed the phone to Kelly. "If they ever answer, you tell them. I'm going to look in the back yard."

Kelly stared at her. "Are you crazy? What if someone's back there?"

"What if someone's hurt?"

More than anything, Claudia wanted to know whether Annabelle was in that house. She got out of the car and walked across the grass on the other side of the house from the driveway, where she could see a gate at the side of an overgrown six-foot hedge.

When she reached over to open the latch, the dilapidated hasp broke off and fell to the ground. The gate groaned in protest as she pushed it open. She glanced around to see whether any of the neighbors was watching. The old man from next door was nowhere to be seen and the street appeared empty.

Just a quick peek through the windows, she told herself. Breaking and entering wasn't part of the plan. Not that she *had* a plan, but something was urging her on.

Weeds ran riot in the yard and vied with the crabgrass for control. Two chains hung forlornly from the crossbar of a rusty swing set, remnants of a weathered canvas swing seat dangling from one of them. It all added up to a picture of inattention and neglect.

The sudden loud beep of a car horn startled her—Kelly. Had the 911 call been answered? Then the rustle of leaves and an explosion of sound.

Claudia spun around, her heart pounding against her chest wall like a jackhammer on steroids. The elderly neighbor was peering through a gap in the hedge that he had just created with his hedge trimmers. "Yer friend's car ain't back there," he yelled.

Ignoring him, Claudia went on toward the back porch, where a stack of battered cardboard boxes made luxury accommodations for what smelled like a thriving community of rats.

The broken glass in the windowpane of the back door was her first warning. The stench was the second.

A wave of nausea nearly sent her running back to Kelly's car. But Annabelle's pale little face nagged at her without mercy. The self-portrait she had drawn depicted her as alone, faceless, turning away from the world. A child abandoned by everyone.

A feeling of resolve hardened in her, stiffened her backbone and pushed her forward. *You are not alone this time, kiddo,* she muttered under her breath. Yet, despite her brave words, her mouth dried up. Each step screamed at her that something horrible waited inside.

Pulling a tissue from the pocket of her jeans, she pinched her nostrils and covered her mouth in an attempt to block the smell of decay. Claudia had been in the presence of death before. Standing on that porch, she had no doubt that it was about to happen again.

The back door had been left ajar. Conscious that she was trembling all over, she nudged the door open with her foot and stepped across the shards of broken glass. She passed an antiquated Kelvinator washer and dryer on the service porch, then went through the kitchen and into the living room. The odor was making her eyes water.

It was early afternoon, but little light penetrated the house and left the interior shrouded in gloom. Although she felt certain that no living thing occupied the place, Claudia walked softly as she moved through the living room. Coming to a short hallway with a closed door on either side, she realized that door number one on her left must be the front bedroom she had seen from the porch. On her right would be the master bedroom, which faced the back yard.

As she reached for the knob of door number two she heard the sound of glass crunching underfoot and Kelly's quivery voice calling her name. She twisted the doorknob and opened the door.

From behind her came a scream that chilled the blood in her veins, a scream that seemed to go on and on.

Kelly stood there, her eyes dilated with shock, staring into the room. She clapped her hand over her mouth, but that didn't stop the shrieks emanating from it.

Claudia turned to the bloated, discolored thing lying on the floor that had once been Paige Sorensen. Her dazzling blue eyes were now empty in death. The tongue protruded, purple and swollen, from the mouth.

At the instant of recognition, a black, buzzing cloud rose from the eyes.

Flies.

Kelly ran for the door, still screaming, then retched up her breakfast on the grass. Claudia followed, bile flooding her mouth as she tasted what she had seen, felt it permeating her skin. She leaned on the old gatepost for a dozen heartbeats, gulping clean air.

Shock had given her a brief reprieve from the horror, but now it caught up with her.

Oh my God, Paige. Poor, poor Paige.

Then came relief tinged with guilt: *Thank God Annabelle wasn't in there.*

CHAPTER 22

When it was all over—the arrival of the patrol units, the recalling of how they had discovered Paige's body, and all the rest of it, Claudia tried to get everything straight in her head, but the details had melded into one big amnesic blur, and she found herself unable to remember the day with any kind of clarity.

Much later in the evening, long after she had crept upstairs and pressed herself into the comfort of the big, soft cushions of her office sofa huddled in her grandmother's afghan; long after she had stopped weeping for Paige, and long after she had given up on not tormenting herself over Annabelle, she made a focused attempt to recall the order of things.

Once Kelly got past the recording, a black and white unit had arrived within ten minutes of the 911 call. Two more black and whites followed, painting the sunny Sunday morning street with a surreal, zebra-like quality. Claudia had a hazy recollection of that, anyway. *Funny*, she thought, *it felt like there should have been a bigger response.*

In fact, there seemed to be more media than law enforcement, with the news helicopters overhead and satellite trucks nudging as close to the yellow crime scene tape as they were allowed.

The brass arrived later in unmarked Crown Vics, the detectives in their own vehicles. Between them, the Sorensen and Giordano names were big enough to roll out the big shots. They stood around looking important, pretending to know what was going on, while the detectives and the crime scene team got down to the serious business of investigating a brutal murder.

The first officer on the scene sat Kelly and Claudia in the backs of separate patrol cars and taken their statements. Their stories would be cross-checked to see if they matched.

By the time a young female officer began unfurling the crime scene tape and marking off a boundary, a flock of neighbors and onlookers had congregated on the street.

The people next door, Lainie and her father, were conspicuously absent, but Claudia saw the curtains twitch in their front window. Was it odd that they had remained cloistered behind closed doors with the two little children while their neighbors packed the sidewalk? She wasn't sure. They wouldn't be able to avoid being interviewed later by detectives.

The detective in charge had identified himself as Investigator Michael Pike. She remembered that because, even in the ghastliness of the situation, she'd had an absurd desire to giggle about his name: Mike Pike. It didn't seem to match his manner, which was cool, businesslike. Like Jovanic when she'd first met him a few months earlier, under circumstances not so very different from these.

Jovanic. If he were here now she would lean into him, feel his arms protecting her. No talking, just his strength comforting her. But he was five hundred miles away, working his case with Alex the Beautiful. He wouldn't be pleased that trouble had found her again, and that it involved Annabelle.

Claudia had repeated everything for Detective Pike in a dull voice. She had not cried then. She had recited it all over again, while in the other patrol car, Kelly had sobbed her heart out. Kelly had never met Paige—not alive, anyway—but it didn't take much to make Kelly cry at the best of times, and this was about the worst it could get. *Unless, of course, Annabelle...* Claudia shut down that thought before it could become whole.

Her mind ricocheted from one image to another, a freaky patchwork that had nothing to do with what she'd seen inside that empty house. Impossible to equate the decomposing corpse with the beautiful, vivacious woman she had come to know and like, despite her foibles.

A heightened alert had been put out on Annabelle, but not an

Amber Alert. While she sat in the patrol car, Claudia overheard Pike talking with another detective. Like everyone else she had spoken with, the cops didn't believe Annabelle had been kidnapped. As a juvenile her records should have been sealed, but somehow they'd dug out her background and she was considered a prime suspect in Paige's death; at the very least, an accessory.

Then the two detectives had started chatting about their personal lives and Claudia listened for ten minutes to Pike complaining about his divorce attorney being too soft on his soon-to-be ex-wife. She listened because it gave her mind something else to do besides gnaw on the question of where Annabelle was now.

Much later, lying on the sofa in her office, bathed in the glow of the desk lamp and the track lighting, she began to stare into the enormity of what she'd witnessed. She couldn't bring herself to get up and turn off the lights. There was already too much darkness in the world.

At eleven-thirty, the phone rang. Again. Jovanic's voice came on after the "leave a message" tape.

"Claudia, are you there? What the hell's going on? Where the hell *are* you?"

He'd called her office number a half-dozen times, her cellular the same. The first messages were tender, concerned: "Claudia, honey, are you okay? I tried your cell phone. Call me, baby." She could hear the frustration in his voice grow with each message but she couldn't bring herself to pick up the handset. Didn't want to hear the stink she was afraid he would raise about Annabelle. Mostly, though, she needed him here physically, not just his voice.

She hadn't answered Pete's calls either, not even Zebediah's. Certainly not the newspapers or the television stations.

She knew she ought to let the people who loved her know she was okay, except that she wasn't, and she couldn't find any words that would not trivialize what she'd witnessed. She couldn't bear to hear the silly comparisons people would make when they learned of Paige's violent death.

I know how you feel, my mother just died. She was ninety-two.
We lost a child at birth.
My friend died of an overdose.
Only someone who had shared violent death could fully

understand how it set you apart.

She would have talked to Kelly, but Kelly had sought her solace at the bottom of a bottle.

Claudia knocked back some of her own solace: a shot of Stoli diluted with a splash of cranberry juice. She would drink enough to blur reality, bend the edges a little, until sleep arrived to afford the protection she needed from her thoughts.

Monday morning brought with it a minor hangover. She took her coffee out to the front deck and swung lethargically in the basket chair, trying to make sense of what had happened.

Around nine, a mustard colored Hummer emblazoned with the Sunmark Studios logo pulled to the curb and Dominic Giordano's driver got out. Juan waved up at her as he climbed the stairs. "Good morning, Ms. Rose."

"Hey, Juan." Her voice sounded as lifeless as she felt. "What's up?"

"Mr. G., sent me to bring you over to the house."

Some nerve "Mr. G." had. How the hell did he know she wasn't working?

Maybe he heard about what happened, dumbshit.

"He's not in the car?"

Juan shook his head. "He's working at the Malibu house today. Those news people, they got the place surrounded. I drove him in from the airport last night. Couldn't barely get through the gates."

"Then why can't we talk on the phone?"

It was an empty question. And the truth was, she had been toying with the idea of calling Giordano. That would have been on her own terms, rather than answering his peremptory summons as if she were one of his employees.

Juan smiled. "I got my orders, you know? It's up to you, Ms. Rose, it's a free country. But he don't give up too easy."

Claudia regarded his polished black lace-up shoes and his chauffeur's uniform and the neatly combed hair. He was just a working stiff, doing what he was paid to do. She unfolded herself from the chair and stretched. "God, I'm thrashed. Tell you what, Juan, you come in, have a cup of coffee, watch a little TV. I have a few things to take care of."

She made him wait for almost an hour, during which time she heard his cell phone ring three or four times. She reckoned Giordano was on the other end, demanding to know what was taking so long.

She remembered the way he had treated Diana Sorensen while Claudia was hiding in the shower and thought, *Tough shit. Let him wait.*

While Juan cooled his heels downstairs, Claudia phoned Jovanic.

"I was worried sick about you," he said angrily. "Couldn't you have picked up the phone and let me know you were okay?"

"I'm sorry, I just couldn't."

"You could've said you didn't feel like talking. I was ready to send a black and white over to check on you, for crissake."

"I *couldn't* talk, Joel. You might be used to seeing dead bodies but I'm not. And this was someone I knew. I needed time to process it."

"Nice try," he said. "But I'm not buying that rationalization. If you'd just called and said, 'Honey, I've been through a terrible ordeal and I need some time alone,' I would have understood. You think I'm such an asshole that you couldn't do that? You left me hanging, imagining…"

"Okay, I apologize again. *I* was being the asshole, not you. But could you cut me a little slack?"

He exhaled, giving up. "Yeah, fine. As long as you're okay."

Then she made the mistake of asking what he knew about the murder and about Annabelle. His tone cooled. "I don't know anything, Claudia. I've been up to my ass in my case here, not to mention worrying about you. I'll bet you my Christmas bonus that Annabelle is hiding out with whatever pals helped her engineer this little escapade gone wrong, trying to figure out how to cover her delinquent ass."

"Damn it, Joel, why are you siding with *them*? I don't believe she had anything to do with this—this—"

The temperature dropped a few more degrees.

"You'd better open your eyes and stop seeing that kid as some poor, wounded creature. She's got big problems. Bigger than you can help her with. Let it go."

Claudia picked up a worry ball from her desk and began squeezing it. "I know she has problems, but I don't believe she's violent. The only times she's taken physical action was to defend herself and to defend me. I don't buy it."

"So now you're a psychologist?"

Claudia's temper flared. "I may not have my doctorate, but I understand human behavior just fine. Handwriting doesn't lie, Joel, and she doesn't have the potential for that kind of behavior. In the news they said Paige was strangled, with a belt, for God's sake—*a belt*. Annabelle doesn't have that kind of strength, and I don't believe she'd do that even if she could."

"You'd be surprised at what people can do—even kids—in a desperate situation," Jovanic said. "These days, kids kill all the time. Hell, I'm not saying she meant for it to happen. Maybe she set it up with some of her gangbanger friends—they'd snatch Paige, hold her for a couple of days and get everyone good and scared—get media attention, some money, whatever. But something went wrong. She couldn't control the situation anymore, or Paige tried to escape, or... Look, Claudia, I gotta go. Alex needs me. Let's drop it, okay?"

I need you, dammit! She said a frosty goodbye. There was a certain irony in their exchange, she realized. He had reached out to her the night before and she'd rejected him by not answering his calls. Now she needed him, but he was forced to choose Alex. She replaced the phone in its base, unsettled and resentful, feeling isolated and alone in her support of Annabelle.

CHAPTER 23

The drive from Playa del Reina to Dominic Giordano's Point Dume home in Malibu took close to an hour along the busy Pacific Coast Highway. Juan dodged and wove through traffic, bullying smaller vehicles with the big Hummer. He kept glancing at the dashboard clock, nervous about the reception he would get from his boss for taking too long.

"You married, Juan?" Claudia asked, trying to distract him.

He shook his head. "Nah, but I got me a real nice girlfriend. We been talking about it."

"Want me to look at her handwriting? Tell you if she's a secret axe murderer?"

"You can tell stuff like that?"

"Nope. Handwriting can't predict what someone's going to do, it shows *potential* for behavior." She smiled. "I'm sure your girlfriend will keep the axe in the tool shed."

"Gee thanks, Ms. Rose, now I feel *much* better."

They drove past the Country Mart at Cross Creek, with its low-key chic and trendy shops. Here, where a greater number of celebrities lived than in any other town in the country, including Beverly Hills, the views of the coastline seemed even more impossibly beautiful than the one Claudia saw from her own deck every day.

When he'd said that the media had the place surrounded, Juan had not exaggerated the situation. As they rounded the corner onto the private road leading to the Giordano house, Claudia could see that the estate was under siege.

Television trucks on stakeout ringed the ten-foot walls surrounding the property. Cameramen milled on the street, conferring with their producers, mini-cams ready for action.

They drove past Michelle Gillette, the reporter who had broken the news of Paige and Annabelle's disappearance, primping in a TV monitor. Claudia surmised she was preparing for the next important update: *Who Killed the Headmistress?* and, *Where is the missing student? Special Report, coming up next. Don't miss it!*

A security camera mounted on top of the wall panned its electronic eye over them as Juan cruised up to the gates. Taking advantage of the slowdown, the reporters rushed the car.

"Has Mister Giordano's daughter been found?"

"Anything new on the Sorensen murder?"

A reporter from Channel Four, a slight blond guy in a windbreaker, rapped on the tinted window, and shouted, "Is Mr. Giordano inside?"

Juan hit the brakes to avoid slamming into him.

"Are they crazy?" Claudia cried out.

"I think so, Ms. Rose. Don't even look at them."

The immense iron gates swung inward and the reporters fell away as the Hummer picked up speed and plowed through. Claudia looked straight ahead, refusing to make eye contact. Let them wonder who she was, if they could see her through the tinted glass. God knew, they were trying.

Behind them, the gates closed with a satisfying *clang*. They bumped along a dirt road that took them up a gentle incline for about a half-mile before the house came into view: A sweeping lawn, blue-gray slate roof, a magenta thicket of bougainvillea caressing shell-pink stucco. In front was a one-story section with rounded walls. The rear section rose two levels. A grove of avocados fringed one side of the house; a rose garden, the other.

They were high enough on the hill to afford a clear view of the ocean across the Coast Highway. From here, the surfers sitting on their boards waiting for a wave were nothing more than dots in the water.

It would have been on that private stretch of beach where Annabelle had made her suicide attempt a few months ago.

The thought of Annabelle made her stomach flip-flop. Every day that passed reduced the chances that she would be found alive. Juan came to a stop in front of a four-car garage whose open doors revealed a Lexus, a Mercedes, and a magnificent restored Stutz Bearcat. *Rich man's toys.*

In the circular driveway was another Mercedes. As Juan cut the engine the front door to the house opened. A man came out and slammed the door. He was short and beefy, a fireplug in a black suit. Even from this distance, Claudia could see the scowl on his face. He strode along the path toward his car with rapid, angry steps.

"Hold up a second, Ms. Rose," Juan said, urgency in his voice. "Don't get out yet." Waiting until the man had driven away, kicking up gravel as he went, the chauffeur hurried around to open Claudia's door.

"Go on up," he said. "I'll be right here when you're ready to leave."

I'm ready now, she thought, climbing out into the cool, still morning. The birds were noisy in the trees. Movement caught the corner of her eye and a young deer appeared, staring at her for a moment, its nose quivering before bounding off across the lawn.

For some reason, the sight of the deer seemed to bring the world back into balance again. Claudia smiled. "Thanks, Juan. This shouldn't take long."

"Good luck, Ms. Rose." He touched the bill of his chauffeur's hat in a salute.

Good luck? Was she going need it, dealing with Dominic Giordano?

Dwarf lemon trees lined the path to the front door, their branches heavy with fruit, perfuming the air with citrus. The door opened and a woman as brown and wrinkled as a walnut came out, wearing a maid's uniform. She gave Claudia a broad, welcoming smile and nodded at her. "Good morning, Miz Rose, come on in. Mr. G's waitin' for you on the terrace."

Claudia followed her into a room straight out of *Architectural Digest*. Filled with light and space; limestone floors and huge skylights that brought the outdoors inside. At close to noon, sky and clouds poured in. She could imagine looking up at the stars at midnight, diamonds on black velvet.

The furniture was sparse: a celadon pot of bromeliads on a chunky spruce table, an oversized khaki sofa and chairs that had been designed for comfort; sisal rugs. Understated Asian motif artwork. At the center of the room, the branches of a large ficus stretched toward the high-beamed ceiling like Jack's beanstalk. The splashing of a waterfall completed a picture that spoke of money and power, plenty of it.

Anyone could hire a decorator and create a beautiful environment, but they couldn't mask the heavy energy that infused the place.

Claudia followed the maid past a tiled bar that overlooked the beach through floor-to-ceiling windows. They exited through French doors to a terrace where Dominic Giordano was seated at a table, his back to the door. He spoke without turning around, sounding peevish. "What took you so long? Sit down."

Claudia crossed the terrace and rounded the table. "I'm not your employee, Mr. Giordano, I don't have to account to you for my time."

Midday in his own back yard—if that's what you called the rolling lawns with tennis courts and a swimming pool in the distance—the silver-streaked hair was as meticulously styled as the evening she'd met him in his limousine. A blinding white Ralph Lauren polo shirt and tennis shorts reflected off his deep tan.

When Claudia came around the table she saw with a jolt of shock that Giordano's left leg was a steel prosthesis attached above the knee. The artificial limb had been hidden beneath his trousers when they'd met in his limo. She pulled out a chair and sat down opposite him.

"So, why am I here, Mr. Giordano?"

He gave her a look of cynical amusement. "You want to ask about my leg, don't you?"

A slight flush of embarrassment colored her cheeks. "Do you want me to ask?"

"I figure you gotta be curious, right? Here's this rich guy who's got all the shit anyone could ever want, and he's a *gimp*. You're wondering. Let's get it out of the way."

Claudia leveled a glance at him. "I thought you wanted to talk about Annabelle, but if you want to tell me what happened to your leg, go right ahead."

"Whoa!" he said, a hint of admiration. "You're one cool bitch."

She shot him a silent look of contempt at his choice of words and waited for his story.

"It happened surfing," he said, and she could tell that he enjoyed having a captive audience. "I've surfed some of the best beaches in the world—Hawaii, Australia, you name it. I fucking *lived* in the water." He pushed back his chair and stood up smoothly with practiced ease, beckoning Claudia to follow. "Come with me. I want you to see something."

He walked without any discernable limp toward an area enclosed by a wall about fifty yards from the terrace.

Feeling uneasy, Claudia crossed the lawn with him, wondering why he chose to display such an obvious prosthesis, rather than a realistic-looking limb. From what she knew of him it was intended to make others uncomfortable.

Dominic Giordano unlocked a pair of riveted steel doors and led her through to an enormous in-ground tank. Her stomach churned with a sick premonition as she peered into the water.

The flat grey blade of a dorsal fin sliced the surface, moving in lazy circles. Claudia turned to Giordano, who was closely observing her reaction. "Why are you showing me this?" she asked, a little breathless. *JAWS* had never been her favorite movie.

"He took my freedom," Giordano said. "I took his."

"You lost your leg to a shark?"

"Yeah, he was a big mutha—six-footer. Bit my board in half, got my leg with it."

Claudia's eyes widened in horror. She took a step back from the water. "My God, that's horrible. How did you get away?"

"Hammered his goddamn nose with my fist until he let go. Made it to shore with one leg. He had my other one for lunch."

The thought made her stomach curl. "So, you captured another shark for what—revenge?"

"You got it."

"What good did that do?"

He gave her a smile that was halfway between a leer and

a grimace. "Shows the world that *nobody* fucks with Dominic Giordano and gets away with it." Giordano grinned at her and went over to a large barrel standing on the pool deck. He lifted the lid, reached inside, hauled out a hunk of raw meat dripping with blood and tossed it into the pool.

With stunning speed the shark raised out of the water, its powerful jaws spread wide. The razor-edged teeth clamped onto the flesh. A split-second later nothing more than a red stain remained in the water.

"What did you feed it?" Claudia asked, afraid of the answer.

Giordano grabbed another hunk of meat from the barrel and held it up so she could see the sleek black pelt before he tossed it to the shark. "Baby seal."

"I'm sorry I asked," she said, resolving to find out which organization protected seals and report him.

"They hang out down on the rocks in the cove," he said, pointing toward the beach. "Just club one a couple of times and *ecco*, my shark has dinner."

"Stop it," she protested angrily. "I don't want to know."

Giordano took a folded cloth from the top of a pile of damask napkins on a small table beside the barrel, and wiped the seal blood from his hands, observing her distress with amusement.

Claudia met his gaze with a stony glare. "What's your point, Mr. Giordano?"

"Claudia, *prego*, call me *Dominic*," he said in an ingratiating tone. "Aren't we friends?"

"No," she snapped. "We are *not* friends. I want to know why you're showing me this."

"I want to impress you, Claudia," he said in a voice as smooth as silk.

"Well, this sure as hell won't do it."

He reached over and stroked her bare arm. The fine hairs rose and her breath caught in surprise. Then she got hold of herself. She wasn't a teen actress or a young nanny in his employ, or Diana Sorensen who apparently had fallen under his spell. Claudia knew what he was capable of, but she wasn't beholden to him. He had no power over her like he did the shark. She swung around and started back to the terrace.

"Hey," he called after her with a mocking laugh. "You gonna leave a poor crip to fend for himself?"

She spun back to face him. "You're no cripple."

"You got that right," he admitted with a great deal of pride. He lengthened his stride to catch up with her. "By the way, I still surf. No fucking shark is gonna take that away from me."

Giordano walked beside her in silence for a dozen paces, then he said, "Listen, Claudia, I know you're worried about the kid—my sources tell me the two of you were pretty tight. I need to find her too, before the cops do. You can help Annabelle by telling me how you came to find the Sorensen woman's body."

Claudia narrowed her eyes in suspicion. "How's that supposed to help Annabelle?"

"I got better investigators than the cops. You tell me everything you know, I'll find her faster than they do."

The January sun was warm. They arrived at the terrace and the maid magically appeared and poured ice teas. Giordano sat down at the table and leaned his forearms on the glass. "I want to know what the cops know, and you can tell me."

Claudia drank some tea and considered what he had said. "What *I* want to know," she said, "is who took Paige to that house and why did they kill her? And don't tell me it was Annabelle."

A disturbing notion struck her. What if Giordano himself was behind the killing and he just wanted to know how much she knew? A motive didn't surface right away. Then she remembered the man who had stormed out of the house when she and Juan arrived. He looked like he could be a hit man for the mob. At least, a central casting image of one.

Giordano held her gaze so piercingly and for so long that she got the distinct impression he knew what she was thinking. It was all she could do not to squirm.

He carefully unfolded a napkin and wiped condensation from his glass. "You got any kids, Claudia?"

"I'm sure you already know I don't."

Giordano shook his head. "They make you *insano*, kids. And this one's had a lot of practice. Started running away when she was seven. You know she's got a rap sheet for shoplifting and car boosting?"

Even now that it didn't make any difference, Claudia wasn't going to admit that Paige had shared that information with her.

She said, "So what? When I was her age I got picked up with kids shoplifting, too. I got past it."

Giordano's brows lifted in surprise. "You? I wouldn't have guessed that."

"I was with the wrong people at the wrong time." The memory of the fear and humiliation of that weekend was still strong. Being left in juvenile detention because her mother refused to allow her to come home was one of the worst experiences of her life. She didn't tell him that she had never stolen anything. The older kids who took her along for cover were the ones stuffing their pockets with candy.

"Annabelle's problems are a lot bigger than being with the wrong people," Giordano said.

"Losing her mother at such a young age had to be hard on her."

"Her mother?" His lips twisted. "She's better off without that ungrateful slut."

Giordano's words shocked Claudia into silence. Then she found her voice. "What's that supposed to mean?"

"What do you think it means? She screwed around on me. That bitch was nothing but a teeny bopper bit player when I found her. I sent her to the best acting school, voice lessons, you name it. I put up money for films she could star in." His voice heated up and his complexion suffused a dark crimson as old anger kicked in. "When she insists on this bozo, Tony Belmont to co-star, I look into it and find out she'd been screwing him for over a year."

"I don't know about that," Claudia said. "But I saw a picture of her in Annabelle's room at school. It was obvious from the way she looked at her how much she loved Annabelle. Doesn't that mean anything to you?"

"Who the fuck knows if she's even my kid?" Giordano sucked in a deep breath, looking as though he were trying to bring his bitter anger under control.

"Is that why you're so cold to her?" Claudia asked.

He threw her a scornful look. "What the hell do you know? You show up a few times, give her handwriting lessons, go home. You don't know a goddamn thing about it."

Claudia knew it would be better if she let it go, but something compelled her to keep pushing the issue. She knew it was foolish, but it felt like defending Annabelle's mother would help to draw the girl back.

"If you think she's not your child, why don't you have DNA testing done?" she asked.

The look he turned on her made her regret the question. Maybe for some reason of his own, he didn't want to know. "Listen, lady," he said. "I don't need you psychoanalyzing me. I need to find that kid before she does any more damage."

Handwriting didn't lie, and Claudia had studied Annabelle's until her eyes hurt. If she listened to Giordano, he was telling her that his daughter was a raving sociopath. She said, "If you'd seen Paige's body, there's no way you could believe Annabelle was involved in her death."

He shook his head in what she judged to be mock sadness. "Claudia, Claudia, you think I'm a cold-hearted monster like that bastard out there in the tank? You got no idea what I've been through with her." He broke off and stood up. "Come with me."

"What now?"

His laugh grated. "No more sharks, just Annabelle's room."

Claudia followed him upstairs to a large bedroom made bright by a bank of windows overlooking the grove of avocado trees. Taking in the flat panel television, the iMac on a built-in computer desk, the DVD surround sound system, she couldn't fault Giordano for the material comforts he'd provided. Annabelle appeared to have it all.

All except what she really needs.

Giordano crossed to a large cardboard box that had been placed on a chair. Ripped open, strips of peeled back adhesive tape hanging loose. "Sorensen Academy sent all her shit home," he said, reaching in and taking out a leather bound book. Claudia remembered his conversation with Diana in Annabelle's room and guessed he had been there to pick up her possessions.

"She won't be going back there," he said, handing the book to Claudia. "Read the last entry."

Taking the book, she saw that it was a diary, the broken lock violating its secrets. Nothing could be more invasive than breaking into a young girl's diary. But these were extraordinary circumstances. Claudia flipped through the pages. She caught her breath at the date on the last written page: Christmas Eve, the last day Annabelle and Paige were seen alive.

She noted with frustration that the positive changes she had observed, both in personality and handwriting, had regressed under the stress of Annabelle's mental state at the time of writing. Annabelle's handwriting had begun to open up, expand a little. This writing was more like what Claudia had seen in the first sample from weeks earlier, with its narrow letters and squeezed spaces.

"I have to talk to Cruz," Annabelle had written, underlining the words. *"He cares about me more than that bitch Paige. He's so awesome—I'm gonna give him his present tonight. I can't wait to see him. Neil was mad about the belt, but too bad. He asked if it was for my father—as if! Then he guessed who it was for but too bad. I don't care what he thinks. It's my art project. When Cruz finds out I made it myself he'll like me even better."*

Typical teenage stuff. Except that Paige had been strangled with a belt.

"She *did* go over there," Claudia said. "But she didn't give him the belt. She didn't get a chance."

"You *know* about this Cruz character?"

She nodded. "I'm sure you know, he's the athletic director at the school." She filled him in on some of what Annabelle had seen at Cruz's cottage on Christmas Eve.

"This is the first I've heard about the sonofabitch being involved with her," he said, jabbing a finger at the diary. "If he's laid so much as a pinkie on her, that fucker's gonna get whacked."

Given his own rumored involvement with young girls, Claudia found his rage ironic. "He was sleeping with Paige," she hurried to assure him. "Cruz doesn't have the profile of a pedophile."

But even as she said it, she wondered whether she could be wrong about Cruz. She had seen his handwriting in the gift card Annabelle had lifted from Paige, and that had not sent up any red flags. He had yet to return the form she had e-mailed him, which would give her a better fix on his motivations.

Claudia had seen plenty of cases where publicly upstanding

adults had secretly used children in ways that sickened her. Still, Cruz displayed confidence with adult women, which suggested he wasn't the type to go for a troubled young teen.

Giordano moved in close, looking over her shoulder at what Annabelle had written. Too close. She could feel the heat coming off his skin; became aware of his aftershave, the warmth of his breath on her neck. He might be boorish at times and lacking in social graces but there was no denying his good looks and, at this moment, his sheer animal magnetism.

Claudia's heart was racing as she stepped away and turned toward him. "I, uh—the handwriting shows that she was upset when she wrote this."

For a moment, Giordano looked at her as if she were speaking a foreign language. Then he interrupted, ignoring her comment. "What about the belt? She says she was giving this clown a belt. Don't you *get* it?"

"I get it, Dominic, I get it. You're thinking she used the belt to strangle Paige. Well, I told you, Paige was with Cruz that night. Cruz said they played sex games that involved a belt around the neck. Don't you think it's a little more reasonable that *he* might have killed her accidentally? If he was that wasted, he might not even remember it."

Giordano paced to the window and back, putting the weight on his prosthesis so that it thumped on the hardwood floor. "If she's not involved, why is she hiding?"

Claudia looked at him for a long moment, hardly daring to voice her fear. "Maybe she's not hiding."

"He killed Paige and then he killed Annabelle and hid her body somewhere? If that's how it went down, he doesn't know who he's dealing with. Nah, something doesn't smell right here."

He was right about one thing, it made no sense for Cruz to have told Claudia about his and Paige's experimentation with autoerotic asphyxiation if it had resulted in her death.

Unless he blocked it out.

Giordano's face crumpled for a moment, then his jaw set into a hard line. "Goddammit, *I'll* choke the life outta the little bitch. We have to find her before the cops start sniffing around. I've got a lot riding on…"

He broke off, and with a rush of aversion Claudia realized that he was talking about his reputation. She held up the diary. "Would you mind if I hold onto this for a while?"

"Sure, why not." Giordano looked at her with speculation in his eyes. "I want to hire you to help me find her."

She shook her head. "You don't need to hire me, I'm already involved up to my eyeballs."

"I want you on my payroll. At least then you'd have to keep me in the fucking loop."

"I'm not interested in your money," Claudia said, determined that he wasn't going to control her the way he did other people. "And there's one thing you can be sure of, I won't betray her, not to you nor anyone else."

Giordano turned and aimed a vicious blow at the bedroom door, leaving an indentation in the wood from his knuckles. "This is getting out of hand," he shouted. "We gotta bring her in."

When Juan dropped her at home, Claudia checked her voicemail. There were no calls from Jovanic, but there were two hang-ups listed as *Out of Area*.

She worked through the afternoon, analyzing a handwriting sample for a client who was hiring a new employee, breaking at six to watch the news.

She heated a frozen dinner while they rolled tape of Juan driving her in and out of the Giordano estate in the Hummer, then she logged on to the Internet and surfed the web for a couple of hours, searching out news stories about Paige and answering e-mails that had stacked up over the previous week.

When the phone rang around eleven, she grabbed the receiver, hoping to see Jovanic's cellular number on caller ID. Instead, the display read *Out of Area*.

She pressed the 'Talk' button. "Hello?"

The sound of rapid, ragged breathing on the line.

"Who is it?" Claudia asked, somehow *knowing*.

A voice whispered, "It's me, Annabelle."

CHAPTER 24

Claudia closed her eyes, dizzy with relief. Then her mind started clicking into gear. She mentally checked the gas gauge of the Jag, grabbed pen and paper, ready to note an address. "Annabelle, honey, where *are* you?"

"I didn't mean what I said about hurting her," Annabelle whimpered, choking on tears. Her disembodied voice sounded slurred, as if she had trouble getting her tongue around the words. "It's all my fault."

Claudia's heart sank. Could she have been wrong all along? She put on the Adult Authority Voice. "Annabelle, tell me where you are. I'll come get you right now."

"They're gonna lock me up," the girl said dully. "But I didn't hurt her, I swear I didn't. He said the cops won't believe me because I was in trouble before."

"*Who* said..." Time enough for that later. "Annabelle, you've got to tell me where you are. I promise, I'll help you."

Annabelle broke into strangled sobs. "I think—a hospital. It's dark all the time. Claudia, I don't feel good."

"Can you give me an address? Are you in L.A.?"

"Oh no!" Annabelle gasped. "No!"

The line went dead.

Dominic Giordano's rant wound down. "Goddammit, you got

nothing! What the hell hospital? Where?"

"If I knew that, I'd have called the cops, not you."

"Did you try Call Return?"

"Dominic, you've asked me that eighty times already. Maybe you should reconsider your attitude. I'm not the enemy, remember?"

She heard him draw a sharp breath. "*Merda*," he muttered. "I'm up to *here* with this shit."

Claudia rested her head against the back of her chair and pressed her toes into the carpet, rocking back and forth. The movement comforted her in some small way. "She said someone told her she would be blamed. It doesn't sound to me like she killed Paige."

"*Jesus*, Claudia. You think the cops are gonna buy that?"

"She sounded drugged."

"She's done a lot of stupid things, but not drugs."

Apparently he didn't know about the pot in Annabelle's backpack.

"If she's in a hospital she could have been *given* drugs," Claudia said.

"Now I have to get someone checking every fucking medical office in the state. *Goddamn it.*"

Callous bastard.

Annabelle's drawing lay atop Claudia's desk, the clever sketch of her father pushing a car over the edge of a cliff.

Her mother died in a car wreck.

Keeping half an ear on his diatribe, Claudia opened a web browser and Googled Annabelle's mother. The first of the twenty-five links listed was titled, *An Inside Look at Valerie Vale's Life.* She clicked on the link, murmuring "Uh huh" at appropriate intervals so Giordano would know she was still on the line.

"*The young actress was the only child in a show business family,*" she read. "*Her mother was a model and her father an orchestra leader. On her seventeenth birthday, with the permission of her parents, Vale married thirty-two-year-old movie mogul Dominic Giordano, the producer of her debut film,* City of Light."

I guess he always liked them young, Claudia thought, feeling sad for Valerie Vale. She read on, "*Giordano, whose Sunmark Studios has long been rumored to have ties to organized crime, took full charge of his young wife's career, casting her in a string of highly profitable starring vehicles which showcased her youthful glamour.*

"However, Vale told our reporter that acting was not her first priority, and the role she really wanted to play was wife and mother. Four years later, she got her wish when her daughter, Annabelle Lee Giordano, was born."

Annabelle Lee.

Had Vale been a fan of Poe? Claudia wondered, or had she just heard the name and liked it? Already, the child's life had been as ill-fated as her namesake. It sounded to her that Dominic had used his beautiful young bride more as a puppet whose strings he played to his own tune; a trophy wife.

Like Paige had been to Torg Sorensen.

She scrolled down the screen as the article continued, *"Misfortune followed when Giordano lost a leg in a rare shark attack while surfing on Maui's West Coast. After his recovery, Valerie complained to friends of his increasingly morose behavior, which eventually escalated to alleged physical abuse. Police were called out to the Malibu estate on more than one occasion for domestic disturbances.*

"Tragically, Valerie Vale's life was cut short when the brakes of her convertible apparently failed and she lost control of the car. The twenty-seven-year-old Vale suffered severe head injuries after a horrifying plunge off a cliff on Pacific Coast Highway only a short distance from her home, and died after lingering in a coma for nearly a week. Annabelle Lee, who was six-years-old at the time, was in the car with her mother, but escaped serious injury.

"Vale's other passenger, Tony Belmont, her leading man in the film she was making at the time of her death, described what could have been a scene in one of his movies as he told investigators how he grabbed the child and leapt from the car just prior to the accident. Devastated by his inability to save Vale, Belmont refused to talk with reporters. Yet, the tragic story does not end here.

"Shortly after Vale's death, Tony Belmont was mysteriously attacked in his home by unidentified intruders and was left with disfiguring facial lacerations that ended a promising acting career."

"Claudia, are you listening to me?" Giordano snapped.

"What? Yeah, of course." Wrapped up in the story on her monitor, she had tuned him out and had no idea what he'd been saying. She pulled her attention back to the conversation and tried to pick up the thread.

"...looking at this Montenegro prick—the one she wrote about in the diary."

"You're checking out Cruz? The police are already doing that."

"What's that got to do with me?" said Giordano. "I intend to find out for myself how he's involved."

"Cruz *likes* Annabelle," Claudia said, concerned about the menace in his voice. "I don't believe he'd hurt her."

The line went silent except for Giordano's breathing. She asked herself why she hadn't called the police. The answer was, Giordano was a jerk, but Annabelle stood a better chance with him than if the police found her first.

When he finally spoke, his words were a *non sequitur*. "How can she be in a hospital? No friggin' hospital contacted *me*."

"Dominic, what about the police?"

"Forget it. I'm not telling them, and neither are you."

Irritation surged through Claudia like an electric shock. "You know what? I've had it up to here with you telling me what I'm going to do or not do. I think the police need to know she called."

"Yeah? What good's that? You didn't get a location, you didn't find out who she's with; you didn't get anything useful out of her."

Claudia didn't wait to compose herself before responding. "You have balls the size of grapefruits to talk to me that way," she shouted into the phone. "I *care* about Annabelle, and I don't need *you* hassling me."

With a charge of intense satisfaction she slammed the instrument back into its cradle and stood there for a moment, steadying her breathing. She'd had more than her fill of Annabelle's father.

She went downstairs to the service porch. The laundry basket was on top of the washing machine, filled with the clothes she'd sorted and left unwashed when Kelly dragged her to the mall.

After making the gruesome discovery of Paige's body she had been in such a hurry to get out of her clothes and into the shower, she'd shed them without emptying the pockets. Digging through the dirty clothes, she uncovered the jeans she'd worn the day before.

Detective Pike's business card was folded in with the cash and credit card she had intended to use on the abortive shopping trip.

She stared at his phone number, sucking on her lower lip. It was well past midnight. Could he do anything if she called him tonight? As Giordano had so crudely pointed out, she had no concrete information to supply.

Except that Annabelle is alive.

She hesitated to wake Pike. Giordano was right; the cops weren't going to buy Annabelle's tale, whatever it was. She decided to compromise and leave a message at the police station. Pike would get it in the morning.

The next call was an easier decision, but Cruz' answering machine picked up after four rings. Wondering whether he had heard from her too, Claudia left him a voicemail that Annabelle had phoned.

Later, lying in bed alone, chasing sleep, she wondered what Jovanic was doing and why he hadn't called. She closed her eyes and tried meditation breathing for a while, but that didn't help. She realized that she was longing for him to be there, holding her, comforting her with his warmth.

Deep down, she understood that his brusque attitude arose out of his concern for her and she forgave him for it. He believed she had become overly involved with Annabelle and he wanted her to avoid getting hurt.

Well, she *had* gotten hurt, but that didn't make her care any less about what happened to the girl.

She sat up and punched her pillow into submission, then lay back, yearning for the sound of his breathing, slow and steady at first, accelerating as his hands moved over her body, arousing her. With an almost perverse melancholy, she let herself imagine the sensation of him nibbling her ear, whispering loving promises of what he would do to please her. The more she fantasized, the stronger the longing for him grew, until sheer exhaustion overcame her and with it, sleep.

The cell phone rang, startling her awake. Blurry-eyed in the semidarkness, Claudia fumbled to answer. "Hello?"

"Claudia." Annabelle's voice. Tense, urgent, still whispering, but clearer than in her earlier call.

Claudia sat up and swung her legs over the edge of the bed, shaking sleep from her brain. "Are you okay? Do you know what hospital you're in?" She grabbed for the notepad and pen.

"I'm in Las Vegas."

The pen dropped to the floor and rolled under the bed. "Las Vegas? What the—"

"They'll be back in a few minutes. Please help me! I don't want them to catch me on the phone."

"*Who'll* be back? Annabelle, *what's going on?*"

"I'm gonna get out of here. Will you come get me, *please?*"

Claudia blinked, wondering if she were still asleep and this was all part of a dream. "You want me to come to Las Vegas?"

"You promised. You said you'd help me!"

"Of course I'll help you."

Am I nuts? How am I supposed to help her?

"I've gotta get out of here. He's weirding me out, the way he keeps looking at me. Will you *pleeeease* come?"

"Yes, Annabelle, yes, I'll come, but Las Vegas is three hundred miles away. I have to get a flight."

"Claudia, hurry, I'm scared." Although she was whispering, Annabelle's voice was accelerating towards hysteria.

Claudia hurried into her office, considering her choices: call Giordano, call the cops, don't call anyone, just go. She sat at her desk and launched a browser, keyed in the Southwest Airlines website. "Okay. There's a flight at seven forty-five. That gives me ninety minutes if I can get on it. I could be in Vegas before nine. Where do I find you?"

"I don't know yet. I'm someplace high up right now—I can see that tall tower thing from the window. But I'm going to get out of here. Hurry, Claudia, he's coming. *Hurry.* I'll call you later."

"Annabelle—*Annabelle?* Hello?" She was speaking to dead air.

CHAPTER 25

On a foggy Tuesday morning the flight was half empty. Claudia threw her purse onto the empty seat next to her, grateful to have a row to herself, questioning the wisdom of giving in to Annabelle's pleas and jetting off to Nevada. She didn't even know where, or if, she would find the girl.

Maybe it was that unfulfilled-motherhood thing. She was a sucker for a kid with a sad story.

If I had any brains I'd have called Pike.

Claudia leaned her forehead against the cold porthole glass and stared down at the blue lights flanking the tarmac as the engines thundered to life. The big wheels began to turn and the aircraft was pushed away from the gate and moved out to the runway.

After the usual safety briefing, the flight attendants strapped themselves into their seats at the bulkhead, casually chatting with each other, unaware that the passenger in 7C was on a rescue mission.

The Boeing 737 rolled along the runway, almost languidly at first; gathering momentum. Then the jets were screaming, the nose lifted, and the aircraft thrust upward like an enormous whale breeching.

Or a shark, Claudia thought, remembering with a shudder the way the marine beast had clamped its teeth on that piece of flesh.

A few minutes later they were above the marine layer that hid the coastline. They flew toward the sun, throwing long shadows across the endless rows of houses and commercial properties spread out below. Los Angeles County—more than four thousand square miles, a mushrooming population in excess of ten million. A tangled web of freeways loaded with morning-drive commuters, still miniature from this faraway perspective.

Las Vegas. What the hell is she doing there? How will I find her?

When the flight attendants came around with the beverage cart Claudia refused the offer of coffee. She didn't need caffeine jitters adding to the misgivings already playing ping-pong with her insides.

Her thoughts scudded to Paige, of Annabelle's assertion that *"it's all my fault."* She had brought along the girl's diary, hoping to find something significant that Giordano had missed in his reading of his daughter's private thoughts. She turned to the final entry and re-read the words that had returned to her again and again like a recurring nightmare.

"Neil was mad about the belt, but too bad. He asked if it was for my father–as if! Then he guessed who it was for but I don't care what he thinks. It's my art project. When Cruz finds out I made it myself he'll like me even better."

It was Cruz' word that he and Paige never saw Annabelle that night. Now Paige was dead and somehow Annabelle had ended up in Las Vegas. Assuming she was telling the truth, all this time she had been in a hospital under some kind of guard. The questions kept coming: What phone had she used to call Monica, and now, Claudia? Why had she waited so long to make contact? And the million dollar question: how in God's name was she going to escape and meet up with Claudia?

A sudden drop into an air pocket jerked her out of her musings and Annabelle's diary slipped onto the floor. Claudia reached for it under the seat in front of her, chagrined to see that some of the pages at the back of the book had become folded over in the fall.

With the book open flat so she could smooth the pages, her eye was drawn to a slit along the edge of the binding. A hiding place.

With the edge of her fingernail Claudia felt paper. It slid it out easily, a sheet of notepaper folded into quarters, its creases so frayed they had almost separated. Annabelle must have read these words many times.

The first stanza of the poem for which Poe was so well known had been copied in violet-colored ink. Around the margins, a skillful hand had drawn garlands of pink roses that looked so alive you could detect their perfume.

It was many and many a year ago,
*   In a kingdom by the sea,*
That a maiden there lived whom you may know
*   By the name of ANNABEL LEE;—*
And this maiden she lived with no other thought
*   Than to love and be loved by me.*

Following the poem was a letter from a young mother to her child:

"Dearest Beautiful Baby Girl,
"This is my favorite poem. When I read it, I knew I was going to name you Annabelle Lee because I love you so much, the way the girl in the poem is loved. You are the only one in the world who loves me just because I'm me, not because I'm rich or pretty or because I can help them get a part in a movie. Even when everything else is falling apart, my life is worth living because of you.
"One day, when you're grown up, I'm going to tell you all about how you got to be the little Giordano princess. You deserve to know the truth about your daddy. But before that happens, we're going to have a whole lot of fun together. I love being your mama, and when"

The letter ended abruptly mid-sentence. What else had Valerie Vale intended to say? And what had interrupted her?

The handwriting itself was large and round, the words spaced close together—a young woman with a profound need to love and be loved, and one who would habitually draw an abuser to her. The attention and approval of a man would be of primary importance in her life, yet she was ill-equipped to choose a man who would be good for her.

She had a feeling that the approval of the Dominic Giordano she knew would last about as long as the attention his trophy wife brought him.

She reread the letter, curious about the reference to "the truth" about Annabelle's daddy. Was Giordano correct in his belief that she was not his child? If that's what Vale had intended to reveal to her daughter, her death had put an end to that. Claudia flashed on Annabelle's drawing and found herself wondering how thoroughly Vale's death had been investigated before it had been closed as an 'accident.'

Feeling like a voyeur, Claudia carefully refolded the letter and replaced it in its hiding place. This tangible connection to her mother must mean a great deal to Annabelle, and Claudia was glad the girl had it.

The plane's nose leveled out as it reached altitude, then soon made a subtle downward movement for the descent into Las Vegas. Less than an hour after leaving L.A., Claudia was looking down at the crayon-colored turrets of Excalibur; the mini Eiffel Tower of Paris Las Vegas; the massive black pyramid of Luxor. In the morning light it resembled a sprawling amusement park.

Yet, the remarkable skyline failed to hold Claudia's attention. Her thoughts were riveted on where in that neon jungle she might find Annabelle Giordano.

CHAPTER 26

Neon lights pulsing, slot machines endlessly pinging. Terminal C of McCarran Field at Las Vegas International was an extension of the casinos on the strip. Even first thing in the morning—or what was probably more accurate, the butt end of the evening for last-minute gamblers awaiting the call for flights out of town, they crammed dollar bills into insatiable electronic bandits.

Claudia powered on her cell phone the instant the plane taxied up to the gate, and checked her voicemail. She had two messages. The first was from Jovanic.

"Hey, babe, sorry I didn't call last night, I fell asleep early. You're not still pissed, are you? I'll be unreachable for most of the day, so don't call me back. I'll catch you later when I can." Hearing his voice made her smile with relief.

The second message was from Dominic Giordano, who sounded mad enough to spit glass.

"Where the fuck are you? That asshole, Pike, called me. Did you talk to him? They're talking about an arrest warrant for Annabelle. Goddammit, Claudia, call me back. I'm with my lawyer, tell Louise to interrupt."

Claudia set the phone to vibrate so as not to miss Annabelle's call and slipped it into her pocket. Giordano would have to wait until she had a handle on the situation here.

After stopping at an ATM machine to pick up some extra cash for a cab, Claudia strode along the concourse to the baggage claim area and through the Exit doors. Outside the terminal the desert air was cool and crisp, unlike the relentless blistering heat that would turn the summer months into hell.

Her last trip here had been during Thanksgiving. For once, she had screwed up the courage to blow off the big family dinner, which invariably ended up in bitter recriminations from her mother anyway, and drove to Vegas with Jovanic. She smiled, remembering the long, uninterrupted nights of lovemaking, pagers and cell phones switched off for once.

Then her phone rang and wiped away the smile. She answered without checking the source.

"Annabelle?"

"Ms. Rose?" An unfamiliar male voice. "This is detective Pike. I got your message. I've been trying to call you, but I've been getting voicemail."

Shit! She'd forgotten about him.

"Oh, uh, yes, my phone was off for a while," she said, trying to sound cool and knowing she had failed. She had not told him about Annabelle in her message, only asked him to call her back. "Er, thanks for returning my call, but I, er, actually, I'm in the middle of something. I need to get back to you a little later."

"Is everything all right, Ms. Rose? Sounds like you've been running."

"Uh—yes, I've been running. Call you back."

She clicked off before he could question her further, wishing she could enlist his help. At least Pike could have taken the burden.

Who was she kidding? Her voluntary participation in Annabelle's current drama might well be viewed as obstruction of justice. Or even worse, accessory to murder if they charged the girl, as Giordano claimed.

One way or another she was going to be in deep shit, and she wasn't at all sure that Jovanic would be able to help her out of it this time. Until she knew more about what had happened to Paige, sharing information with the police seemed like a very bad idea.

Not sure what to do next, she strolled in the direction of the taxi stand, where a crowd of French-speaking tourists milled around, waiting for a bus. A dispatcher with a clipboard and walkie-talkie started toward Claudia, but she waved him away. Where could she tell him she was going?

Call me, Annabelle, dammit, call me!

She checked her watch. Nine o'clock. How long would she have to wait for the girl to call?

What if she doesn't call at all?

The baggage claim doors slid open, disgorging another wave of travelers swarming to the parking garages and taxis. They hurried past her rolling suitcases, ready to jump-start vacations; hauling laptops to business meetings or conventions.

Claudia paced the pavement, checking the cellular in case she had missed a call; checking voicemail. *Nothing.* She looked at her watch for the ninetieth time. Nine-ten. Time seemed to be moving backwards.

Going back into the terminal she picked up a shot of caffeine and a cinnamon scone at a Starbucks, then claimed a table in the food court and watched the local news on TV while she ate. Same old crap she could view any day in L.A.: *Man's death and woman's disappearance link pair to slaying suspect; traffic deaths climbing; pilot error cited in crash.*

In the ladies room, she tried out a series of arguments in her head as she washed her hands, searching for something that might convince Pike of Annabelle's innocence. The girl *had* to be innocent. Despite any evidence to the contrary, Claudia couldn't bear it any other way.

Yet, she hadn't even been able to convince Jovanic, and he was supposed to be on her side. Why would Pike listen to her?

When she activated the automatic faucet again and realized she had washed her hands twice, Claudia dropped the crumpled paper towel into the overflowing trash bin, took a last glance in the mirror and returned to the concourse. *What next?*

Window shopping gave her something to do while she waited for Annabelle to call, but the concession stands hawked the same shot glasses and magnets as every other airport she had ever visited; a different name on the same kitsch. She browsed magazines, ridiculously high-priced clothing, the duty free shop. *Killing time.*

An hour later she couldn't stand it anymore and left the terminal again to resume pacing near the taxi stand. The French group had given way to a busload of Japanese, and the sidewalk was alive with tourists. Two hours had passed since she'd landed.

Had Annabelle managed to escape? Or had her getaway attempt been scotched? Fear for the girl's safety fused with irritation at her own forced impotence. Decision time: If Annabelle didn't phone in the next ten minutes she would call Pike and let him take over.

But what if she didn't call at all? *What then?*

Thirty seconds later, her cell phone rang.

CHAPTER 27

"Annabelle, I can't hear you, you're breaking up. Where are you?" Every other word disappeared into some cellular black hole. Claudia's phone showed two bars.

"...did it...needle...away..."

There couldn't have been a worse time for a weak signal if a master planner had arranged it. Claudia strained to understand what she was saying.

"...don't...the number...the phone."

"Where are you?"

"...go...that pyramid...starving..."

"Did you say pyramid? The Luxor?"

Her voice sounded hyper. "Yeah, the Luxor. Can you meet me...I'm go..."

"I'll meet you there. Ask for me at the front desk. I'll get a room. Annabelle, can you hear me?" Claudia heard three electronic beeps and the call dropped.

Dammit! She scrolled to the list of incoming calls, but the number Annabelle had called from was blocked. Redial produced an "invalid number" message. At least now she had a destination: *The Luxor.*

As she started toward the taxi stand, the cellular rang again. The display showed *Sorensen Acad.* Bert Falkenberg.

"I've been trying to reach you," Bert said.

"What's up, Bert?" Claudia moved close to the wall, sheltering her phone ear, straining to hear over the street noise.

"There's been a development. Cruz was arrested last night."

"Are you serious? He's been charged with—"

"Paige's murder," Bert finished for her. His tone dropped a couple of levels, turning somber. "I'm afraid things don't look so good for Annabelle. He hasn't confessed yet, but the police believe he probably killed her, too."

That put the lie to Giordano's claim that they were about to issue a warrant for her arrest. What was going on here?

"No, Bert, she's alive. I talked to her." Claudia heard a sharp intake of breath.

"You *what?*"

"She called me this morning from Las Vegas. I flew out; I'm here to take her home."

"But…you're in *Vegas?* I don't understand. What did she say?"

"Her phone kept cutting out, I couldn't understand anything except she's escaped. I'm on my way to meet her at the Luxor."

"Wait a minute…" Bert sounded bewildered. "I don't–"

"Bert, I have to go. I want to be at the hotel when she gets there. I need to grab a cab."

"Wait, Claudia. I'm in Las Vegas, too. I'll pick you up. I'm not far from the airport."

"What are *you* doing here?"

"I had to get away from everything, thought a little Blackjack would take my mind off it all. Drove out last night. I can be at the airport in fifteen minutes. You're near the taxis? Watch for a black Escalade."

Claudia rang off, her thoughts churning. Bert wasn't her first choice for confidante, but it was a relief to know she could share the responsibility with someone.

A beep sounded from her phone indicating that she had received a voicemail during her conversation with Bert. Dialing in, she listened to Annabelle complaining that the battery on the phone she was using was about to die. She planned to hitchhike to the Luxor.

Hitchhike? Claudia didn't think her anxiety level could get any higher. She stepped to the curb, craning to see Bert Falkenberg. A few minutes later, his SUV pulled to the curb beside her and he was beckoning her from the driver's side.

She slid into the luxurious leather seat and told him about Annabelle's voicemail. He shifted into gear and joined the slow moving line of traffic on Swensen Boulevard, his fingers drumming impatiently on the steering wheel. "Depending on traffic, we ought to make the Luxor in about ten minutes," he said. "Now, here's the plan—"

"There's a plan?" Claudia interrupted. "I'm glad to hear *you* have a plan, because I have *no* idea what's going on."

Bert swung left onto Tropicana Avenue. "We'll go ahead and check into the hotel and debrief Annabelle in private. After I see what condition she's in, I'll decide what to do from there."

"What do you mean, *you'll* decide?"

"I'm in charge of the school now, so she's my responsibility."

Claudia shook her head. "She's not a Sorensen pupil anymore. Her belongings were sent home, remember? Besides, her father has involved me, so any decisions about Annabelle are *at least* going to be joint ones."

His jaw bunched and his knuckles whitened on the steering wheel. "I'm not about to argue with you," he said in a tight voice. "Let's get the girl back first before we start going off half-cocked."

They traveled west in silence for several minutes, threading through traffic as heavy as any L.A. rush hour.

"That must have been what Annabelle was talking about," Claudia said, pointing to the eleven-hundred-foot Stratosphere hotel at the north end of the Strip. "She said she could see it from where she was being held. She said she was in a hospital."

Bert jerked a sideways glance at her. "A *hospital*? How the hell did she get out?"

"I don't know; the phone connection sucked. We'll find out when we see her."

He made a left onto Las Vegas Boulevard, where most of the eye-popping resorts claimed space. "Who else knows you're here? Her father?"

"Nobody," Claudia said. "Detective Pike called about an hour ago, but I blew him off. I didn't want him asking questions I can't answer."

"Good. That's the way to keep this thing under control. Keep that barn door closed."

"It's a bit late to worry about that, don't you think?"

Bert made an impatient sound and shook his head, looking like he wanted to say something poisonous. He clamped his teeth together and stared straight ahead.

Claudia gazed out at the wide boulevards of the world-famous Strip with its towering palm trees and as many taxis as downtown Manhattan. Finding someone who had a compelling need to hide themselves in this town would be about as easy as winning a progressive jackpot in one of the big casinos.

The larger-than-life-size Sphinx loomed as they drove up the avenue of stone lions. At mid-morning the immense black pyramid of Luxor hid secrets. After dark, the brightest beam in the world would project ten miles into space from the top of the obsidian glass structure.

Bypassing the weary vacationers in rumpled Hawaiian shirts queuing in the valet line outside the lobby doors, Bert headed for the self-park. He squeezed the big vehicle into a parking space far from the hotel entrance, muttering about valets taking all day.

Claudia couldn't care less where they parked. A feeling of anticipation had her nerves jumping. God knew what Annabelle had been through over the last ten days. She would insist that Bert not press the girl too hard. Give her some time to decompress.

They had walked a few yards from the vehicle when Bert stopped abruptly. "Damn! I forgot my phone. Wait for me." He hurried back to the SUV, returning a moment later. "Can't leave home without it."

"Come *on*, Bert. She might already be here looking for me."

They took the people mover to the lobby, which was close to deserted at this time of day. In another hour, the place would be crammed with travelers checking out.

Claudia was on her way to the registration desk when Bert caught her arm. "Wait, Claudia. Uh, would you mind putting this on your credit card?" He looked a little sheepish, cleared his throat. "I don't want it showing up on my corporate card. I'll reimburse you," he hastened to add.

"No problem," Claudia said. Something in his voice made her look closer. His face was pale, with a light sheen of perspiration.

"Are you okay, Bert? You don't look well."

He took out a handkerchief and mopped his forehead, where pearls of sweat had gathered. "It's the stress of everything—Paige, the school, Annabelle. You have no idea how relieved I am to know we're going to get her back."

Claudia nodded agreement. "I'll be happier when we see her for ourselves."

Bert started to reply, but was interrupted by his phone. He excused himself and walked away to answer it. Claudia stepped over to one of the empty stations at the long stretch of registration desks and requested a double room. If they needed to stay overnight, she and Annabelle would take the room. Bert said he had come out the night before, so he must have booked a room somewhere.

Annabelle had said she was starving. Before making arrangements to return to Los Angeles they would order room service and give her a chance to rest. Once Dominic Giordano learned she had been rescued, he would want to join them in Las Vegas, Claudia was sure, and take charge of escorting his daughter home.

She asked the reservationist who was running the charge on her credit card to leave a message for "her niece, Annabelle," to come up to the room. After all the media coverage of Paige's death and Annabelle's disappearance, it was too risky to give her surname, which was uncommon enough to draw attention.

The reservationist gave Claudia a professional smile and slipped two key cards into an envelope. "Certainly, Ms. Rose, with pleasure. You're in room 1408. Take the Inclinator to the fourteenth floor."

Claudia thanked her and glanced around. Bert had disappeared from view. She wandered through the massive lobby looking for him, imagining that the Pharaohs seated on their colossal thrones staring down at her with cold, impassive faces were challenging her right to be there.

Caring about Annabelle gives me the right, she thought with a touch of defiance, as if the stone Rameses could read her mind.

She spotted Bert on a marble seat near the entrance to the casino. He was faced away from her, elbows leaning on his knees, his body language giving off waves of tension.

As Claudia came near she could hear him. "…really deep shit

now," he was saying with rising agitation. "I gotta go. I'll call you later, when I get everything arranged." He rang off and his head slumped, giving him a look of utter despair.

Wondering who he was talking to, Claudia reached out to touch his shoulder. Bert swung around, eyes wild, his hands going up in a defensive stance. The cell phone clattered to the floor.

Then he saw it was her. "Goddamn it, Claudia! Don't ever sneak up on me like that!"

"Jeez, Bert," she said, unprepared for his reaction. "I didn't mean to scare you. I'm sorry."

He bent down with some effort and retrieved the phone. His hand trembled noticeably as he shoved the cellular into his pocket. "The Sorensens are trying to get a court order," he said, scrubbing a hand through his hair, leaving it standing on end. "They want to freeze operations at the school until there's a hearing." He shook his head, ridding himself of the Sorensen family and their machinations. "Forget that. Did you get a room? Let's get going. I could use a drink."

The odd sensation of the special elevator slanting up the side of the pyramid gave Claudia a slight sense of vertigo, and she was glad when the doors opened at the fourteenth floor. "I don't like being up this high," she said, glancing at the open balcony overlooking the Galleria far below. "It was the best I could do without a reservation."

"It'll be fine," Bert said. "It'll serve the purpose."

He looks unwell, Claudia thought, taking in the greyish cast to his face, the trunk-size bags under his eyes. Then an uncharitable flash: *He'd better not have a heart attack.*

She slid the card key into the electronic reader on the door and stepped into a room with the expected Egyptian-themed decor. To the left of the entry was a standard bath. The room had two queen size beds and an armoire, a small round table with two side chairs and an armchair.

Claudia already felt drained and had a tension headache. She shrugged out of her blazer and laid it across one of the beds, then dropped into the armchair. "Let me know if you find any painkillers," she said to Bert, who had made a beeline for the mini-bar and was pawing through it.

"Liquor, soda, candy," he said, squatting in front of the cabinet. An airline-sized bottle of tequila disappeared in his meaty fist. "What do you want?"

"Diet Coke if they have it. We can order room service when Annabelle gets here. Poor kid, she said she was starving."

Bert handed her a can of soda. "God, what a week." Sighing with the exaggerated kind of relief one might expect from a parched man at an oasis, he uncapped the tequila and chugalugged the little bottle, then tossed the empty into the trash can beside the desk.

Claudia popped the top on her soda and drank. "Tell me about Cruz getting arrested."

"That asshole," Bert said bitterly. "Pardon my French. He had no alibi. Admitted he'd been with her, but he claimed he couldn't remember anything, *including* whether he'd hurt her. And the belt that…it has Cruz' initials engraved on the buckle."

"How do you know about that?"

"Detective Pike came and talked to me about it. He had questions…I can't…Paige was…" His shoulders shaking with emotion, Bert turned his face to the window. For a moment he said nothing and Claudia allowed him time to gain hold of himself.

When he spoke again, his voice was soft, but the words harsh. "That piece of shit took her away from me. He deserves what's coming to him. I've lost everything. Paige, the school."

"You and Paige—"

"Torg was out of the way, she was ready for a younger man." He stopped, seeing the appalled look on Claudia's face. "Oh come on, Claudia. Don't pretend you didn't know she was sick and tired of being tied to that old geezer. It was making her old, too. Everything was peachy between her and me until Cruz showed up."

His words had set her mind racing. Surely he wasn't saying that Paige somehow hastened Torg's demise? "She said she loved Torg. Why wouldn't I believe her?"

Bert returned to the mini-bar for seconds. "Dammit, no more tequila," he grumbled, grabbing a mini-bottle of Southern Comfort and one of Tanqueray. He cracked open the whiskey and stood the gin on the nightstand. Downing his second drink in a couple of gulps, he stretched out on one of the beds, clasping his hands behind his head. A few seconds later he bobbed up again and grabbed the third bottle.

I'll bet he got started before he came here, Claudia thought, wanting to slap the bottle out of his hand. She said, "I'm not your mother, Bert, but would you knock off the booze? It'd be nice if you weren't totally bombed when Annabelle gets here."

He gazed at Claudia through eyes gone glassy and downed the Tanqueray. "Don't worry," he said with a look that dared her to challenge him. "I can hold my liquor."

"So why are your hands shaking?"

He glanced down at the empty bottle in his hand, which was trembling conspicuously, and stared at it as if it didn't belong to him. He tossed the bottle into the trash, where it *plinked* against its mates. "It's been a tough week. Cut me some slack, okay?"

Claudia wanted to yell at him but contented herself with a scornful look. "You think you're the only one who's had a bad time? It's been tough on *all* of us, Annabelle most of all. She needs us to be the adults, *okay*?"

"Yeah, sure." Bert glanced at the bedside clock. "Where the hell is she?" He hauled himself to his feet and walked over to the window, which was slanted at the extreme angle of the pyramid.

"Shit! Ouch!" He turned back, rubbing his forehead. "Goddamned slanted windows."

"Take it easy, Bert. Calm down."

"Easier said than done, Miss Claudia," he said with a lopsided smile. He turned back to the window, taking care not to hit his head again. "You know, I liked Annabelle, right from the start. She's a plucky kid. She wouldn't trust anyone for the time of day, but I was the one she warmed up to. Before Cruz, she used to come to my office when she had a problem, confide in me. She doesn't think much of her old man. I guess she saw me as a reasonable facsimile." He half-turned to Claudia with a wry look. "Her judgment pretty much stinks, huh?"

What could she say to that? "I expect you helped her a lot, Bert."

"But then Cruz—"

An urgent pounding at the door silenced him. Claudia sprang out of her chair and started across the room. Bert rushed past her, but instead of opening the door to admit Annabelle, he swerved into the bathroom and shut the door behind him.

For a heartbeat, Claudia stared after him. Then she opened the door.

A small, dark cannonball launched itself into the room, and then Annabelle was gripping her as if she would never let go, her slight body wracked with sobs.

Claudia shepherded her into the room, keeping a protective arm around her shoulder. She pulled a couple of tissues from her pocket, handed one to Annabelle and blotted her own tears.

She tried not to let on how disturbed she was by the pallor of the heart-shaped face, the dull hair, scarecrow-thin arms. Annabelle had lost weight that she couldn't afford to lose. Where she had been thin before, now she looked anorexic.

What did they do to her?

Claudia sat her in the armchair and pulled up a chair from the desk. She sat down and took hold of Annabelle's hand. The back was mottled purple with bruises. "Annabelle, what happened to you?"

"Can I please have something to eat first, Claudia? I'm so hungry."

"Anything you want. I'll call room service."

"Burger and extra fries," Annabelle said without hesitation. "I haven't eaten in forever."

Claudia went to the nightstand. "Bert's in the bathroom," she said, picking up the phone. "He'll be—"

"*What?*" Annabelle's face registered shock, disbelief, then, utter horror. "What did you *do?*"

The bathroom door opened and Bert Falkenberg stepped out, wielding a gun.

CHAPTER 28

Annabelle was out of the chair, screaming, "No! No! No!" She whirled on Claudia, shock and confusion in her eyes. "What's he doing here? Are you crazy?"

Bert stood by the door, staring at them, panting a little. Blocking the exit. Above the bushy salt-and-pepper beard, his eyes were wide, and Claudia realized that he was as scared as she was. Pushing down her fear, she struggled to process what she was seeing. "What the *hell*, Bert?"

"He killed her! He *killed* her!" Annabelle's voice rose on a note of hysteria. She fell to her knees, huddling into a fetal position, wailing. "My belt—*he* took it and he killed her. He killed her."

Bert's voice shook. "Anna, I'm sorry; I didn't mean to. I was— she made me crazy. I didn't know what I was doing." He turned to Claudia, who was trying to figure out when she had stepped into the Twilight Zone. "Would you get me another drink, please, Claudia? Anything."

His request sounded so normal and polite, but it was the gun that sent her to the mini-bar, grabbing the first bottle within reach. He told her to open it before she handed it to him. He gulped it down, never taking his eyes, or the gun, off her.

Bert must have gotten the gun when he returned to the car, claiming he'd forgotten his cell phone. Cursing herself for being a blind fool, Claudia knelt beside Annabelle and put her arms around the girl, who was silent now, rocking herself.

"My God, Annabelle, I had no idea. He picked me up at the airport."

"We're dead now," Annabelle said dully. "He's gonna kill us, too."

"No!" Bert said, full of righteous indignation, as if he hadn't already committed murder. "No, it's not true. If I wanted to kill you, you'd be dead already. But I didn't, did I? I'm not a killer. I don't want to hurt you."

Annabelle glared up at him through strands of long, black hair that covered her face like a shroud. "You're a liar," she screamed at him. "You killed Paige, I saw you do it! And you tied me up and drugged me. Don't say you don't want to hurt me!"

Claudia drew the girl up off the floor, holding her close. Trying to somehow shield her from this insanity. "What now, Bert?" she asked, her mind whirling back over their encounters, looking for the clues she might have missed.

Sweat trickled from his forehead. With the gun in one hand, he felt in his pocket for his handkerchief, swiped it at his face. "I don't know yet," he said, desperation in his voice. "I don't fucking know! First I have to get you both out of here." He turned to Annabelle, his mouth compressed into a grim line. "I don't know how you got away, but I'm gonna tell you this one time, you little smartass. If you put *one toe* out of line, Claudia is toast. Then you'll have her blood on your hands, too."

Annabelle shrank against her with a little mewling sound. Claudia whirled on him. "You sonofabitch, *you* murdered Paige, not Annabelle! Don't you dare try and push your guilt off onto her."

Watching the gamut of emotions that chased across his face: shame, anger, fear, desperation, Claudia saw a tiny glimmer of hope. She had learned from studying criminal psychology that it's easier to kill somebody you know in a fit of rage, rather than in cold blood. The fact that Bert had cared for Annabelle worked in their favor. She tried to remember his handwriting, but realized she had only seen his signature witnessing Torg Sorensen's will, and a signature was pretty limited evidence. One thing she knew, he slanted his writing far to the left—a slingshot of emotion waiting to be triggered.

"We're going down to the car," Bert said, refusing to meet Claudia's eyes. He stopped with his hand on the doorknob. "I'm trying to work this so no one else gets hurt, but at this point, I've got nothing to lose. If I have to—" He let the threat hang there, somehow made worse by their imagining.

CHAPTER 29

Annabelle stood silent and sullen between them as they rode the Inclinator to the lobby. Bert kept one hand under his windbreaker, holding the gun. There was no doubt in Claudia's mind that he was desperate enough to follow through on his implied threat.

Outside, the early afternoon sun threw shadows across the pavement as they walked to the parking lot—to the casual observer, an All-American family on vacation. Except that none of them was smiling.

"Think, Bert," said Claudia, walking beside him. "Her father will come after you, I guarantee it. You know as well as I do that he's *connected*."

"He wouldn't care," Annabelle broke in. "It doesn't matter to him if I'm dead or alive. He already killed my mother."

Claudia squeezed her hand. "Hush, he's doing everything he can to find you." She touched Bert's sleeve. "You can let us go. You can walk away, go anywhere in the world, right now. I won't call anyone until tomorrow, I promise. That should give you enough time."

For a moment his face went still and she could see that he was actually considering her offer. Then he laughed without humor. "Too bad it's not that easy."

When they reached the Escalade, Bert pointed the alarm key at the SUV and turned to Claudia. "You drive. Annabelle in the passenger seat up front."

Claudia held her hand out for the key but he shook his head.

"Keyless ignition. I'll start the engine. You just drive."

After watching Claudia and Annabelle climb in, Bert heaved his bulk into the back. He wrapped his left arm around the driver's seat. "Don't forget I've got my buddy here."

"Like I could forget someone's got a gun stuck in my side," Claudia retorted, wondering if she was making a big mistake, following his orders. Maybe they would stand a better chance if they refused to go with him.

Bert leaned close to her ear. "If you try anything stupid, I'll shoot Annabelle," he said softly.

She flicked a glance at him through the rearview mirror. His desperate face made her believe he would follow through on his threat. That settled it.

"Where are we going?" she asked.

He exhaled loudly and pointed the key fob. The engine turned over. "Just start driving. I need to think about this."

Claudia took her time to get settled behind the wheel and adjust the seat forward, getting a feel for the cockpit controls. Big and fancy, but it wasn't a 747. It would be like driving a bus compared to the Jag, but she could do this. Her eyes lit on the navigation system screen, and she was considering how she might use it to her advantage when Bert said, "Annabelle, turn off the GPS."

Annabelle twisted in the bucket seat to face him. "Fuck you. I'm not doing anything you say."

Bert narrowed his eyes. "You want Claudia to get hurt?"

"Who's gonna drive if you hurt her?"

He leaned between the seats and backhanded her across the face. "Shut your smart mouth and turn off the goddamn GPS like I told you to."

Annabelle recoiled with a gasp. Her hand flew to her cheek. "You asshole!"

He raised his hand again, threatening. "Don't you touch her again!" Claudia shouted. "Or you can shoot me right here in the parking lot, and where's that gonna get you? Now leave her the hell alone!"

Bert's head swiveled from one to the other, like watching a tennis match. "Stop it, both of you!" He sounded frantic. "Claudia, drive out of the lot and turn left. *Now!*"

"Okay, okay. Take it easy, Bert. This is scary for all of us."

"Yeah, chill out," Annabelle said with an echo of her old tartness, glowering as she followed his order to power off the GPS system.

Claudia shifted into reverse and eased her foot onto the accelerator, her mind buzzing in a dozen directions. Bert had murdered Paige because of his jealousy over Cruz, but Cruz was the one who was under arrest for the murder. What did that mean for their chances of a rescue?

"Take the I-15 North," Bert ordered as they passed a highway sign.

"Where are we going?"

"Don't worry about it. Just drive." He leaned down, keeping his eyes toward the front, and felt around under the driver's seat. Claudia heard the crackle of a paper bag and in the rearview mirror saw that he was holding a liquor bottle. A moment later she caught a whiff of something that made her think of liquid salt—tequila.

She drove up the ramp onto the I-15 North, noticing from the corner of her eye that Annabelle was looking out the passenger window, scanning the cars as they zipped by.

"Face front, Annabelle," Bert ordered, noticing, too. "Don't even *think* about signaling for help."

Annabelle flopped back against her seat with a muttered, "Fuck you."

"Take it easy, Bert," Claudia said. "How many people do you think would pay attention, anyway?"

Her disgust for him bubbled up and spilled over onto herself. She had made it easy for him; led him to Annabelle as if she were a sacrificial lamb on the altar. She would never forgive herself for that. *Assuming she survived to worry about it.*

Maybe she could skid off the roadway and make him drop the gun, she considered in desperation, but abandoned the idea as too risky.

Soon after they entered the highway, Bert instructed her to exit at Tropicana.

Annabelle pointed to four towers rising in the distance. They appeared to be taller than any of the hotels on the Strip. "That's where I was," she said. "That's where I escaped from."

"You should have stayed put," Bert said. "It would have been so much easier."

She ignored him and spoke to Claudia. "I *thought* it was a hospital. They tied me up in one of those beds like they have in hospitals and kept it dark all the time."

"What did you do to Henry?" Bert broke in. "How did you get away?"

Claudia snapped her head around. "Who's Henry?"

"This old dude who was guarding me."

"What did you do to him?" Bert repeated.

"I stuck him with the needle, like that lady did to me," Annabelle answered, all defiance.

Claudia's confusion was growing, and her headache made it worse. "*What* lady?"

"Some skanky bitch. She was s'posed to be a nurse." She jerked her chin at Bert in the back seat, not deigning to say his name. "*He* said she was a nurse. She drugged me with an IV. It made me sleep all the time."

"How did you get loose?" Bert demanded.

"The old dude messed up the needle and the stuff dripped on the bed. Last night when they left, I called you, Claudia. The old dude left his phone on the chair. When he came back and fell asleep I stuck him with the needle." She turned and glared at Bert with loathing. "I hope he dies."

"You'd better hope he doesn't," Bert said grimly.

Annabelle squeezed her eyes shut but tears dribbled down her cheeks. "Why'd you have to do it?" she cried, a torrent of anguish and grief bursting out of her. "Why did you have to *kill* her?"

"I didn't *mean* to," Bert snapped. He was breathing heavily through his mouth and the sour smell of his fear saturated the cabin of the SUV.

Brusquely, he ordered Claudia to take the gated entrance to a subterranean parking garage and told her to use the key card to open the gate. Slowing to cross the tire shredders she glanced over at Annabelle, and noticed her complexion had turned a shade of green.

"Annabelle, are you okay?"

The girl hunched over in her seat, holding her stomach and moaning. "I think I'm gonna hurl."

"Park by the elevator," Bert ordered, grabbing the back of Claudia's seat. "Hurry! I don't want her puking in the car."

"Damn you, Bert," she snapped, parking the Escalade where he indicated. "You've kept her on nothing but IV for days? After what you've put her through, no wonder she's sick. *Deal* with it." Glancing in the rearview mirror she could see that his face was splotched red and damp with sweat. Now she wished he *would* have a heart attack. He deserved it, the murdering bastard.

Claudia told Annabelle to put her head between her knees and asked Bert if he kept any water in the vehicle. He came up with a plastic bottle of Penta and passed it between the seats.

"What are we doing here, Bert?" Claudia asked, as Annabelle twisted off the top and took a sip.

"We're here to follow through on some travel arrangements I made for this young lady before she left us," he said. The calculating look in his eyes frightened Claudia all over again.

"What travel arrangements? What are you talking about?"

Ignoring her question, Bert touched the girl's shoulder. "You feeling better, Anna? Let's go. Remember, I've got my eye on you."

"She needs something to eat," said Claudia.

"There's food in the condo."

"Too bad you didn't give her any sooner."

He threw her a dirty look and shut off the engine, then got out of the vehicle.

The garage was deserted. Claudia's hopes of getting help from that source went into a free fall. There were security cameras, but by the time all the pieces got put together, she was certain it would be too late for her and Annabelle.

She jumped down from the SUV and went around to the passenger side where Bert was opening the door. Annabelle's legs wobbled when she got out and Claudia put an arm around her waist, helping her to walk.

Bert also put his arm around Annabelle, who was too weak to protest, and led them to the elevator. There were no buttons to push, just a slot for the key card. Bert took the card from Claudia and slid it into the slot. The doors closed behind them and the elevator ascended rapidly, stopping at the 35th floor.

When the doors parted they stepped directly into the vestibule of a condo.

Bert walked Annabelle into the great room and parked her on a sofa. "Wait here," he ordered. He veered off to the right, through the kitchen and along a hallway, calling out, "Henry—hey, Henry!"

It looked as though someone had half-moved in. The great room was partially furnished with a black leather sofa, an Eames lounge chair. On the back wall was a built-in black-and-granite wet bar. Floor-to-ceiling windows overlooked the city with a view that reached all the way to the distant mountains. High in the clear Nevada air the sky, empty of clouds, was the blue of eternity.

Claudia left Annabelle lying on the sofa and told her she was going to scrounge up some food. Adrenalin had kept the girl going for the past few hours, but she needed to eat if she was going to be strong enough to make it through whatever was coming next.

She found the kitchen. First things first: check the drawers and countertops for sharp knives. It didn't take long for her to conclude that Bert was not stupid enough to leave her unattended if there had been anything she could use as a weapon. Most of the drawers were empty. The cutlery was plastic picnic ware.

Damn!

Feeling beaten down, she checked the refrigerator. It might as well have been empty. It contained a Pizza Hut box with three dried up slices of sausage and mushroom, a couple of Chinese food cartons with contents that looked like something out of a slasher film, and a long out-of-date container of milk.

Claudia sniffed the milk carton and gagged on the sour odor. She emptied the spoiled milk into the sink and dumped the carton into the trash compactor. There was a hanging metal basket with a bunch of overripe bananas, an orange, and a couple of limes, and she resigned herself to the fact that the pickings were slim.

She peeled a banana and the orange and wrapped them in a paper towel, then returned to the great room.

While Annabelle devoured the fruit, Claudia leaned close to her, lowering her voice a whisper. "Don't let on when you're feeling better. If he thinks you're still sick..."

"Move away from her, Claudia." Bert spoke from behind. When

she turned around, he had the gun pointed at her. She didn't know firearms, but to her it looked similar to what Jovanic carried—a nine millimeter. The deadly black hole was pointed directly at her heart. She wondered dismally whether he was a good shot.

Then her mouth dropped open in shock. "*You!*"

Shuffling along behind Bert was an old man she had seen before. The neighbor with the hedge trimmers from the house next door to where Paige's body had been found.

He glowered at her. "Trouble-makin' bitch. I shoulda taken care o' you back at the house." Then he caught sight of Annabelle, and his features screwed into hatred. "And *you*, ya little—"

Annabelle stuck her chin out defiantly as he went for her, his body language promising violence. Bert put out a restraining hand and grabbed the old man.

"Leave it be, Henry. There's no time." He stepped in front of him and crossed over to Annabelle, demanding that she return the cell phone she had stolen from Henry.

She took it from her pocket and flung it in the direction of his head.

"Piece of shit doesn't even work," she said with contempt.

Bert reached out his hand and caught the phone before it hit him. "You don't have to use that kind of language," he said in a stern voice, as he might have had they been at the Sorensen Academy.

"Under the circumstances, I hardly think her language matters," said Claudia, watching him plug the phone into a charger on the bar. "And you don't deserve the courtesy."

"What do you hear from Lainie?" Bert asked Henry.

"You're all in this together?" Claudia said, figuring Lainie must have been the nurse Annabelle had mentioned.

"She oughtta be hittin' the state line pretty soon," Henry said, ignoring her. "You hear anything from her yet?"

"She called earlier," Bert replied. "But I don't want anything discussed on a cell phone. You never know who might be listening."

As if on cue, the 007 James Bond theme sounded. Claudia had assigned it to Jovanic's phone number as a joke. All eyes turned to the phone clipped to her belt.

"My boyfriend. He knows I'm expecting this call," she lied, struggling to keep the hope out of her voice. "If I don't answer it, he'll know something's wrong."

"Okay, answer it," Bert said. "But you'd better watch what you say."

I certainly will, she thought, turning her back on him. She took a deep breath in an effort to quell the fear she was feeling and flipped open the phone. "Hello?"

"Hey, baby," Jovanic said. "I'm at your place. Where are you?"

The sound of his voice made her want to cry. How could she tell him how much she needed him, with Bert's gun pointed at her back?

"I–I–er, I had to go out of town."

"Out of town?"

"I'm with Annabelle. She's–" She broke off as the jab of the gun stopped her from going down that path. In a flash of memory, she recalled that she had printed a copy of her Southwest Airlines itinerary to Las Vegas. It was on her desk from booking that morning's flight. "Hey, uh, Joey, I uh, there's a...er, phone message for you on my desk."

"*Joey?* What's going on, Claudia? Who would call me at your number?"

"Uh huh."

His detective's ear, or maybe his lover's ear, connected with the distress in her voice. "You can't talk?"

"Boy, is that the truth."

"Okay, I'm on my way upstairs. Are you in trouble?"

"*Yeah.* I—"

"Hang up," Bert demanded in a loud whisper. "Hang up now."

"Uh, honey, I have to go now."

Annabelle jumped up and screamed, "WE'RE IN LAS VEGAS."

Henry reached over and slapped her hard across the face. Then he grabbed her by the hair, snapping her head backwards. She fell back against the sofa with a cry as blood blossomed from her lip.

At the same instant, Bert snatched the cell phone out of Claudia's hand and ended the call. In a rush of panic, she watched him hurl it to the floor and grind her connection to the outside world into a useless piece of trash.

All at once, the smoldering fear and anger that Claudia had been holding in exploded into a solid ball of fury. She didn't spare a thought for the fact that he was holding a gun, nor that the old man, his ally, was a few feet away. Her hand clenched into a fist and slammed into Bert's chest with all the force she could muster.

"You goddamn bastard!" she cried, breathless with anger as she struck him over and over. He was a large target and taller than Claudia by several inches. The gun went thudding to the floor while Bert stood there, looking stunned, doing nothing to stop her blows.

All at once, Henry, Annabelle, and Bert burst into action, the three of them scrambling for the weapon.

Claudia turned away, shaking all over. There was yelling behind her, then something heavy struck the back of her head and she pitched forward, knees sagging. Her vision went dark as she hit the floor.

CHAPTER 30

The first thing Claudia became aware of as she regained consciousness was the sound of a kitten mewing near her ear. No, that wasn't it. Someone was crying. *Who?*

"Claudia, Claudia," Annabelle sobbed, shaking her by the shoulders, patting her face. "Don't be dead, please don't be dead. Wake *up. Please*, wake up!"

Groaning, Claudia opened her eyes, squinting against the throbbing at the base of her skull. She was face down on beige carpeting that smelled new. Its fibers tickled her cheek and made it itch. Her head felt too heavy to lift. She put her hand up and tentatively probed the back of her head. Her fingertips met an egg-sized lump. It felt as if the moorings of her brain had come loose, but her fingers came away clean, the skin wasn't broken.

She pushed herself onto her back with effort, flinching as her head made contact with the floor. "I'm not dead…yet…I think," she gasped. Staring up at the vaulted ceiling, she noticed that everything seemed fuzzy, off kilter. *Concussion*, she decided, making an attempt to get her bearings.

It took a few moments before her surroundings began to make more sense. Gradually, it all started to come back: *Bert—Henry—the gun*. She listened to the condo but heard no sounds aside from Annabelle, who was sobbing beside her.

Slowly, laboriously, fighting a wave of vertigo that nearly felled her, Claudia struggled onto her side, then her knees. "What happened?"

"That old guy slugged you with the gun. If I could have got it first, I would have shot them both."

"That's all we need to make a perfect day complete."

"I was glad when you hit Bert. I wish you'd hurt him."

"Yeah, me, too." Claudia sat back on her heels and looked at her watch through blurred vision. "How long was I unconscious?"

"It felt like forever." Distress filled the girl's eyes in her tear-stained face. "I thought he killed you."

"Not yet, anyway," Claudia muttered as she dragged herself to the sofa and crawled onto it. Her head still felt heavy and her hands went up to support it. She wasn't any too sure about standing up. "Where did they go?"

"I think they're in that bedroom where they kept me locked up." Annabelle sat down beside her and laid her head against Claudia's shoulder like the little kid that she really was. "They're gonna kill us, aren't they?"

Claudia reached up and held her hand. "Don't worry, kiddo, I'll think of something. We're gonna be fine."

She wished she felt as confident as she sounded. She wondered whether Jovanic would be able to trace her through her broken cell phone. Didn't most cell phones have GPS these days? If that was so, the longer they stayed in this place, the better.

"What did Bert do with his card key after we got out of the elevator?" she asked.

The girl thought for a moment. "I think he put it in his pocket."

"Damn." Claudia rolled over and slowly climbed to her feet. "Maybe there's an emergency exit somewhere. I'm going to look around. Don't piss him off if he comes back before I do."

In the foyer, she could hear muffled voices coming from a room down the hall. Moving in the opposite direction, she peeked into the first door on her right. An entryway led to a master bedroom, walk-in wardrobe and master bath. Locking herself in the bathroom she began a rapid check of the drawers and cabinets under the sink, looking for scissors, razorblades, anything that might be used as a weapon.

All she found was the basics: extra toilet paper, toothpaste, toothbrushes, soap, shampoo and conditioner.

The wall-wide mirror reflected a pale face framed by thick auburn hair that currently looked like she had been pulled through a hedge backwards. The normally bright emerald eyes were dull and lined with worry.

"You've got to get her out of this," Claudia admonished her reflection sternly. "Don't be a wimp, you've been in rough spots before. Figure it out!"

In the medicine cabinet she found an interesting item: a prescription bottle in the name of Elaine Falkenberg. *Bert's wife?* Was he living a double life—a wife in Las Vegas, while acting the bachelor in L.A., in love with Paige? He didn't seem the type. But then, he didn't seem like a murderer, either.

Elaine must be Lainie, Henry's daughter, the skinny chain-smoker. The prescription was for an anti-anxiety medication. Apparently, the prospect of kidnapping and accessory to murder charges made Lainie anxious. *Go figure.*

When she had finished exploring the bathroom, Claudia took another turn around the kitchen, looking for a service door, not finding any. If there was an alternate way out of the condo, it was eluding her. She completed her inspection and returned to the great room and sat with Annabelle, her hopes of finding anything useful fading fast.

Now the voices of the men could be heard coming along the hall, and she worried about what they might have planned. Somehow, she had to protect the girl.

"Oh, you're awake," Bert said. "Are you okay, Claudia? Sorry Henry had to get rough with you."

"Yeah, I'll bet you're *real* sorry."

He moved over to the bar and laid the gun on it while he took a tall glass from the overhead rack. He dropped in a couple of ice cubes, then took a bottle of Gordon's from the freezer and poured himself a double shot.

"Can I get you something?" he asked, behaving as if this were a social event and Claudia was his guest.

"I don't think it would help the *concussion.*"

Bert cut a twist of lime with an expert hand and placed it lovingly in the glass. "Regardless of what you think," he said, after gulping down half the drink, "I *am* sorry. I'm sorry about *all* of this, but it happened, and now I have to deal with it the best I can."

"What are you going to do with us?"

"Don't worry, you'll be fine."

"What about those 'travel plans' you mentioned for Annabelle? Travel where?"

"You don't have to be concerned with that. It's all been taken care of."

He seemed to have gained some confidence. Maybe the presence of an accomplice fortified him. More likely, the weasel wanted the old man to see him in charge. Or maybe it was the booze.

Claudia knew in her heart there was no way Bert could let them go. She had read somewhere that the desert was littered with the bodies of murder victims who would never be found, their bones soon picked clean by birds of prey and other animals. And there was plenty of desert around Las Vegas. Was that the fate that awaited her and Annabelle?

"Bert," she pleaded. "You care about Annabelle, I know you do. You've *got* to let her go." She closed her eyes, beyond despair.

"Stop worrying, Claudia. Nothing's going to happen. She'll be fine. I've got a little babysitting job for her, that's all."

"What are you talking about? What babysitting job?"

"Those little kids, I bet," Annabelle said with an accusatory glare. She turned to Claudia and spoke urgently. "At that nasty old house where *he* lives—" she jerked her head in Henry's direction. "They locked me up with these two little kids—I think they were Russian or something—I listened through the wall. They were talking about *selling* those kids for a whole bunch of money."

Claudia remembered the two small children Lainie had ordered into the house. It dawned on her that he was probably planning to sell Annabelle into slavery along with them. She had never been drawn to Bert, but this appalling scheme sickened her.

She tried to get him to look her in the eye. "Bert, you can't do this!"

He refused to meet her gaze, focusing instead on his drink. "I don't have a choice," he said, his voice tense. "Get yourselves together. We have a schedule to meet." He turned to the old man. "Your cell phone ought to be charged enough to give Lainie a call and find out when she's arriving. I'll meet her at the airstrip."

The old man cocked his head, narrowing his eyes. "You sure you don't want me to come along? These two might try to give you grief."

Bert gulped down the rest of his drink. "Drop it, Henry. They know if either of them pulls anything, it's going to be a big problem for the other one. I need you to wait here for Lainie." He brandished his weapon carelessly, deepening Claudia's unease. By now his blood alcohol level had to be well over the legal limit of .08, yet despite the large amount he had consumed throughout the afternoon, he did not appear drunk. His ability to function with so much booze in his system was the sign of a serious drinker.

Pointing the weapon at the two women, he said, "Okay, let's go."

Claudia tried to stand, but the pounding in her head made her feel as though she were in a cave of echoes. She sank back onto the sofa. "I'm dizzy, Bert. Let me sit for a little longer, please."

He strode over and grabbed her arm, yanked her up. "Nice try, Claudia, but it's time to go." He took the key card from his pocket. "Ladies, after you."

CHAPTER 31

Bert unlocked the Escalade and fired up the engine with the keyless remote. "You drive," he ordered Claudia.

"I feel like shit. How about *you* drive?"

"So I can get pulled over for a DUI? No, thanks."

Now, there's the perfect irony, Claudia thought, privately wishing they would get stopped. The strobe of a black and white LV Metro police cruiser behind them would be an answer to a prayer.

"Maybe you shouldn't have drunk so damned much," she snapped, slamming the SUV into gear.

Back on the highway, the wind had kicked up. Desert sand swirled around the car in dusty eddies. Getting through town at rush hour absorbed the better part of thirty minutes. By the time they made the city limits and Bert directed Claudia to take Highway 95, the sun was dropping fast over the outlying hills to their left—not that she could *see* the sun through the furious brume. Most drivers had their headlights on. A glance at the dashboard clock told her that sundown wasn't far off.

Claudia's hopes of attracting attention were soon dashed. There were few other travelers sharing the 95 with them. The smart folks were safe at home, not out in this twilight nightmare.

The hollow feeling in her head was starting to subside. Now she just wanted to cry. Concussed people sometimes got overemotional, didn't they? And so did someone racing toward their own death. *How would you tell the difference?*

She wondered about their destination. Bert was withholding specifics, but she recalled his mention of an airstrip to Henry. It had to be a private airstrip, she realized with a stab of fear, as they were many miles from any public airport. She assumed they were heading to the kind of place you saw in movies—the kind of place that would be hidden away, far off the beaten track where drug traffickers, or in this case, human traffickers could make their vile bargains in perfect privacy.

On the open road the wind gusted stronger. Claudia tightened her grip on the wheel, fighting the unpredictable blasts that rocked the vehicle. Sand whipped across the windshield, obscuring her vision. A harsh sound like radio static filled her ears as the storm slammed a million tiny grains against the body of the SUV.

Chancing a glance in the rearview mirror, her eyes met Bert's. "How can you work at a school and sell children? Paige would be appalled."

His eyes, bleary and red-rimmed, slid away from hers. "*I* don't sell children. I have nothing to do with that."

"Oh, you're just an innocent bystander?"

"It's Lainie's gig," he retorted with a petulant edge. "None of this would have happened if it wasn't for the thing that happened with Paige."

Contempt surged in Claudia for the way he spoke of Paige's death as if it had nothing to do with him. "What do you mean, 'the *thing* that happened'? It didn't just happen, you asshole, you made it happen!"

"For crissake, this is better than the alternative, isn't it?

"You really think so?" She thought of the future that awaited the children and Annabelle if Bert and Lainie got their way. The most likely scenario was that they would disappear into Asia and be forced into prostitution or pornography. The prospect made her shudder.

She thought of the gun he held; of the way he had been drinking all day. Pissing him off might not be a good idea, but Claudia was fresh out of ideas. "Your wife doesn't seem smart enough to pull this off by herself," she said. "Who's the brains behind it?"

"Don't go there, Claudia," Bert warned. "Leave it alone."

"Human trafficking is big business, isn't it, Bert? I saw a documentary on it. A child can bring forty-five grand. How much do you get for destroying those little lives, Bert?"

He struck his fist against the back of the driver seat, startling Claudia. The blow reverberated in her head and started it buzzing. It took all her concentration to keep the Escalade in its proper lane.

"Those kids were going to be the last ones," Bert said. He put his forehead against Claudia's headrest. His voice was a mumble. "My gambling—I had to find a way to pay off the debt."

She struggled to keep her mind focused on the road. What she was hearing was hard to take, impossible to believe of someone she knew, even though she did not know him well. "Where did you get them? They're not from this country, are they?"

She was surprised when he answered her questions. The alcohol must have loosened his tongue. "Ukraine," he said, his words beginning to slur. "We have a contact. The parents think it's a scholarship to the Sorensen Academy."

"*What?* You're not saying that Paige was in on this, are you?"

"Of course not, we use the school letterhead."

"Does Lainie know about you and Paige?"

"It's none of her business. We only stayed married so we couldn't be forced to testify against each other." Bert gave a wretched sob that caught in his throat. "I didn't want to hurt anybody."

"Oh, poor baby. I guess you were *forced* to kidnap children and murder Paige." The windows were shut tight, but Claudia tasted grit in her mouth, dry and choking. Visibility was worsening.

"You don't understand! She made me crazy, coming to me right from *his* bed."

"So plead temporary insanity. It's better than compounding what you've already done."

"It's all my fault," Annabelle broke in, tearfully. "If I hadn't gone to Cruz' house that night, Paige would be alive and we wouldn't be here with this whacked-out freak."

Claudia shook her head, then regretted the action, as it made the buzzing worse. "It's *not* your fault, Annabelle." She jerked her thumb violently in the direction of the back seat. "*He's* the one who did it. Nobody else."

Annabelle hung her head low and her hair tumbled around her face. "I was so stupid," she said, her voice nearly lost in the noise of the dust storm. "I thought Cruz cared about me."

"Sweetie, he does care about you. And he cared about Paige in a different way."

Annabelle went on as if Claudia hadn't spoken. "I made him a belt in art class. I wanted to give it to him for Christmas. He didn't come to the door when I knocked. I was going to leave his present for him." Her voice dropped even lower. "The door was unlocked and I heard them in the bedroom. The bedroom door was open. I got really mad, seeing him with her like that. It freaked me out. I kept getting madder and madder."

"*He* was in his office and he heard me." She spoke rapidly, with the fervor of a confession, refusing to acknowledge Bert by name. "He acted all nice, like he wanted to know what was wrong. Then he used *my* phone and called Paige and said I was in trouble and she had to come back right away."

"I was just going to *talk* to her," Bert blurted. He had remained silent while Annabelle told what happened, but now, his voice choked with emotion as he took up the story. "I wanted to make her see how much she hurt people. I wanted to make her care about what she was doing to me. I loved her. You don't understand."

"You used her feelings for Annabelle to ambush her," Claudia said. "You knew she'd come if she thought Annabelle was in trouble. That's why you used her phone. She wouldn't have answered if it had been your number showing up."

"Yeah, she came. But she wasn't interested in anything I had to say."

His inner torment made his voice raw and ragged, but Claudia could feel no sympathy. After what he had done, his whining made her want to stop the car and beat the shit out of him, gun or no gun. Whether he had planned it or not, the man was a killer, and he was going to kill again, that much was clear. Even if he sold Annabelle into slavery, he couldn't afford to let Claudia go. She knew it as undeniably as she was piloting this behemoth along the dark highway in a howling wind.

Bert kept on talking. Maybe he thought words could exorcize his demons. "She wouldn't let me into her bed anymore, but that didn't stop her from using me when she wanted something. As soon as she laid eyes on Cruz, it was over between us. It didn't mean diddly that she was breaking my balls."

"So you killed her."

"It wasn't like that!" he protested weakly. "It wasn't like that at all."

"Yes, it was," Annabelle shouted at him, twisting in her seat. Her voice was pitched high with torment. "It was *just* like that! Paige was yelling at you about Cruz and—and you grabbed the belt from me and you put it 'round her neck and you kept twisting and twisting and she was choking and her face turned a funny color and I couldn't make you stop and—and I kept screaming at you to stop, but you wouldn't listen, and she was kneeling on the ground and—" The words ran together as the child relived the horror of Paige's final moments. Annabelle covered her face with her hands and sobbed.

Claudia's foot touched the brake, preparing to pull over to the side of the road and comfort the girl, but Bert pressed his hand on her shoulder. "Don't slow down, we've got a schedule to meet."

The gun he was holding made him dangerous, but contempt overrode Claudia's fear. "Bert, for crissake, you've put her through the wringer. Don't you have a shred of humanity left?"

His cell phone bleated, saving him from having to respond.

"Yeah, Henry? *Yeah*, there's a sandstorm, we're right in middle of it. I know he can't fly in this weather, but you tell your idiot daughter to get her ass back on the road or there's gon' be hell to pay! If we're drivin' in this shit, so can Lainie." His voice was showing the drag of too much booze. He clicked off with a muttered curse and tapped the back of Claudia's seat with the cellular.

"Keep an eye out for a private road, it ought' be comin' up any second. We gott' turn there."

About five minutes down the highway he grabbed the back of the driver's seat again. "Slow down, I think tha's it."

The wind had abated for a fleeting moment, and like the parting of the Red Sea, made a turnoff visible about fifty yards ahead. Claudia slowed the SUV, left with impotent rage at the situation Bert had created. Braking onto the dirt track he had called a road, she sought for a way to frustrate his plans.

Through the rearview mirror, she saw him lift the three-quarters-empty tequila bottle to his lips and take a hearty swig. Liquid dribbled down his chin into his beard. He swiped at it with the back of his hand.

The next time she glanced in the mirror, Bert's eyes drooped at half-mast. He leaned his head back against the seat with a gusty exhale and closed them.

"What now?" she asked, backing her foot off the accelerator. There was no response from the back seat. She waited for ten breaths, then, softer, "Where to, Bert?"

Nothing. Annabelle was curled up in the passenger seat, crying softly. Now she sat up, her eyes wide. She and Claudia exchanged a glance and Annabelle crossed her fingers on both hands.

They drove at a crawl for about another half-mile before Claudia checked the mirror again. Bert's mouth had dropped open and saliva dribbled from his lip. The day's consumption of alcohol had caught up with him in time to give them hope.

Claudia gradually applied the brakes and then they were motionless. Tapping a finger to her lips, warning Annabelle not to say anything, she moved the gear lever into the Park position. Without the keyless remote, she would not be able to switch off the engine, but leaving it running would be less likely to disturb Bert's stupor.

He was snoring now in noisy gusts. Holding her breath, Claudia released her seatbelt and turned to look at him. *Definitely out cold.* But for how long? His fingers were curled loosely around the butt of the gun, which lay across his crotch. If she could get it away from him—but she didn't dare. If he awoke with a start, one of them was certain to get shot.

The SUV's headlamps leaked through the blizzard of sand, the only illumination on the narrow ribbon of road in front of them. She switched off the lights and leaned over to Annabelle, beckoning her close. "Stay put until I come around to your door," she whispered in her ear. Hardly daring to breathe, she opened the driver's door.

Instantly, the wind whipped the door away from her. She heard Bert stir and do a double-snore. She jumped from the vehicle, not looking back. If he roused, it would take him a moment to figure out what was going on.

A light flashed on the ground about a half-mile further down the road. Bert's intended destination: the airstrip where Annabelle and the children were to be whisked away to face another kind of nightmare, and Claudia would disappear, too.

Cold air sliced through her blazer and the wind slammed sand and dirt in her face, blinding her. Struggling to keep her footing, she ran around the front end of the SUV and dragged open the passenger door to help Annabelle out.

Lowering their heads against the pummeling wind, they ran behind the Escalade and started back along what Claudia hoped was the road. Without the beam of the headlights to guide them, and sand in her eyes, the sand blown trail was invisible. The resistance of the hardened dirt under her feet told her that they were on the right track.

Sand swiftly filled their shoes and stung their eyes, their mouths, their noses, making it impossible to speak. Annabelle was shivering violently in her light tee shirt. Claudia pulled off her blazer and wrapped it around the girl, covering the lower part of her face. She pulled the neck of her own tee shirt up over her nose and mouth.

They started off again down the road. The girl's icy fingers grasped Claudia's with the jaw strength of a Komodo dragon. Her small hands were vibrating with cold and fear and, Claudia guessed, the adrenalin rush of escaping from Bert Falkenberg for a second time.

The unwelcome thought crawled into her head that Bert would eventually waken and find them gone. He definitely had the advantage with the Escalade. She would have to ensure that they were far enough away when that happened to get help.

She wished she could be certain they were moving in the right direction, back to the highway. The darkness and whirling clouds of dust, and the concussion, too, left her feeling disoriented, as if flying an aircraft that had lost the horizon.

She estimated that before she and Annabelle had left the SUV they had traveled approximately a mile from the highway. In normal weather it would take twenty minutes to cover that distance on foot. Tonight, in these conditions, it could take an hour or more.

Please God, make the wind stop.

Astoundingly, as the thought entered her head, the wind died down and a sudden, uncanny silence fell as the airborne grains of sand drifted and fell to the ground. A crescent moon emerged from the clouds and stars appeared, incandescent in the inky sky after the haze.

Claudia pulled her tee shirt off her face and spat onto the ground. Her mouth tasted like the sole of an old army boot, and a gallon of water wouldn't have been enough to wash the grit out of her throat.

"Fresh air never tasted so good," she said, filling her lungs from the cold night. Too cold, now that they had stopped running. They needed to get someplace warmer or Bert wouldn't need to kill her; she might succumb to hypothermia.

Wrapped in Claudia's too-large jacket, Annabelle tugged at her with an urgency borne of near-panic. "Come *on*, let's go! We have to get further away."

Glancing over her shoulder, Claudia could still see the Escalade. It looked like a toy from their vantage point, but they hadn't come far enough to elude Bert if he awoke. And from the side of the conversation she had overheard, Lainie was apt to appear on this road at any moment.

"You're right, kiddo," she said, picking up the pace. "Let's move it; the highway's not all that far." In fact, she could now see it in the distance, maybe a quarter mile off, a long dark gash in the desert landscape, the occasional headlight sweeping the road, coming from the north lanes. The sight of it renewed her spirit.

The sound of an engine above them was something she somehow felt, even before she heard it with her ears. Looking up, she saw no lights in the sky, but from behind them on the ground, quick flashes of alternating white and green showed the aircraft where to land. Seconds later, the roar of a twin engine plane became audible, growing louder as it closed the distance to the ground.

Annabelle heard it, too. She pulled on Claudia's hand, her face a pale mask of pure terror in the darkness. "They're going to come after us. They're going to kill us!"

And then, another engine, even more unnerving because it was on the ground. The Escalade was on the road and moving toward them, fast.

"Run, Annabelle!" Claudia urged her. "Get off the road. Cross the highway and flag down a car."

"But what about you?"

"If we split up, he can't chase both of us. *Go!* Now!"

"Be careful, Claudia," Annabelle pleaded over her shoulder and started running diagonal to their original heading. In her dark clothing and with her dark hair, she disappeared into the shadows as completely as if her presence had been a figment of Claudia's imagination.

On the road, the intensifying growl of the Escalade's engine was a growing menace in the otherwise silent night—a concrete jungle cat, preparing to pounce on its prey.

Bert's steering was erratic as the Escalade closed the distance between them. Under the influence, he must be running on adrenalin. God knew, Claudia was. She felt a piercing pain in her right side and her ribs felt squeezed in an iron grip. Her breath started to come in shallow gasps as the pain expanded. The Escalade bore down on her and she knew she couldn't run much further.

Bert had her pinned like a bug in the headlights. He slowed his speed, toying with her now. Was he going to run her down or just shoot her? There was no hurry for him, she had nowhere to go.

This is it, she thought, gasping. *The end.* Maybe Annabelle at least would have a chance to get away.

"You goddamn worthless piece of shit," Claudia screamed with what little breath she had left. She dug deep for a final burst of speed. With the front bumper inches away from her heels, every cell in her body straining to keep going, she plunged off the narrow road, following the direction Annabelle had taken.

Tires spun in the sand as Bert drove the SUV off the road after her.

Without the density of the packed dirt track under her feet her calves were soon aching as much as her lungs were. The highway was about a hundred yards away. Claudia knew she had to keep pushing, but she was winded, had no choice. She pulled up short, panting and coughing up grit that had made its way down her throat.

Thank God it's too cold and dark for snakes and scorpions, she thought, sucking in some air.

Then she noticed that the night had become silent. Hands on

her knees, still breathing hard, she looked back. The Escalade's headlights were pointing downwards. The SUV was tipped, ass-end up at a slight angle.

When he drove off the road in pursuit of her, Bert had become stuck in a shallow gully in the sand. Now she could hear him gunning the engine, could hear the back tires spinning as he tried to use the all-wheel drive to pull out. She could picture the plume of sand flying behind the SUV as he dug himself farther in, and almost laughed with relief. Then she saw the driver's door jerk open, and it was no longer funny. He still had the gun.

Taking a last big gulp of air, she poised to sprint to the finish line. She couldn't outrun a bullet, but maybe his aim would be off in the dark, or maybe—

A howl of pain and rage reverberated across the desert floor. Claudia swung around and saw a small form separate itself from the shadows in front of the Escalade.

Bert was on the ground, holding his leg and sobbing a string of curses.

"You asshole! I hope you die!" Annabelle's young voice carried across the expanse, ringing with triumph. It looked like she had taken advantage of the opportunity to slam the door on Bert as he attempted to exit the SUV.

Claudia made a wild guess and concluded that instead of following instructions, the girl had stayed close by and watched Bert drive off the road after her.

Claudia ran back toward the Escalade and was in time to witness Annabelle aim a vicious kick at the injured leg. Bert gave a great howl again and grabbed at her. He made it to his feet, but the weight on his leg made him cry out and he collapsed back into the dirt, writhing like the snake he was.

"Annabelle, come on!" Claudia shouted, frantic with the awareness that Lainie might come upon them at any moment. "Let's go, before someone comes looking for him." *Or before he recovers enough to remember the gun.*

CHAPTER 32

Their savior arrived in an eighteen-wheel semi.

After dashing across the empty lanes of the highway, Claudia and Annabelle started walking south, trudging in the dirt, following the macadam at the edge of the road. How long it would take to get to the nearest lights and people Claudia had no idea, but one thing she did know, every step was taking them farther away from danger.

About a mile into their trek, the high glare of headlights picked them out of the shadows and the double blast of an air horn ruptured the silence. As the big truck rumbled to a stop alongside them, Claudia suffered a momentary pang of alarm. Was it possible that Bert could have flagged down a trucker and—*No*, she told herself. *It's* not *possible.*

Annabelle glanced nervously at her as the passenger door swung open. Her face relaxed when the driver leaned across the seats. "You gals need a ride?"

She was a chunky blonde in her fifties with a Claymation face arranged in a grin. She looked downright pleased with herself for being a Good Samaritan, and was probably glad of some company, too.

Not waiting for a second invitation, Annabelle hopped up into the cab and Claudia climbed up after her, congratulating herself on the turn of their luck. When the trucker said she was driving to L.A., she could have shrieked with joy.

In a smoky voice that came as a surprise, the driver said her name was Roberta. Not just booze and cigarettes, it had a sultry Southern flavor that was at odds with her looks.

Maybe she has a sideline talking dirty on dial-a-porn, thought Claudia.

Dwarfed behind the wheel, Roberta commanded the semi from a purple swivel chair fit for a top-of-the-line motor home. She couldn't have been more than five-three at a stretch, but her sneakered feet looked at home on the pedals, and the tough set to her shoulders said she had more miles on her than a dozen coast-to-coast rigs.

"Didja have car trouble?" she asked. "I was *that* surprised when I saw you, 'cause I didn't see any car back there on the road. You gals been walkin' long?" She talked fast and her eyes were the kind of bright that comes from chemical assistance.

"This asshole's trying to kill us," Annabelle blurted before Claudia could stop her. "But I slammed his leg in the car and we left him in the desert." Then, in typical teenage fashion, "Do you have anything to eat?"

Roberta said there was food in the sleeper cabin behind the seat. After the door had closed behind the girl, she guided the massive beast back onto the highway, silent for maybe ten seconds. Then she said, "I don't wanna know anything about it. I'll take you t' L.A., but I don't want any part of whatever trouble you're in."

That was fine with Claudia, but before she could enjoy her relief, she spotted a white sedan that flew past them going north. Something told her that Lainie was driving it. Even in the darkness she could make out that it was a Saturn like the one in Henry's driveway. The crumpled front fender sealed it. Her chest tightened with dread.

"So, does that mean I can't ask to make a 911 call?" she asked.

"You sure as shit better not," Roberta said. Whatever neighborly urge had persuaded her to pull over for two stranded females seemed to have evaporated. "I c'n just as easy leave you off at the next truck stop."

Claudia's head was spinning. Bert and Lainie would get away. The two young children in their hands would end up in the hell that Annabelle had only just managed to escape. She would never be able to face herself in the mirror if she did nothing to try and stop them. She sucked in a breath and plunged ahead. "Listen, Roberta, if I don't call the cops right now, two little kids are going to suffer in the worst possible way."

The trucker made a sound in her throat like grinding gears. "I *said* I don't wanna know."

"All right, all right, I got it. The next truck stop will be fine. I'll use a payphone. We won't trouble you any further."

"Listen, doll, don't try to twang my conscience. This point in life, ain't got one."

The sleeper door opened and Annabelle stuck her head out, the corners of her mouth dusted with powdered sugar. Krispy Kremes might not top the list of nutritious foods, but they were in no position to be choosy and the donuts would boost her energy for a while.

"Are the cops coming?" Annabelle asked, wriggling her way into the front seat and squeezing in next to Claudia. She began working to open the plastic wrapping on a Beef 'n Cheese Slim Jim.

There was a brief hush while she nibbled. "Roberta's taking us to a truck stop," Claudia said. "We'll call the cops from there."

Annabelle bit off a chunk of Slim Jim and stared at her in amazement. "But they'll get away! You can't let them get away. Why didn't you call them?"

"Cool it, Annabelle."

"These people are trying to sell some little kids for sex slaves," Annabelle persisted, addressing Roberta. "I think they were gonna sell me, too, but the fucktard got drunk and passed out. That's when I slammed the door on his leg and we got away before the plane came."

The trucker's eyebrows shot up into her hairline.

"Annabelle, *shut up!*" Claudia said, putting steel into her tone.

"But what about..." The girl's words trailed into silence as headlights from behind the truck flashed on and off, reflecting in the side view mirrors. A car horn blared: *beep, beeeeeeep, beep beep beep.*

Roberta growled, "What the hell?"

Claudia saw her glance in the side view mirror; knew she had surmised that the driver of the white car trying to get her to pull over was in pursuit of her and Annabelle.

"Please, *please* don't stop."

"God*dammit.*" Roberta pulled the truck over to the side of the road. "I need this like I need a third tit." The truck shuddered to a halt.

"Don't give us away," Claudia begged. She twisted around and pushed Annabelle back through the sleeper door, going in after her. She closed the door and locked it before the girl could say anything. "It's Lainie," she whispered into the semi-darkness. "Shhhh."

Annabelle's fingers gripped Claudia's arm painfully. She gulped rapid breaths, well on her way to hyperventilating. Claudia took one icy hand in her own and squeezed it with as much reassurance as she could manage, but she was trembling, too.

They sat on the edge of the bunk, clutching one another. The pungent tang of the Slim Jim still clenched in the girl's fist filled Claudia's nostrils and made her want to puke.

The sound of voices reached them, too indistinct to make out the words. They waited in silence for the exchange to be over and Roberta to slam the door, for the truck to start moving. Waited an eternity, but the voices continued.

Claudia's eyes had adjusted to the semi-darkness and she glanced up, looking for a window. An air vent was above them, the lever in the closed position. She got to her feet, reached up to raise it, hoping it wouldn't make any noise.

The women's voices outside became audible and erased any lingering doubt that Claudia might have harbored that it was Lainie.

"...worth your while," she was saying in her raspy voice.

Oh shit; she's offering her money.

Considering what the trucker had said about her lack of conscience, Claudia was none too optimistic about their chances.

"I don't make a habit of picking up hitchers." That was Roberta. Maybe there was hope after all.

Lainie said, "I know they were walking on this road; they couldn't have got all that far. They were involved in a hit-and-run. My husband's injured."

"Maybe you oughta leave that to the cops."

"Listen, for argument's sake, let's say you did pick 'em up. Maybe I could make it worth your while to just drop 'em back off again, right here and now."

"What makes you think I'd tell *you*, if I did pick 'em up?"

"Let's cut the crap. Would fifty bucks do anything for you?"

There was a snort of derision. "I may be a whore, but I ain't a *cheap* whore."

Lainie's voice came back: "Now, I know everyone has their price."

"Well, sister, mine's a lot higher than fifty bucks."

Claudia's heart was thumping as she leaned down and whispered in Annabelle's ear. "Come on, kiddo, we gotta go. Now."

"What—"

"Shhh. Follow me."

Despite the cold, Claudia's hands were clammy as she unlocked the door to the cab and pushed it open wide enough to peek around. Through the windshield, she could see the top of Lainie's red hair near the front wheel well, her back to the truck. Roberta was too short to be seen.

With Annabelle holding onto the belt loop of Claudia's jeans they moved around the passenger seat, keeping their heads down. Cautiously, Claudia pushed the passenger door, hoping Roberta would not choose this moment to end the conversation.

Roberta's cell phone was Velcroed to the dash. Claudia reached for it and stuffed it into her pocket. Right now, they needed it more than the trucker did. Let Roberta buy herself a new one with her thirty pieces of silver.

Then they were on the ground.

The rumble of the semi's engine idling was a godsend and covered the sound of their exit from the truck. They hurried to the back of the eighteen-wheeler, crouching every few feet to look under the trailer. Lainie's and Roberta's feet were visible near the front of the truck, where they were still haggling over the price of betrayal.

At the rear of the semi, Claudia crouched down low and took a cautious glimpse. The steady ding-ding-ding of an open door reached her. The white car was idling with its headlights on. She whispered her intention into Annabelle's ear. Her eyes feverish with excitement, the girl nodded agreement.

First Annabelle, then Claudia made her move. They crept behind the sedan, staying low until they reached the open driver's side door. Then their luck wavered.

As if pulled by an invisible string, Lainie's head swiveled in their direction. "Hey! What the—"

The rest of her shout was lost as Claudia hustled Annabelle into the car. The girl scrambled across the seat, all legs and arms.

Claudia wedged herself behind the steering wheel and slammed the door shut. The seat was pushed up uncomfortably close, cramping her long legs and pressing the steering wheel against her belly, but there was no time to make adjustments.

Reaching for the panel of electric locks, her hands were shaking so hard, she accidentally hit the button that slid the rear window down. *Shit! Shit! Roll it up!*

Lainie was running toward them.

"Go Claudia, go!" Annabelle cried, bouncing in her seat.

Lainie threw herself at the door, grabbing the handle at the same instant the lock engaged. Claudia released the brake, jammed the transmission into gear and hit the gas. Lainie hammered on the glass, screaming for her to stop.

They skimmed past Roberta, who flattened herself against the truck, gaping at them; Lainie clamped onto the handle, trying to keep pace.

The speedometer needle rose and Lainie was forced to let go. Her skinny body swung away from the car, her legs still moving as she stumbled and went down on the roadway with a shrill cry of anger and pain.

"She landed on her face," Annabelle cried out.

Claudia watched in the mirror as their enemy receded in the distance. The highway opened up in front of her—once again, the road to freedom. Her breathing was as labored as if she'd run a mile, but she started to laugh, knowing it was sheer nerves. She put out her right hand and high-fived Annabelle, who promptly burst into tears of relief.

Then, a low sob from the back seat shocked them both into silence.

CHAPTER 33

Annabelle twisted around and stuck her head through the space between the seats. "Omigod! Claudia, you won't believe it."

But Claudia guessed, even before she saw the two little towheads in the mirror. She offered a silent *Thank You* to whatever forces had allowed this miracle.

Daring to breathe a little easier, she adjusted the seat into a more comfortable position, then dug Roberta's cell phone out of her pocket and had Annabelle punch in Jovanic's number for her.

He answered in a voice filled with tension. Of course he wouldn't recognize Roberta's number on his caller ID.

"It's me," she said.

"Claudia! *Thank God.* Are you safe?"

She gave him the quick and dirty version of what had happened. Just the basics, while Annabelle tried to reassure the two scared children. They might not understand her words, but seemed to be reassured by her manner.

Jovanic told Claudia that when Annabelle had yelled they were in Las Vegas, he had alerted LVPD and the FBI, since Annabelle was a minor who had been transported across state lines. He had not known about the two little ones, of course.

He had raced off to Nevada in his Jeep while the FBI worked to get a fix on Claudia's location from the phone call Jovanic had made to her. They were able to identify a general area and were canvassing the neighborhood where Bert had his condo.

Jovanic was now passing Primm, an outlet mall forty miles outside the city of Las Vegas, three hours from home.

He must have driven like a madman, Claudia thought, tears of gratitude welling up. But there was no time to get weepy. She still needed to keep her wits about her and get them all a safe distance from harm's way.

Jovanic wanted a description of the car she was driving so local authorities could spot her when he alerted them. She told him it was a white Saturn. "But don't ask me what model or year because I have no clue. It has a damaged front bumper."

"Okay, forget that. You're on I-95 south? About how far from Vegas?"

"Maybe fifty miles. We just passed a sign for Indian Springs. It's deserted out here."

"Okay, I'll contact Nevada HP—"

The glare of headlights in the rearview mirror told her that a vehicle was moving up on them fast.

"Oh God, Joel, it's Bert. He got out of the ditch. What do I do? *What do I do?*"

"Claudia, listen to me—" Jovanic's voice was urgent. "Hang up and have Annabelle call 911, right now. I'll call too, but she can give a better description of what's happening. Do it. *Now!*"

Behind them, Bert flicked on his high beams, filling the Saturn's mirrors with reflected light, blinding her with the glare. Claudia reached up and switched to night view, but then it was harder to gauge his distance. Batting the mirror upwards in frustration, she tossed the phone to Annabelle.

"Call 911," she said, pushing the speedometer to eighty-five. "I need both hands."

Ninety.

Annabelle punched in the numbers.

The speedometer hit ninety-five.

The Escalade swerved in the lane, hugging the Saturn's rear bumper. Its driver seemed impaired, maybe as much by the injury to his leg as the booze in his system.

One hundred.

The accelerator was almost on the floor. Still, she could not seem to lose him.

Watching the scenery fly past, Claudia's senses felt more acute than normal. Maybe it was the concussion, but she could *feel* the sounds—the steady hum of the engine, the muted rush of air hitting the car, their dangerous speed on the dark road—and she found herself mesmerized by them. She could almost imagine that none of this was reality, that they were actors in an action movie.

Then Annabelle's voice broke through the surrealness of the experience as she got the emergency operator on the line. "There's a guy chasing us," she said, sounding more excited than scared. "He's got a gun!"

Claudia coached her on their location as best she could, but with few signs along the road, and at the speed she was driving, it was too hard to read them.

She chanced a glance in the side mirror. The Escalade was a higher profile vehicle and more powerful, and Bert was staying on their tail with ease. She could tell he was playing with her, viciously mocking when the Escalade kissed the Saturn's bumper.

The speedometer hit one-o-five and she couldn't push the Saturn any more. With the low visibility, they might end up in a ditch.

A movement in the side mirror caught her eye. Bert, leaning out the driver's window. Too late, Claudia remembered he was left-handed.

Sparks flashed on the road ahead of them. Could he hit a moving target?

The next shot smashed the side view mirror.

"Get down low and get those kids on the floor," Claudia yelled to Annabelle, instinctively yanking the wheel to the right. The children in the back seat would be vulnerable if a bullet came through the trunk. The accelerator was mashed to the floor. How could she hope to outrun him when their vehicles were so mismatched?

The Escalade started to move to their left, but instead of coming alongside them it nudged the edge of the Saturn's bumper. The steering wheel wrenched to the left. Annabelle screamed and dropped the cellular to the floor. The two little ones started crying.

Struggling to regain control, Claudia hit the brakes. The ABS kicked in and the brake pedal vibrated madly under her foot.

Boom! The SUV slammed into them again, harder, pushing the

Saturn across the lane. She fought for control but they were sliding left, toward the metal rail at the side of the road. Less than a foot from the rail, she jerked hard on the wheel, swerving back toward the center of the roadway.

"*Shit! Shit! Shit!*" Her jaw was clenched so tight her teeth hurt. Pulling the rear view mirror down, she saw the Escalade veer across the lane, coming straight at them like something from a nightmare.

The Escalade bumped them, then Bert lost control and the SUV was spinning—once, twice. It brushed the metal guard rail and the wheels on the driver's side went airborne. In slow motion, the Escalade's left side lifted, flipped and came down on its roof, sliding...sliding...sliding.

It all seemed to happen in eerie silence as metal buckled and glass shattered. Fifty yards down the road, Claudia hit the brakes.

She was shaking uncontrollably as she popped the trunk lever and opened her door. "Stay in the car with the kids," she ordered Annabelle, who was already halfway onto the road. "Call 911 back and tell them to send an ambulance."

"No way," the old defiant Annabelle shot back, "I want to see."

"Please don't give me a hard time."

"That's bogus! I'm not staying–"

"*Annabelle!* This is *not* a fucking game. I need you to take care of those kids, and I need you to call the cops. *Do you understand me?*"

Annabelle flounced back into the car, her mouth set in a sullen pout. "*Fine!* But I don't think it's *fair.*"

"Your objection is duly noted," Claudia muttered, slamming the door shut and pocketing the keys. In the trunk's wheel well, along with the spare tire, was the jack, a tire iron, and a heavy maglite like the one Jovanic kept in his car. She found some flares and took them, along with the tire iron in case she needed a weapon, and the flashlight.

Slamming the trunk shut, she sucked down a few calming breaths, then started back down the road to the accident scene, where the SUV had come to rest on its roof.

The terrain was sand, dirt, and sagebrush that snagged on the legs of her jeans as she walked. The only illumination came from the cars, the starlight, and the moonlight.

From a hundred feet away, she could see the upturned Escalade's wheels still spinning. At fifty-feet it became evident that the front window had blown out. At twenty-five feet she made out a dark shape on the roadway.

She swung the maglite in a wide arc. Bert lay face down, his body bent in an angle that it hadn't been designed to accommodate. He wasn't moving.

Shivering and numb, not just from the low temperature, Claudia lit a flare and laid it on the road. She approached the Escalade with caution and pointed the flashlight at the passenger window. Lainie's head lolled upside down against it, the blood blending with her red hair. Her eyes were open, as unseeing as Paige's when Claudia had found her.

From the distance, headlights appeared; lights located up high. The hulking form of a big rig lumbered along the highway. Claudia stood in the road and waved her arms, yelling for the trucker to stop, until she realized it had to be Roberta, the lady Judas. She dropped her arms and stepped back onto the dirt.

The truck slowed as it neared the smashed-up SUV, and Roberta leaned out of the window to get a look. After she'd rubber-necked long enough to satisfy her curiosity, the truck picked up speed and left the scene.

CHAPTER 34

The woman from Child Protective Services closed her car door and turned to face Claudia. "Those kids have no idea how lucky they are."

Claudia looked through the window at the children and smiled at them. They were huddled as close as their seat restraints would allow. They stared back at her with eyes drooping with fatigue.

"I'm sure they'll feel a lot luckier once they're home with their families," she said. "Any idea where they belong?"

The social worker shook her head. "No, but I'm sure we will soon. I'm gonna get them to UMD and have them checked out, get them something to eat and a bed for tonight." She held out her hand. "You're a brave gal."

"Sometimes you don't get a choice," Claudia said, returning the handshake. As the social worker drove off toward Las Vegas, she didn't feel at all brave. For a moment she stood alone at the side of the road, grateful to be alive and physically unscathed, but still rattled from the too-close encounter with death.

A few yards away, the fire services, paramedics, and police vehicles were strobe-lit in a string of flashes from the police photographer's camera. A skinny photographer in a navy windbreaker with LVPD stenciled across it walked backwards with his camera, continuing to fire across the southbound lane where the Escalade had come to rest.

Claudia watched him for a couple of minutes, then started to return to the dark blue Nevada Highway Patrol car where she had left Annabelle wrapped in a blanket, telling her adventures to a good-looking young state trooper.

The photographer shot another blast. In the light, a Jeep could be seen approaching the first of the emergency flares a trooper had added to the ones Claudia had placed on the road. The Jeep pulled over and Jovanic got out. Claudia saw him extend his badge wallet to one of the investigating officers, who gestured in her direction.

As his arms drew her to him all the air seemed to rush out of her. She sank against him, too overcome to speak. Jovanic rested his cheek against the top of her head and she felt his warm breath in her hair. They stood together in silence, clinging to each other. Then he lifted her face and covered it with kisses. Between them was the enormity of knowing that if Bert Falkenberg's machinations had been successful, this opportunity would have been denied them forever.

His presence infused her with new energy, but Jovanic kept his arm around Claudia as they strolled over to see Annabelle. The young trooper straightened and moved away from the vehicle, giving them some privacy.

"Seems I owe you an apology," Jovanic said to Annabelle. "I should have listened to Claudia. She's obviously a better judge of character than I am."

Annabelle stared up at him, suspicion in her eyes, taken by surprise at his words. She said nothing, but she could not hide the pleased little smile that touched the edges of her lips.

"This is one amazing young woman," Claudia said. "Annabelle, you can be my backup any day."

Jovanic nodded approval, then said he needed to talk to the commander. As he walked away, Annabelle looked back at the SUV. "What about *them*?"

"You don't have to worry about them anymore."

"Are they dead?"

"Bert's pretty badly hurt."

Lainie had been killed on impact, but drunk drivers tend to survive the crashes they cause. The paramedics had talked about Bert having sustained a spinal cord injury, possible brain damage.

A tear slid down Annabelle's nose and over her upper lip and she swiped it away. "Why do they all have to be so bad?"

Claudia knew instinctively that she was talking about all the men in her young life who had let her down. Dominic Giordano, Cruz Montenegro, and this most monstrous of all betrayals by a man in whom she had trusted and confided.

Crouching on her heels, Claudia gently touched her cheek. "I know it seems like that right now, but they're not *all* that way. I promise."

"Yeah, like I'm s'posed to believe *that.*"

"Give it some time, kiddo. You'll see."

Together they watched a couple of EMTs take out a stretcher and wheel it over to where Bert lay. The coroner's van would come later for Lainie. No hurry for her.

Claudia wanted to tell Annabelle not to watch as they loaded Bert onto the stretcher, but something told her she needed to see it. Maybe some of the bad dreams that were apt to follow this real-life nightmare would be a little less intense if she saw with her own eyes that he was no longer capable of hurting her.

Annabelle gave a little shudder, but not for Bert. "Ugh, I feel so gross. I haven't had a bath in days. My hair is all greasy."

Claudia produced a small comb from her jacket pocket. "Here, at least you can comb your hair, if that will make you feel a little better."

Annabelle took the comb from her and started vigorously tugging at the snarls. Too vigorously. Turning her frustration, anger, fear, on herself.

"Hey, don't attack it, you need to keep some of that hair on your head."

Annabelle made a scornful sound at Claudia's lame attempt at humor. She handed back the comb. "What about Cruz?"

The question came out of left field. "What about him?"

"Do you think he'll blame me about Paige?"

All at once, Claudia realized that Annabelle was unaware of what had happened to the athletic director the night before. According to Jovanic, Bert's tale of Cruz' arrest was only part of the story.

The police had arrived at the guest cottage with an arrest warrant to discover Cruz bloodied and beaten. He refused to name his assailants and was currently hospitalized in the jail ward. Now that the truth had come out about Bert, he would be released.

Claudia looked at Annabelle and decided that the girl had been through enough. She did not need to hear the whole truth about what her father had undoubtedly ordered done, and for no good reason.

"What happened to Paige had *nothing* to do with you. Cruz will understand that. He cares about you, Annabelle. I think you're one of his favorite students."

"I don't wanna go home, Claudia. I don't want to see Dominic."

"Sweetie, he's your father."

"Don't make me go back there; I'll run away again. Can't I stay with you?"

"Joel is talking to the officer in charge right now, to see if we can at least take you home." She glanced up as Jovanic approached, looking unhappy.

"We can't take her without a court order," he said, after pulling Claudia aside. "I thought maybe I could get around it, but Lieutenant Estevez isn't going for it. She's responsible for what happens to her. If it were L.A., we wouldn't do it, either."

"But Dominic *asked* me to be involved."

"Claudia, honey, arguing with me doesn't do any good. Talk to the Lieutenant. She'll tell you the same as she told me."

"So, what happens next?"

"They'll take her to the hospital to be checked out, then if she can be released, juvenile hall until Giordano picks her up. We won't be allowed any contact once she leaves for the hospital. It's the HIPPA law. It's supposed to protect a patient's privacy."

A knot of anger started in her stomach and made its way up to the throbbing contusion at the back of Claudia's head. "That's fucked up," she said.

Jovanic smiled. "Now you sound like Annabelle."

Claudia shot him a *'that's not funny'* look. The girl's emotional state was fragile, at best. The thought of having to leave her with strangers, even the 'good guys,' worried her. The last time she'd spent time in juvenile hall she had attempted suicide.

Leaving Jovanic at the Jeep, Claudia went back to the patrol car where Annabelle waited. The distress on her face made Claudia feel as if she were about to personally perpetrate yet another betrayal on the girl.

Annabelle began shaking her head from side to side in protest. "No! No! No!" She jumped out of the patrol car, throwing off the blanket and pushing past Claudia. "I'm not going with them," she shouted, drawing the attention of the emergency personnel who were trying to extract Lainie's body from the SUV, and the troopers who were taking measurements and sketching the scene.

Claudia caught her arm as she started to storm off. "We're in the middle of the desert, Annabelle, there's no place to go."

"Fuck that! If you won't help me, I'll—"

"Do we have a problem here?"

The two stripes on her sleeve said she was a lieutenant. Her badge identified her as Angela Estevez. She had a pretty face and a trim body, but thirty pounds of utility belt around her waist added some bulk. Annabelle glared at her with her chin jutting defiantly, but she kept her mouth shut.

"Get back in the car, please," the lieutenant said. "It's time to go."

Annabelle stared around wildly, like a panicked animal caught in a trap, knowing there was nowhere to go but still looking for a means of escape.

"Get in the car, Annabelle," Estevez repeated, firm but not unkind.

"No! I want to go with Claudia!"

Estevez gave a nod to the young trooper. He pinned Annabelle's arms and forced her into the back of the patrol car behind the cage, doing his best to avoid her kicks.

Claudia stood rooted to the ground, impotent tears of frustration and anger choking her.

The crunch of dirt under the patrol car's tires echoed in her ears as they drove away, Annabelle clawing at the back window, her mouth silently forming Claudia's name.

CHAPTER 35

The next morning, Claudia stared out the window as they cruised past hotels and casinos lining the Strip on their return to L.A. Even at nine a.m. Las Vegas Boulevard swarmed with visitors ready to risk their hard-earned cash on the tables or video slots.

She'd had a lot of explaining to do before Lieutenant Estevez had released her. She hadn't even had identification, as her purse had been left in the hotel room. Lucky for her that Jovanic had the credentials and was able to vouch for her, or she might have been booked for larceny of a vehicle in her commandeering of the Saturn.

Back in their room at the Luxor, Claudia wanted to let Jovanic's touch caress her into arousal. Despite the emotional and physical exhaustion that had threatened to overtake her she had wanted his touch to erase the last memory of Annabelle's desperate face from her mind. But her ghosts refused to leave, and they brought with them guilt and a sense of failure, making sleep a distant promise, unkept until the wee hours.

Now she felt weary and depressed, like she had let Annabelle down. Logic told her that they had done everything they could, but logic didn't ease the feeling that Jovanic could have done something more for her.

On top of it all, Dominic Giordano was pissing her off on the cell phone.

"I'm already talking movie of the week," he was saying, sounding positively cheerful.

Claudia snapped Jovanic's cellular shut, cutting him off mid-sentence. She shook her head, her lip curling into a moue of disgust. "Unbelievable bastard. After all Annabelle's gone through, he's thinking about how to get mileage out of it."

"A real prince of a guy," Jovanic said in a dry voice. "No wonder Annabelle's got problems."

"He sees a way he can use her to his advantage, so he's hot to come out here and play loving daddy for the cameras. *We* could have brought her home if he'd had his lawyer get a court order. *Goddamn* it!" Unwelcome tears welled up and she swallowed hard. She didn't do vulnerable well, and at this moment she was feeling far *too* vulnerable.

It must be the concussion, she told herself, struggling to contain the kind of emotion that she rarely shared with anyone, even Zebediah. Long ago, she had learned that it was safer not to let anyone too close. With a jolt, she realized that this was the kind of thing that Jovanic had been complaining about—her emotional unavailability. She firmly pushed the thought aside to deal with later.

Claudia corralled her emotions and made sure any trace of tears was gone from her voice. "I'm so worried about Annabelle," she said. "I can't get it out of my mind—her little face pressed up against the window."

Jovanic's tone was cool and flat as usual, but she was learning to detect the subtle undertones that told her he cared. "She'll be home by this afternoon."

"Dominic is such a rotten influence. You know the news keeps saying he has ties to the mob? What kind of environment is that for a kid? Particularly a hypersensitive kid like Annabelle. Can't you do *anything*?"

"Like what, Claudia, drop Social Services a note that Giordano's running a racket? I can tell you right now that dog won't hunt."

"*That dog won't hunt*? Where'd you get that from?"

Jovanic flashed her the skinny eyes. She flapped a hand and said, "Never mind. Help me figure out what we can do for Annabelle."

He glanced over his shoulder to check traffic, then passed a blue-haired matron in the fast lane doing forty-five. "Do you know how dangerous that is?" he bellowed, as if the matron could hear him. "They oughta revoke her license. Okay, look, Giordano says

Annabelle's not his child. So, who's he think is the father? Maybe you can start there."

"Tony Belmont," Claudia mused. "He was her leading man at the time and Dominic said Valerie was having an affair with him. Belmont was with her in the car when she was killed."

"Shouldn't be hard to track him down and see if he's willing to talk about it. You're a computer geek. Why don't you start with the Internet?"

"The accident was eight years ago, but you'd think there would be *something* about him out there in cyberspace."

"You'd think," echoed Jovanic.

The idea of doing something proactive for Annabelle lifted Claudia's mood. She dug a notepad from his glove compartment and started a list of keywords that she would use in her search for Tony Belmont.

The story of Annabelle's rescue was plastered all over the six o'clock news. Various versions with a similar theme: *Major studio owner's daughter returned safely to the arms of her loving father.* Photo of Dominic Giordano hugging Annabelle, who was scowling in disgust.

His publicity machine juiced that story for all it was worth, Claudia thought cynically, flipping stations. She stopped at channel 5.

A bank of microphones had been set up outside Sunmark Studios' office for a news conference. Claudia watched Giordano shamelessly exploit the girl he had earlier claimed was not his biological child. She muted the sound, unable to listen to his voice.

Annabelle had her sullen face on and turned her back on the reporters who shouted questions at her. She looked toothpick-thin after her ten-day ordeal, and Claudia felt an impulse to reach through the television screen and snatch her up, give her a good meal and tuck her in bed.

Claudia's name was left out of the story, which was fine with her. But Giordano had not returned the messages she left on his voicemail, and that was *not* fine. He didn't need her anymore, and she figured he was still incensed that she had hung up on him.

She went up to the office and sat at the computer. Starting with the Internet Movie Database seemed to make the most sense. She opened a web browser and pointed it to IMDB dot com, then clicked in the 'Search' box and typed "Tony Belmont."

A handful of credits appeared for B movies in which Belmont had parts, including three with Valerie Vale. The one in which he had co-starred with Vale was listed, and some walk-on parts in television shows over a decade old. Claudia noted that in his earlier listings he was sometimes credited as Antonio Belmonte. There was nothing after the accident.

A drawing of a shadow in the box where his head shot should have been indicated that no photo had been uploaded to the site. Disappointed, she clicked on the link to Valerie Vale's name, which took her to a gallery of publicity shots from Vale's films.

Enlarging one after the other, at length, she came across a gallery that included a thumbnail of Valerie Vale on the arm of Tony Belmont.

Bingo! She clicked on the photo to enlarge it.

"Oh my God!" Claudia stared at the actor whose picture emerged, and the autograph he had written across it, her heart pounding with excitement.

She gave the computer the 'print' command and began pawing through the stacks of files on her desk until she found the one labeled *Sorensen Academy.* Opening it, she took out the item she was looking for and laid it next to Tony Belmont's autographed photo.

The answer had been there all along.

CHAPTER 36

Claudia banged on the door of Cruz Montenegro's guesthouse.

"Cruz, I know you're here," she called to the staccato beat of her fist meeting solid oak. "Open the door, I need to talk to you."

She heard a voice, but couldn't make out what it was saying. The door opened and her eyes popped wide. "Holy shit!"

When Detective Pike informed her that Cruz had checked himself out of the hospital as soon as he understood that he was released from custody, he had not described the extent of Cruz' injuries.

His eyes were swollen almost shut. A patchwork of purple stains beginning to yellow around the edges stained his face. There were a dozen stitches crisscrossing an angry-looking gash along his neck from his right ear, disappearing into his tee shirt, like a latter-day Frankenstein. The old scar across his mouth stood out more than usual on lips still puffy from the beating he had taken. A wide spandex belt supported his ribs.

"Hey," he mumbled, hardly opening his mouth. He moved aside for her to enter, then limped over to the armchair and lowered himself gingerly into it.

Claudia took the same chair she had occupied on her last visit. "You look worse than Rocky after the big fight."

"Looks worse than it is."

"Don't you think you should have stayed in the hospital?"

"Hate 'em."

"Tough guy, huh? You ought to be where someone can take care of you, at least for a day or two."

"Thanks for worrying." He tried to say it in a light tone, but it came out pitiful. "Saw 'belle on TV."

Claudia grinned. "She didn't have much to say, did she?"

Cruz tried a laugh, winced. "They bleeped her 'fuck you' to the camera. So, straight up, what happened?"

But Claudia wasn't ready to go there yet. There was something more pressing on her mind. She reached into her purse and produced the handwriting sample that had come from her file, and the autographed photo she had printed off the Internet, and leaned across to drop them in his lap.

"You're Annabelle's biological father, aren't you, *Antonio*?"

Cruz' body jerked in surprise. He leaned his head back against the chair and sighed, releasing the long-held secret that must have felt like dragging a boulder around on his back.

"What are you, a detective?" he said with grudging admiration. "Val told me she was mine and I believed it. Annabelle is a lot like me."

"I don't know why I didn't see it before," Claudia said. "Her eyes aren't blue like yours, but they're the exact same shape, and so is her mouth."

"How'd you figure it out?"

She told him about searching for Tony Belmont on the Internet. "Your face looks different now, but in the photo the resemblance to Annabelle was amazing."

"Plastic surgery," Cruz said. His hand went up automatically to touch the old scar and Claudia wondered whether it was a result of the accident in which Valerie Vale had died.

"It was your handwriting that clinched it," she said. "When I saw the writing and the autograph on the photo and I compared it to the sample you faxed me the other day, I knew it was the same writer."

His eyes lifted to meet Claudia's. "We couldn't stop loving each other, but she always said he'd never let her go." Cruz bent forward, his head hanging low. "She'd told Giordano she was gonna file for divorce, that she would fight to keep Annabelle. The next day she went over that cliff." He choked on his words and began to sob.

Feeling helpless, Claudia got up and went into the tiny kitchen, took a clean glass from the drainer and filled it with water. "Why didn't she leave him sooner?" she asked, handing the glass to Cruz, who had his fists pressed to his eyes.

He cleared his throat and thanked her, then took a careful sip through his swollen lips. "She was scared; he'd made threats, been violent before." His eyes dimmed with anguish as he remembered. "Giordano married her when she was sixteen and pregnant. He would have gone to jail if it came out he'd seduced her. He bullied her parents into agreeing to keep her mouth shut. Then he forced her to get an abortion. We met after they'd been married for a few years and the marriage was already over."

Feeling helpless in the face of Cruz' grief, Claudia desperately wanted to say something that would make a difference, but she knew there was nothing. Nothing could bring back his lover.

Cruz shook his head, looking defeated. "She's beautiful, inside and out. Giordano always knew Annabelle wasn't his daughter. But he was legally the father, so he held it over her head, to punish her. Said he wouldn't let her have custody."

"Annabelle believes he was behind the accident," Claudia said.

Cruz nodded. "She's a smart kid, but Giordano is smart, too. The cops checked the car; they didn't find anything." A tear slid down his nose. He swiped at it angrily, in precisely the same way Claudia had seen Annabelle do. "Goddamn it, I wish it had been me driving, instead of Val. Maybe she'd still be here."

"Don't beat yourself up, Cruz. I think somebody else has already done that for you. A *couple* of times."

He half-smiled but there was no humor in it. "Yeah, his goons paid me a visit right after the accident; cut up my face pretty good. It was a real clear message."

"And *now*? He caught on to who you are?"

"What else?"

Claudia thought about Dominic Giordano's reaction to what he had read in Annabelle's diary. He'd said he was investigating Cruz. It would have been as easy for him to follow the trail backward to Tony Belmont as it had been for her. He'd been hiding in plain sight.

She said, "I suppose it's not a coincidence that you work at the Sorensen Academy?"

Cruz shook his head. "I've kept tabs on Annabelle ever since

Val's death. When she came to Sorensen I was working at Gold's Gym, Venice Beach. I got the word they were looking for a gym teacher here. Oh, 'scuse me—*athletic director*. Lucky break, huh? Put in my application, got hired. Worked out real good for me. I got to see my kid every day."

"And Paige, too."

"Yeah, Paige, too. That fucking Bert; what a whack job."

"I guess the Sorensens never knew about the arrangement he had with his ex-wife. Unbelievable how he used the school name to recruit children for slavery. He always seemed so mild-mannered, in a smarmy way."

"Mild? Lady, you got no idea."

"What's that mean?"

"One Saturday night, Paige was here with me. We woke up next morning, Bert was standing over us with a gun at my head."

"Jesus, Cruz! What did you do?"

"Laid there like a turkey. What could I do? Lucky for Paige and me, he turned around and walked out. He wanted to feel like a big man, scaring us that way."

"And Paige still let him work here?"

"I wanted her to get rid of him, get a restraining order. But she wouldn't do it; she felt bad about dumping him after he helped her out."

"Did you tell the cops about that after she was killed?"

"Of course. But the only other witness couldn't speak for herself. It sounded like I was trying to cover my ass. That morning when he had the gun, I didn't think he had the balls to do it. But I guess he musta grown the balls, 'cause now Paige is—"

His voice had grown thick, and Claudia looked away, embarrassed for him. She began to talk about what had transpired in Las Vegas. He listened in silence until she reached Annabelle's description of Paige's murder.

A sound like a wounded animal escaped his throat. Cruz dragged himself from the chair and stumbled to the bathroom. The sound of his dry heaving and sobbing squeezed Claudia's heart. She had been an insensitive jerk, blurting out the story so baldly. It was obvious that he had cared deeply for Paige, the second woman he had loved to face a violent death.

"I fucked up big time," Cruz said when he returned. "I get this job so I can watch out for Annabelle, and Paige ends up getting murdered and my daughter kidnapped by a jealous psycho. Now she's back under Giordano's dirty thumb."

"How about DNA? If you can prove paternity, you could sue for custody."

"How the hell am I gonna get her DNA? Giordano hates me for making a chump of him with his wife."

Claudia grinned at him, feeling the first glimmer of optimism since she had walked through the door. "I gotcha DNA right heah," she said, handing him an envelope that she took from her purse. "Annabelle used my comb last night. Hair follicles are a good source of DNA. I checked the Internet before I came over. You can send this to a private lab and get paternity results overnight."

Despite his swollen lips, Cruz cracked a pained smile. "Claudia, if my face didn't hurt so freakin' much, I'd kiss you."

CHAPTER 37

Jovanic turned the Jaguar onto the private road that led to the Giordano estate. It was four days after Annabelle's return home, and the media had decamped once again.

"Did you bring the lab results?" Jovanic asked.

Claudia patted her purse. "Of course. And the letter from Cruz. It's too bad he's not in good enough shape to be here himself."

"Are you sure about this? It's not like you've heard from the kid since she came home."

"Not hearing from her is why we're here. Something's wrong, I can *feel* it. I know she would have contacted me if she could."

Jovanic's lips gave a wry twist. "Maybe she's changed her mind about wanting to be friends with you."

"Hey, remember what you told her that night in Nevada." Claudia gave him a smug look and reached over to pat his knee. "I'm a better judge of character than you, that's what you said; so trust me, okay?"

"I knew I shouldn't have said that. Are you going to tell her that Cruz is her real father?"

"No, that's Cruz' privilege," Claudia said. "I think, somehow, she won't be all that surprised. Everyone thought she had a romantic crush on him because that's what we expected, but I think it's hero worship, a natural bond, maybe.

"Dominic doesn't want her. She's a constant reminder that he couldn't control his wife. If he can get past the power thing, I think

262

he'd be glad to give up custody."

"You think Montenegro can take better care of her?"

Claudia gave him a look that said, *Are you nuts*? "Maybe he doesn't have money like Dominic, but at least he cares about her."

They rounded the last turn and saw the Sunmark Humvee squatting in the driveway next to a copper-colored Mercedes that Claudia recognized from her last visit. Jovanic pulled in and parked to the right of the Humvee, whose large body hid the Jaguar.

"Looks like he's got company," Claudia said. "Maybe he won't make a scene in front of someone else."

Jovanic looked dubious. "From what you've told me about this guy, I doubt he'd care. How about I go in with you?"

"I want to see what his attitude is first. Wait here for me, okay? If I'm gone more than ten minutes, come looking." She leaned over and gave him a lingering kiss, parting her lips with a promise. "I'll be back, hopefully with Annabelle, to collect some more of those."

The front door stood open, the house silent. Claudia knocked, but there was no response. With a shrug at Jovanic, who was eyeing the expensive vehicles parked in the open garage, she went inside the house, calling out.

Across the living room, she could see Dominic Giordano through the glass patio doors, seated in his chair at the table. Two black-suited men stood on either side of him. One of them was holding a gun at his side.

One thought entered her mind: *Annabelle.*

The house was the size of a small hotel. Claudia tried to remember the way Giordano had taken her to Annabelle's bedroom. On the second floor, an open balcony wound around the perimeter of the living room, with rooms coming off it.

She took the stairs two at a time, speculating on the significance of the scene on the patio. Whatever it was about, it had looked deadly serious.

Anxiety pressed in on her as she reached the landing. The muffled *thump, thump* of a bass beat warred with an electric guitar and reverberated through the floor. Claudia followed the sounds to the end of the corridor.

"Annabelle!" Claudia knocked on the closed door. "Annabelle!" She rattled the handle, but the door was locked.

The music went silent and a second later she heard Annabelle's muffled voice. "*Claudia?*"

"Yes, it's me. Can I come in?"

"I'm locked in. He won't let me out."

"Do you know where the key is?"

"Kitchen. It should be on the key rack near the fridge."

"Hang tight, kiddo. I'll be right back." Claudia hurried downstairs and into the kitchen. The view from this angle allowed her to see Giordano's tense face; the blood trickling from his hairline and down his tanned skin, staining his white golf shirt.

One of the men was speaking heatedly, gesticulating with the gun. Claudia did not have to hear the words to understand that Giordano was being threatened with worse than he had already suffered.

She had come to the house with the intention of having a reasonable discussion with him. The presence of his two visitors had changed the situation in a big way. Now all she wanted was to get Annabelle out.

The rack of keys was mounted on the wall where Annabelle had told her, but the one key she needed was missing. So completely had she expected it to be there that it took her a moment to reconcile the fact that it was not.

"Claudia?" She swung around and there was Jovanic, the answer to an unspoken prayer.

"Annabelle's locked in her room and there's no key." She pointed out the window. "Dominic's in deep shit. What do we do?"

Jovanic took in the scene outside. "We get her out of here," he said, grim-faced. "Then we call the local cops."

Steering clear of the windows, they hurried upstairs. Jovanic took a small case from his pocket and went to work on the lock with a set of burglar's picks. They were inside in less than a minute.

Annabelle threw herself into Claudia's arms. "I thought you forgot me!"

Claudia hugged her back. "I've been calling every day, but your—Dominic wouldn't let me speak to you. Why are you locked in?"

"I said I was gonna tell the cops that he killed my mother. He started hitting me, and said I had to stay in here till I made some sense. He took my phone."

Now that Claudia stepped away from her she could see a bruise on Annabelle's cheek. For one crazy moment she was so furious, she wanted the man downstairs to use his gun on Giordano.

"Annabelle," Jovanic said. "Just so we're not accused of kidnapping, I have to ask you, do you want to come with us?"

"Oh, hell yeah!"

"Okay, let's go."

"Wait!" Annabelle ran to the closet and grabbed a bulging backpack. "I was gonna climb out the window tonight."

Talk about timing, Claudia thought.

Jovanic turned south onto Pacific Coast Highway. Checking the rearview mirror, he said, "That brown Mercedes is behind us."

Claudia twisted in her seat. "Can you see how many people are in it?"

"The driver in front. I can't see the back. They turned north."

That could mean Dominic Giordano was in the back seat with the other man. As much as she disliked the guy, Claudia felt sickened at the prospect of what might happen to him. "What should we do?"

"My first obligation is to get you and Annabelle away from the scene. I got the license plate, we know the direction they took. With Giordano's name, the local sheriff will get here fast."

Jovanic pressed buttons on his cellular. Two minutes later, an L.A. Sheriff's car passed them heading north with lights and sirens.

"Am I going to live with you?" Annabelle piped in from the back seat, oblivious to what was happening to the man who had claimed her as his daughter.

This was something they had already discussed at length the night before. Jovanic seemed to have resigned himself to the fact that Claudia would do whatever was in her power to help the girl. He had held her close and confessed that the things that aggravated him most about her were the same things that endeared her to him. A prime example was her stubborn need to protect Annabelle against all odds—that the girl's behavior merited that kind of devotion.

Claudia turned to look at her in the back seat. She still looked like a waif in her black tee shirt and black jeans, like she needed a few good meals. "You might be able to stay for a while, but you'd have to agree to some ground rules."

"Like what, I have to go to school?"

"Yep. You'd have to go to school every day, do your homework, and promise not to run away if you don't like something. And no smoking!"

Annabelle seemed to consider this for a long moment. "Do I have to go back to Sorensen Academy?"

"Would you like to?"

She shook her head. "Nobody wants me there, except maybe Cruz. The girls all hate me. I hate them, too. *And* those creepy Sorensen twins."

"I doubt there'll be a school much longer, now that the twins have taken over," Claudia said. "If Dane Sorensen gets his way, they'll be bulldozing it and putting up condos."

"So they got what they wanted," Jovanic said.

"And I got what I wanted." Claudia turned and flashed a smile at Annabelle. "Monica goes to a middle school near me. Maybe you could go there for a while, at least."

"Yeah, maybe."

Her tone was deliberately casual, but Claudia could sense her heightened interest. She glanced over at Jovanic, sending him a look of gratitude for his support in her offer of a home, at least a temporary one, to Annabelle. One thing they both agreed on: for someone so young and so small, the girl wielded a lot of power.

Some couples would be driven apart by her need to nurture this child. She had been the source of so much emotional turmoil. But Claudia had a feeling, now that Annabelle had won Jovanic over, she would bring them even closer together.

She reached out her hand to Jovanic. He grabbed it and didn't let go. A warm glow of happiness spread over Claudia. Taking on the responsibility of a young teen, especially *this* teen, was sure to bring plenty of challenges, maybe more than she had bargained for. But with Jovanic beside her, she was ready for anything.

ABOUT THE AUTHOR

 Like her fictional character, Claudia Rose, in the award-winning *Forensic Handwriting Mysteries* series, Sheila Lowe is a real-life forensic handwriting expert. She holds a Master of Science degree in psychology and has taught forensic handwriting examination at the University of California Riverside Campus in the CSI Certificate program and at the University of California Santa Barbara Campus in the Discovery program.

She's also the author of the internationally acclaimed, "The Complete Idiot's Guide to Handwriting Analysis" and "Handwriting of the Famous & Infamous," as well as the Handwriting Analyzer software. Sheila's analyses of celebrity handwritings are often seen in the media.

Connect with Sheila Lowe at www.claudiaroseseries.com or www.sheilalowe.com.

POISON PEN

BOOK 1: *A FORENSIC HANDWRITING MYSTERY*

Sheila Lowe "wins readers over with her well-developed heroine and the wealth of fascinating detail" (Booklist) in this captivating mystery set in Hollywood, where forensic handwriting expert Claudia Rose knows that, despite the words it forms, a pen will always write the truth.

Before her body is found floating in her Jacuzzi, publicist to the stars Lindsey Alexander had few friends, but plenty of lovers. To her ex-friend Claudia, she was a ruthless, backstabbing manipulator. But even Claudia is shocked by Lindsey's startling final note: *It was fun while it lasted.*

It would be easier on the police—and Claudia—to write off Lindsey's death as suicide, but Claudia's instincts push her to investigate further, and she soon finds herself entangled in a far darker scenario than she had anticipated. Racing to identify the killer, Claudia soon has a price on her head. Unless she can read the handwriting on the wall, she will become the next victim.

"The well-paced plot develops from uneasy suspicions to tightly wound action."

—Front Street

DEAD WRITE

BOOK 3: *A FORENSIC HANDWRITING MYSTERY*

Sheila Lowe's mysteries "just keep getting better," (American Chronicle) thanks to feisty forensic handwriting expert Claudia Rose, who knows that, when it comes to solving a murder, sometimes the pen can be mightier than the sword.

Claudia heads to the Big Apple at the behest of Arusha Olinetsky, the notorious founder of an elite dating service whose members are mysteriously dying. The assignment puts Claudia at odds with her boyfriend, LAPD detective Joel Jovanic, who suspects Grusha herself is trouble.

Drawn into the feckless lives of the rich and single, Claudia finds herself enmeshed in a twisted world of love and lies fueled by desperation. But desperate enough to kill? Clues in the suspects' handwriting might help Claudia save Grusha's already dubious reputation before the names of more victims are scribbled into someone's little black book.

"Sheila Lowe is the Kathy Reichs of forensic handwriting—a rip-roaring read."
—Deborah Crombie, National Bestselling Author of
"Necessary as Blood"

LAST WRITES

BOOK 4: *A FORENSIC HANDWRITING MYSTERY*

Claudia's friend, Kelly, learns that she's an aunt when her estranged half-sister, Erin, shows up at her home in desperate need of help. Erin and her husband have been living quiet lives as members of the Temple of Brighter Light in an isolated compound. But now her husband and young child have disappeared, leaving behind a cryptic note with a terrifying message.

Seizing an opportunity to use her special skills as a forensic handwriting expert, Claudia becomes one of the few outsiders ever to be invited inside the temple's compound. She has only a few days to uncover the truth about Kelly's missing niece before the prophecy of a secret ancient parchment can be fulfilled and a child's life is written off for good...

"A fascinating view into the world of handwriting analysis... captivating."
—Robin Burcell, Author of "The Bone Chamber"

INKSLINGERS BALL

BOOK 5: *A FORENSIC HANDWRITING MYSTERY*

A teenage girl, brutally murdered and left in a trash dumpster; a young man, killed in a firebombing attack; a soccer mom, shot in the living room of her home; vicious thugs whose job is to protect a suspected criminal. Just another week on rotation for LAPD detective Joel Jovanic...until he uncovers a connection between the disturbing series of vicious crimes and Annabelle Giordano, who is in the temporary custody of his soulmate, Claudia Rose.

Annabelle is a troubled and traumatized teen who suffered the tragic loss of her mother and later witnessed the brutal murder of a beloved mentor. Neglected by a father who scarcely acknowledges her existence, it's little wonder the girl makes some disastrous life choices.

But she has one staunch ally in Claudia, a highly regarded forensic graphologist who digs into the darkest of human secrets through the study of handwriting. When Annabelle involves herself with a questionable tattoo artist she re-opens a door to the grim side of life and goes down a path that could get her killed. A distraught Claudia will do anything to save her, even if it means jeopardizing her relationship with Jovanic.

" 'Inkslingers Ball' is the perfect novel for an afternoon by the pool. With vivid characters, smooth writing, and a twisty plot, Sheila Lowe has crafted a mystery that will keep you guessing to the very end."

—Boyd Morrison, International Bestselling Author

WHAT SHE SAW
A STANDALONE NOVEL OF SUSPENSE

Imagine waking up on a train and having no recollection of how you got there. The more you think, the more you realize that you don't have any idea who you are…no name, no memories, no life.

This is the situation you're drawn into in, "What She Saw."

A woman…no name, no memory, no life…only fear.

By chance or fate, she runs into someone who knows her and gives her a ride home.

At her home she finds two IDs, two sets of keys, one face…hers, but two separate lives!

THE COMPLETE IDIOT'S GUIDE TO HANDWRITING ANALYSIS

SECOND EDITION

Space-Form-Movement: A basic course introducing the gestalt method of handwriting analysis. Using hundreds of famous people's handwritings, the CIG2HWA shows you how to understand the core personality of a writer without having to take dozens of measurements. Learn what spatial arrangement reveals about how you arrange your life and time, what writing style says about your ego, and what writing movement reveals about your energy and how you use it.

HANDWRITING OF THE FAMOUS & INFAMOUS

SECOND EDITION

Handwriting communicates much more than what is committed to paper. A quick note, a carefully composed letter, an autograph or a scribble also reveals a great deal about the personality of the writer. What are the clues to look for in a person's writing and what do they reveal? What do they tell experts that the writer might prefer to keep hidden? This fascinating book is a collection of handwriting samples of some of the most influential and notorious people of the past and present.

55198411R00155

Made in the USA
San Bernardino, CA
29 October 2017